Suzanne Jacob has twice won the Governor-General's Award, once for Fiction, and once for Poetry. She is the author of seven novels and three novellas, and has written short fiction, poetry and essays. In 2001, she was inducted to the Academie des lettres du Quebec. She lives in Montreal.

Sheila Fischman has translated into English over one hundred works by major Quebecois authors, among them Roch Carrier, Gaetan Soucy, Anne Hebert, Marie-Claire Blais, Yves Beauchemin and Michel Tremblay. Winner of many awards, she has been nominated on numerous occasions for the Governor-General's Literary Award for Translation and won it in 1998. Sheila Fischman is a Member of the Order of Canada. She lives in Montreal.

Books of Merit

FUGITIVES

FUGITIVES

SUZANNE JACOB

TRANSLATED BY SHEILA FISCHMAN

THOMAS ALLEN PUBLISHERS
TORONTO

Library and Archives Canada Cataloguing in Publication

Jacob, Suzanne, 1943–
[Fugueuses. English]
Fugitives / Suzanne Jacob ; translated by Sheila Fischman.

Translation of: Fugueuses.

ISBN 978-0-88762-280-9

I. Fischman, Sheila II. Title.

PS8569.A286F8313   2008   C843'.54   C2008-900104-4

Editor: Patrick Crean
Cover and text design: Gordon Robertson
Cover image: Beard & Howell / Getty Images

Published by Thomas Allen Publishers,
a division of Thomas Allen & Son Limited,
145 Front Street East, Suite 209,
Toronto, Ontario M5A 1E3 Canada

www.thomas-allen.com

ONTARIO ARTS COUNCIL
CONSEIL DES ARTS DE L'ONTARIO

Canada Council
for the Arts

The publisher gratefully acknowledges the support of
the Ontario Arts Council for its publishing program.

We acknowledge the support of the Canada Council for the Arts, which
last year invested $20.1 million in writing and publishing throughout Canada.

We acknowledge the Government of Ontario through the
Ontario Media Development Corporation's Ontario Book Initiative.

We acknowledge the financial support of the Government of Canada through the Book
Publishing Industry Development Program (BPIDP) for our publishing activities.

12 11 10 09 08   1 2 3 4 5

Printed and bound in Canada

CONTENTS

FUGITIVES

NATHE, SEPTEMBER 13

MY MOTHER FAINTED in the garden one night, it's easy to remember which one because it was the night two days after the one she'd spent glued to the TV set, watching the planes crash into the twin towers of the World Trade Center in New York and saying over and over, "No, no, no, this isn't happening," and pressing the cordless phone against her heart. My mother never makes a move in any room without her cordless. She doesn't take her eyes off its base. Her psyche can't assimilate the cord's disappearance. Same with my father, but in him it takes a different form. He doesn't stop realizing as he strides through rooms and out to the garden, and walks from the back of the garden around the garage, constantly turning his head to check on the miraculous absence of the telephone cord, which proves to me, as I watch him, that he doesn't adapt to technological innovations any faster than my mother.

So: my mother fainted two days after the morning of the day when I'd been able to drive my temperature up high enough to exempt me from leaving for school with my sister Alexa, and two days after the day when Papa and Mama had narrowly avoided a collision between their cars when they were both speeding home from the office, their leaps across the lawn suggesting that the gravity of the events propelling them would oblige the family to stay together, and that I wouldn't be able to avoid the solidarity and join Ulysses for a date we'd been planning for two weeks. My hunch was right. It was impossible to escape the assembling of the troops to go and meet Ulysses, as my parents had forbidden me to stick my nose outside, and so get out of playing the role of witness to their panic attack. As of noon, since all the communications networks had declared war, and since no one had any idea not only of what the next day would bring but even the next minute, my parents had agreed to open a bottle of fine wine, hoping that Alexa would soon be home from school and worrying that she wasn't back inside the family nucleus yet.

Late that afternoon Alexa came home from class reinforced with feelings that diverged from the wave of panicky solidarity that had swept North America—the world, if you want—from east to west, and she openly mocked the stupor and dread in which my parents were still plunged with only me to witness it and despite the bottle they'd consumed at noon. My father couldn't put up with what he first called Alexa's lack of judgment, then insolence, then arrogance, and he'd forbidden her to join her friends on the Net and forced her to "get in line" by fixing us an omelette.

So, it was two days after the evening when my father—exasperated by Alexa's silent but nonetheless flagrant insensitivity—had dragged my mother to the Patrys, the second neighbours to our left, where the Simards were already, after ordering us to go to bed as soon as homework was done and not to open the door to anyone, for any reason—"Do you understand, Nathe, not for any reason?"—as if we were still seven or eight years old. And so it was two days after the day when my mother went into the garden and fainted. It was September 13, 2001, it was just as beautiful as it had been on the eleventh, it will be a year tomorrow. On principle, neither the TV nor the radio are on when we're at the table, but for two days the TV and the radio had stayed on, and that evening my mother rushed into the garden to get some air, she couldn't breathe, we'd eaten halibut, I'd thought that a fishbone might have got stuck in her bronchial tubes, and she fell down. I saw her collapse. It wasn't a halibut bone that had obstructed her lungs, far from it, it was her psyche that had just collided with an antipersonnel mine.

———————

Mama had no symptoms other than a series of fainting spells after September 13, but that was enough to make her consult an army of specialists. Since the fainting spells had occurred in the wake of a televised trauma, my mother had to submit to some psychological tests, an exercise she'd never imagined she might have to do one day. As she was a chartered accountant, my mother never had, as she put it herself, much experience with moods. All the tests accomplished was to tangle up the columns of figures that had always fascinated her. She set about turning it into a disease. I explained to her, patiently and when Alexa wasn't there, that she might have gone beyond her depth a little during the tests, that she'd no doubt tried to give answers in a way that wouldn't allow any intimate clues to get out, which experts could have used to make their diagnosis, just as you're not supposed to leave anything lying around in the house, as if the things we left lying around were inevitably clues to a crime that basically had never been committed. Diagnoses, I explained to my mother, have the same perverse effect as horoscopes do on the will of certain people, even if they're chartered accountants. Suddenly, as I explained it to her, she had felt so exhausted from giving answers in that gentle and reasonable and serene way of hers, which is a way of showing others that no madness could ever even brush against her, that she could no longer hold in the moods that were usually packed so tightly behind the columns of figures—worry, anxiety and tears—and this had led to her being diagnosed with depression, for which they of course had prescribed antidepressants. As a result my mother had started to faint even more, and another specialist, a neurologist this time, had speculated that my mother had a kind of epilepsy, a new variety of epilepsy that was discovered as it was being created but that turned out to be genetic; so, had one of her grandparents, George or Blanche, or one of her parents, Fabienne or Xavier, been epileptic? My mother hadn't the remotest idea. Alexa came out of the bathroom, where I hadn't known she'd been listening, and burst out laughing.

Since long before the war broke out, Alexa has been nagging Mama to make up with her parents—our grandparents. "Stop nagging your mother about your grandmother," Papa has told her a thousand times, but Alexa won't let go. She accuses Mama of depriving us of our maternal grandparents all the way back to the creation of the world. From Alexa's standpoint, the creation of the world happened on the day she was born, three years before me. "And what about your sister Stéphanie and your brother Antoine—why don't we ever see them? Why are we condemned to never see them? Something serious must have happened between you—what was it?" Alexa fumes. She slams her door.

"I'll teach her," says Papa, making as if to get up.

"You can't teach anybody anything," says Mama as she fills the mister so she can spray the split-leaf philodendron.

"They're grotesque," Alexa has been raging for years. "They always talk down to us; why can't they understand that they don't have to?"

It's unlikely that Alexa's rage caused Mama's depression, but it was probably an aggravating factor, as Papa suggested publicly to Alexa, begging her to declare a truce with Mama.

One year after her first fainting spell, my mother doesn't know who she is, doesn't know anything about us, she's taken a leave from her columns of figures, spent the year wandering between the TV set and her room, playing Scrabble and Boogle all by herself and dreaming that she's signed up for a yoga course. She leaves today for a private clinic in Borigine. She's sitting on one of those moulded railway station seats designed for giants. She stubbornly insists on wearing her engagement ring and wedding ring, which she took from her jewellery box and which are too big for her. The diamond keeps slipping and sliding towards the palm of her hand. She decided that she might need her mink too. She hugs it against herself like a stuffed toy. She'll be lost in it, but she insists. Her big pale blue suitcase reeks of mothballs.

When the time comes for farewells, courage means resisting the urge to bury yourself completely in your mother's mink. It means making the leap that grabs panic by the throat so you can ward it off before it erupts through the nerves into the muscles, before it crosses the limit where impassivity cracks. I know that I have a tendency to give in to panic and I'm working at thickening the crust of impassivity that protects me. With exercise that crust, still thin and fragile, will become as tough as a coconut.

"You can take charge of the controls to your own nerves, Nathe, you can do it." I recognize the voice of Alexa, who has a direct line that can connect with my brain at any moment. I push away her voice. I don't need anyone to take my mind off the power I draw from a budding panic, the power that lets me wait for the sequel to events without moving a muscle, without succumbing to the attraction of my mother's coat. If I give in to panic for even a second, all my impassivity will fly away in bits and I'll be back to square one.

Alexa doesn't know the meaning of panic. Her life really did begin on the day she was born. Mine is only hesitantly beginning, mine is only dithering without making any decision. I'm thirteen years old, a black-cat number, an open-umbrella-in-the-house number, the Grim Reaper number, Catherine Piano said so. I am the sleeper cell of my own destiny, unlike Alexa, who was given her mission at her birth, three years before mine.

———

When he realized that the train wasn't leaving at the expected time, my father looked around in search of an explanation. Here's how he searches: he glances to the right, to the left, behind him, and most of the time it pays off, he finds someone who will know what he wants. Today, though, no luck, no one came rushing to explain the delay, no life saver, no one. That took away a fair amount of his courage. He buried his face in Mama's mink. It was not a pretty sight.

As soon as he and I are alone in the car, I'll ask him if he knows the recipe for saving yourself from drowning in case you fall into a river during spring breakup. Maybe he once knew, maybe he's forgotten by now. If you want to escape death by drowning, you mustn't interfere with the movement of the ice. You must follow the movement of the ice and never try to drive it back, which we're always tempted to do; it's the worst temptation when you're caught in a breakup. No! You have to let the ice itself deposit you on the shore, you have to let the ice save you. You have to stop hanging on and persisting in fighting it. I know about that, now I'm grappling with the idea of a *brief stay*, which I'm obsessed with: what exactly is a *brief stay*, and how many days are there in one? Right now, we don't know. If I persist in getting details, panic will be able to pounce on me. If I keep it up, the space between my body and the fur will be replaced by dizziness.

So I sit very straight on the edge of one of the moulded chairs that are screwed to the floor, I step back behind my thoughts so that my spirit can escape very high above the roof of the station. Once it has crossed the limits of the troposphere, my spirit will encounter the being I've created. That's where I will finally be able to start the recapitulations that will take my mind off other things and let me wait for the moment to act while not giving in to panic, while remaining impassive.

———————

No sooner had my spirit crossed the troposphere than my mother's voice brought me back to the station with her inevitable "What are you thinking about, Nathe?" as she tried to forget for the moment that my father had collapsed into her mink. Into her skirts, really. Ridiculous. I told her I was thinking about the troposphere. My mother smiled. She was glad I wasn't judging Papa's behaviour prematurely. "And what exactly is the troposphere, Nathe?"

"It's the bottom layer of the atmosphere, the region closest to the ground, it's from there we draw oxygen, that gas is extracted from my blood, that birds and planes fly, that bombs and missiles are dropped."

"That's nice," said Mama kindly.

That's nice, spoken kindly, means *I've had it up to here, please stop!* She doesn't fool me. My mother always wants to get things over with. Whatever we set out to do from now on, since her fainting spell, it's in order to get something over with.

She crosses her legs, then uncrosses them. I add that I was also thinking about China and about the Chinese female babies abandoned on piles of garbage. My father looks up: "Have you been watching TV for hours at the Pianos' place again?"

I don't reply. I don't ask my father what he's trying to insinuate. I don't tell him that the Pianos don't even have a TV set; that would make him even more jealous of them. All I do is recapitulate the immediate future: they're about to announce that the train is pulling into the station.

We walk Mama to the platform. She's going to kiss me. I'll stay lukewarm and walk away. I don't like getting in the way, I don't like witnessing parents' farewells. I won't get in the way, I won't see them disappear into the train car, I won't witness their embrace. When my father leaves the train, he'll look for me on the platform, he'll find me, we'll wave until the train is out of sight. Now we have to watch the big heap of metal go through towns, forests, countryside, all the way to the Borigine station, where it will stop at dawn. Mama will find a taxi, she'll give the address of the clinic where she will have a brief stay.

"Why don't you check out the newsstand?" my mother suggests.

It's clear that she no longer knows who I am. First of all, it's not a newsstand, it's a store. I get up and tighten the straps of my backpack.

"I can keep an eye on your backpack," she says.

I don't turn around. I just go. Suddenly, with no idea where it's come from, I am overcome by a rage that tries to tear me away from my impassivity. I slow down. My mother doesn't know a thing about me, doesn't know that my legs start to tremble when I get close to the store because I'm bound to be submerged by breasts on the covers of magazines, my mother doesn't know that breasts on magazine covers create enormous ice jams in the river of my life, she doesn't know that if I sink into the river of breasts I'll lose myself in the movement of the breasts so that, by themselves, they'll wash me up onto the shore of my life. If I don't want my eyes to be amazed, if I don't want to betray the thin coating of impassivity that I've built for myself, it will be best for the time being if I head straight for the comics, keeping my eyelids more or less shut. The thought that I sucked at my mother's breasts while Alexa looked on leaves me totally helpless.

Nothing went according to plan, there was a series of movements that opposed one another, we said "Hurry!" but advanced slowly, we said "Pull!" but we had to push, my mother embraced me, but as soon as she did she'd forget that she'd done so, she wanted to kiss me again but I was shivering with fever and already too far away, it doesn't matter, that's one good thing, and here I am, buckled into my seat, my backpack on my lap, behind my mother's empty seat where I refused to sit despite my father's insistence.

To each his own. My mother chose never to be able to drive a car, Alexa chose never to be able to change a light bulb, my father chose never to be able to make mayonnaise, I've chosen never to be able to sit anywhere but in the seat assigned to me in the car, the only one that was free when I was born. What Alexa would have done after the train left if she hadn't had her chemistry class I know perfectly well. She would have grabbed the car keys from my father and run to sit in my mother's seat, she would have started immediately to become the other mother she can't help being with me, with her "Is your seat belt fastened?" and her "Don't put your feet on the leather," and her "Stop pretending you're invisible."

It's been a long time since I've thought about being invisible. I stopped thinking about it years before my mother fell in the garden. If the invisible really did exist, it would see us, that's obvious. Nothing will see me. I want to stay courageous.

My father doesn't start the car. His thoughts may have stayed behind, buried in the scent of Mama's mink. Scents are voices that we can't hear, textures that we can't feel, colours that we can't see, which suspend us in a sort of prison of the air. Some kind of sorrow always comes to the eyes of a person who is suddenly captivated by a scent and tries to identify it. When Alexa and I were little, we often played scents and smells, Mama taught us and she'd learned it from her sister Stéphanie, who'd learned it from her mother, Fabienne, who had learned it from her mother, Blanche. We took turns blindfolding each other and had to guess what scent the other was putting under our nose. We emptied the spice rack and the medicine chest. Once, Alexa put a geranium stem under my nose. Me, a vanilla pod. She, a branch of eucalyptus. Me, Papa's slippers. She, her pillowcase. I never recognized the smell of my own pillowcase. Until the day Alexa made me breathe ether, when I passed out and we were forbidden to play scents and smells.

I don't look in the rear-view mirror. I refuse to meet my father's eyes in the rear-view mirror. Eyes just have to meet and courage is driven away. I won't say anything. I won't breathe a word of what happened to me in the ladies' room a moment ago, just before the final boarding call. Instead of going into the magazine store that's nothing like a newsstand, I went into the ladies' room. I bolted the door to a stall, then I vomited and felt a lot better. I flushed the toilet, I left the stall, I went to the washbasin, I splashed my face and hands. Just as I was pulling some paper towelling out of the dispenser, a woman rushed into the ladies' room and pounced on me. She opened my backpack, threw something in it, closed it again, and pushed me towards the exit: "Get moving! Wait for me in the magazine store!"

I left the ladies' room and hugged the wall to keep from bumping into the two policemen who were running towards me. I went into the magazine store, I started going through the comics and thought about nothing except my mother. I could see her in the waiting room, dozing in her moulded chair, but I was thinking about her anyway. And I began to realize that I was thinking about my mother when she was there, when I would have thought that we only think about our parents when they aren't around. Then I thought that it was quite normal since my mother's new condition consists of being there without being there. And I went over everything again because I was standing motionless in front of the comics shelf and I had no idea what the next instalment of my destiny would be. I went back to the beginning, to the first fainting spell of this woman with blonde, fine, slightly curly hair, with long, dead hands, who is my mother and who for a year now has seemed to be sliding into life through the hands of some ancient clock, what was I saying?, and I had a furious urge to run away and leave my backpack in the magazine store.

Then I noticed the woman from the ladies' room, flanked by two policemen. A long woman, an anorexic spruce tree wearing kohl like the kind Catherine Piano uses, who was looking for me, but I was hiding behind the shelves and letting my heart resume its normal beat. I slid the straps along my arms, picked up the backpack, dragged it behind me like a stuffed toy to the moulded chair where my mother was dozing, and I didn't move at all until I joined the commotion, the rush to the platform. I could have tossed the contents of my backpack into the first garbage container, but I didn't. I should have, but I just couldn't do it. And I won't say anything, I won't breathe a word about the whole business to my father. Anyone just has to feel my bag to realize that it doesn't contain any explosives. It's a bag inside my bag. Drugs maybe. I think to myself that it must be drugs, a package of pure drugs like the drug squads seize on every TV station.

Finally my father lets out a sigh powerful enough to hit the ignition key he's holding, but suddenly the windshield wipers start up. It's a tactical error. There's no rain, no snow, no drizzle, no ice, no wintry weather, no hoarfrost, no hail, but I can understand why he made a tactical error. What better way to get your circulation going than with a pair of windshield wipers ready to beat time indefinitely? I hate metronomes. Totally. And even more than every metronome, I hate the one that belongs to Madame Boismenu, my violin teacher, Madame "You must, you mustn't," Madame "You should, you shouldn't," Madame "You may, you may not." And just as my father puts an end to his tactical error, the woman from the ladies' room comes into view in the parking lot and spots me in the car. She hurls herself at the door, opens it, grabs my backpack, slips her hand inside, finds what belongs to her and says, "Merci, thank you, good evening, monsieur, mademoiselle," with a disgusting wink at me. Then she disappears among the cars in the lot.

Right away, my father gets on his high horse and demands an explanation, as if he's suddenly become the CEO of the police. I tell him the exact truth—not that I vomited, not that I'm overwhelmed by the ice jam of breasts, not that I'm filled with despair over my mother's sickness, not that I may have committed a double murder today—but that the frantic woman with the eyes lit up by kohl jumped on me in the ladies' room. My father's glands produce a fresh dose of adrenaline and the car engine is running for no reason, Mama doesn't like it when the motor keeps running for no reason, everyone has to do his part to fight the pollution of our shared troposphere.

"Just because, excuse me, but just because Mama has gone away, it doesn't mean you should keep the engine running."

"Why didn't you say anything in the station?" my father shouts. "Why didn't you come and look for your mother and me right away, will you tell me?"

I shout back that I can't tell him because I don't know, period, that vicissitudes like this are part of life, that just because somebody spits in the air it doesn't mean that it reaches the comets, which is well put and surprises my father enough that he finally steps on the gas, at full throttle again. I really love to yell like Alexa. It's actually quite soothing when you get right down to it.

You hear yourself saying things you'd never imagined saying or even thinking.

"Apologize," Papa says.

"I apologize, Papa."

Once we're on the expressway, Papa says: "You said 'vicissitudes,' didn't you?" He starts to laugh all alone while he strokes the leather knob of the gear shift. A little later he repeats "vicissitudes" and laughs again, because he'll never stop being amazed that we grow up and that we use the words he gave to me and Alexa.

I wonder if anyone recognized my mother on the train. My first dread is to be recognized on the street by someone from an earlier life. Now there's a second dread, which is to get on a train, because of movies where you see travellers board a train, confident that they'll all find a seat. In that kind of movie more and more travellers board the train, there are no empty seats and the travellers have to crowd in, but still more arrive until they're all suffocated to death. According to Alexa, those travellers are just actors who're paid a lot to be crammed in like that. They could never pay me enough to agree to be suffocated to death in a train before I've had time to recapitulate my life.

Alexa never recapitulates hers. She says that at every moment she is the recapitulation of herself. Except that—as I make a point of telling her—except that she has already lost the memory of her childhood. Which also means that part of my own childhood is already lost. Alexa has a false memory of her birth. She says that when she was born, everyone around her was crying. My mother and father swear that's not true. Catherine Piano says that it isn't unusual, as we grow into adulthood, to remember things that have actually never happened. To her, that proves there is such a thing as previous lives.

Sometimes my brain empties all at once, like a classroom. I can cover kilometres of corridor without having a single thought. I don't have to hang around for centuries like Catherine Piano, sitting cross-legged on a cushion with a swastika embroidered on it, while she waits for her head to empty. When I saw the swastika on her cushion, I screamed: "Catherine!" Catherine assured me that it wasn't what I thought, that this swastika was a symbol sacred to Hindus. Even today, just thinking about it makes the horror catch up with me. I absolutely do not understand why or how I've started thinking about that cushion again. I should calm down. I'm really agitated. Exhale while pushing my shoulders down as if they were going to melt as they descend along the inside of my arms and into my hands. Yesss!

When a car passes us at nightfall, I always wonder if it's guiding us or leading us astray. I often ask myself if the car that we're forced to follow is going to our house, if it will get there before we do. If people arrived at our place before us, would that make it their place, could they keep us from going inside our own house? When a car follows us, I ask myself if it really is following us. I don't know why, but I don't like being followed. Maybe I was followed in a previous life. Catherine Piano believes that our previous lives follow us. Alexa doesn't agree. She thinks it's ridiculous. She says that if previous lives exist, they come before us. Everything that can't be proved by $a + b$ is ridiculous to Alexa, especially since she's been wearing a bra that contains nothing but future. The most striking difference between my sister Alexa and me is that when she discovers what she doesn't have, she's convinced that she'll have it in the future, while for me, I'm convinced that what I don't have, I've had in the past.

A warm mist gradually seeps into my brain. It must be a kind of condensation caused by the physical distance from my mother. I adore numbers that end in *teen*. In four years Alexa won't have *teen* in the name of her age. She's sixteen now. But after she turns twenty, she won't have a *teen* anymore. Words with *teen* are adorable, Ulysses is adorable, little Chinese girls are adorable. If I say "adorable" one more time, a fury will be let loose that will destroy everything that's adorable in my eyes, along with the word *adorable*. My nature wills it.

Everything falls. Night falls. The nights fall earlier and earlier. In a month from now, when I've finished my violin lesson with Madame Boismenu, it will already be night in the Faubourg. All the leaves will have fallen and been picked up, it will be even darker, and with the rain, that darkness will turn gooey and make us fall asleep on our feet. The nights will be darker and darker until, finally, snow will fall.

There's a car following us. Its headlights smash the rear-view mirror. My heart beats faster. A simple nervous reflex, the heart has its own set of nerves. I'll check in the anatomy book to see if the heart has nerves. Alexa says that the vagina isn't innervated. I can't believe that. Alexa shrugs and says that nobody ever believes it. It's knowledge. It's not belief.

"It looks like you're enjoying yourself inside your Nathe-head," says my father to make peace with me and to show me that he understands how shaken I was by the anorexic fury that pounced on me. What I seem to be doing, my father can see in the rear-view mirror. If he could be satisfied with looking at the road ahead of him, he would have noticed that we're being followed, but no, he'd rather try to get inside my Nathe-head.

Ulysses, poor Ulysses, used to say that though his mother and father had had his poop, his pee, his earwax and his boogers, they weren't going to get his thoughts. Except that his parents had hired a therapist whose name was Jax but whom Ulysses called Yuck because Jax's clothes and his breath stank like a yak from Tibet, where Ulysses planned to go into hiding someday. Yuck's mission was to go fishing in Ulysses' thoughts. Yuck had used everything in his power to snatch those thoughts from Ulysses before he'd even had time to know what they were himself. I'd suggested to Ulysses not to resist Yuck, that he confide to him whatever he could invent, everything and anything, all mixed up, in no order whatsoever, like on TV, that it didn't mean his soul was obliged to discharge all the thoughts that were within reach of his mouth. I'd told Ulysses that maybe his refusal to speak excited Yuck the way it excites investigators in movies. Ulysses had replied that the thought of exciting Yuck just made him want to kill someone, Yuck or anyone at all, he didn't exactly know who.

The result of this running around was that Ulysses mutilated his own head so he wouldn't go crazy. I went to see him in the hospital. I sat on the arm of a chair covered in apple-green calfskin and listened to time pass in the room, time that was foreign to the one down the street, on the Plains or along the St. Lawrence, time that smelled of gravy and peroxide, elastic and egg yolk. Ulysses talked for the first time since the attack of muteness that had followed his mutilation. "Nathe," he said, "I don't think I'm going to pull out of this, because my parents have started to eat me, and because here they make me swallow some chemical that eats away at the thoughts in the root of my head."

I cried.

"Nathe," said Ulysses, "I know you won't tell anyone that I stopped being mute when you sat on the arm of the chair. Not Catherine or François Piano."

I swore and we watched time pass between the bed and the apple-green calfskin chair. I think you have to invent several lives on the surface if you want to save your life in depth. Ulysses thinks there's no surface or depth for him. He is his own surface and depth. Every word that he says or hears is spoken or heard on the surface and in the depth of his life.

He finally said that he was going to jump. That he was eaten. That he couldn't take any more. I gave him a piece of paper with the address of someone in Montreal where he could hide out before deciding to jump, if he wanted to think it over. He should tell the man that Nathe had sent him. "Sent," as if he were a letter. Ulysses asked if I knew him very well. I didn't know what to say. Antoine Dumont is my mother's brother, but I've never seen him and I don't know him. He must be around thirty-seven. For no reason, "pure intuition," as Catherine would have said, I was nearly a hundred percent sure that if Antoine agreed to take Ulysses in, he wouldn't start with an investigation into where he was from and what his story was, into his good or bad reasons for leaving the Faubourg.

I told Ulysses that he'd have to build a surface for himself that was as tough as a coconut. Ulysses said that there would always be some retard along the way who would break open the nut. I asked him if he knew that Japanese crows use cars to open nuts and that, if he wanted, I would kill Yuck. He laughed for the first time since the mutilation and the silence.

"How would you kill him? How?" Ulysses asked.

I said: "Help me figure that one out."

So then Ulysses told me where I could find how to kill someone naturally. While he was giving me a detailed explanation, his strength came back. He felt strong enough to clear out of the hospital. I waited for him by the elevators as he'd asked me to do while he got dressed. A thin old woman with dishevelled hair, but pretty anyway because of her emerald eyes, grabbed me by the arm, told me I was her daughter and begged me to take her away. Ulysses appeared, his head snugly fitted inside his lime-green cap, and started gently unfastening the old woman's fingers from my arm. She cried out: "Dirty burrhead!" We took off.

I was worried about Ulysses. Did he have enough money to go somewhere? He didn't have a cent. I gave him my allowance for the month. We didn't exchange another word. We went our separate ways without realizing. Ulysses disappeared. At his age, fourteen, he would have been able to cross the bridge on foot, that's for sure. And once he was on the other side, some truck driver who wasn't prejudiced against lime-green caps would have taken him to Montreal.

His parents had his photo put up all over town and in the newspaper. The cops came to the house. I told the truth, that I'd been sitting on the arm of the apple-green calfskin chair and that Ulysses hadn't said anything. Papa said that he didn't want any trouble. Mama had to start her Scrabble game from scratch. Ulysses' mother told Alexa one day when she ran into her in the Faubourg that she'd gouge my eyes out if she discovered that I knew where Ulysses was. I told Alexa that I had a recipe for killing a person naturally and that I'd kill Ulysses' mother too, if necessary. Alexa laughed very hard and very loud, she cried out: "Is that because you've already killed someone *naturally*, Nathe?"

The reason she was laughing so hard and so loud was that she was trying out a scarlet lipstick. Alexa thinks that lipstick will eventually make your breasts grow. The doctor wouldn't prescribe hormones for her. If her breasts don't come out, Alexa is going to have implants as soon as she's on her own. I told her: "You want to be suckled like Mama."

"Nobody is as totally unbelievable as you," Alexa concluded.

Alexa's right, I know. For instance, every time my age changes, I notice that the airlock between the new age and the old one is not impenetrable, not solid, that it closes badly, opens at the slightest provocation, that my earlier ages come and go inside my present age. And then, years ago, I was a boy for many years, because I was supposed to be a brother. It was as a brother that my father, my mother and Alexa had waited for me to be born. So I was a brother who had the appearance of a sister. I could see what was invisible because I was an invisible brother under the appearance of a visible sister. Visible, I was a girl. Invisible, I was the brother that all three of them had wanted. Alexa told me a thousand times, in minute detail, how atrociously disappointed she'd been when she found out that her brother was going to be her sister, and she had to bite so deeply into the word *atrociously* that I understand she's a carnivore. It may be the remains of an invisible brother inside me that pushes me into the breakup of breasts at the newsstand. But there's no reason for breasts not to push brothers into the ice jam as well as sisters, since at one point they all suckled.

"Would you know how to escape the ice if you were carried away in the river when there were ice jams?"

"I wouldn't struggle, I'd let the big pieces of ice drop me onto the shore," my father replied.

He already knows everything. If everything is known in advance, I wonder what we're doing here—I mean Alexa, Ulysses and me and all the others. Alexa says that children are born precisely so they can bring the parents what they don't know in advance. As for me, I say that without children, parents would have no witnesses.

———

Dear Mama, Nathe began, towing her backpack behind her, dragging it across the lawn to trace a furrow through the leaves that were already dead, red leaves of maples, yellow leaves of ash and poplar, dragging the bag like a stuffed toy to the top of the five front steps, dear Mama, Alexa was waiting for us, the camcorder masking her face, justifiably annoyed because we were late. We should have phoned. Papa put his hand on her head to calm her, as if she were still eight and a half years old. Alexa stepped back to shoot Papa's hand as it floated at the end of his arm.

Dear Mama, Nathe went on, I see an invisible revolver placed against Papa's neck. I can't talk anymore, we have to sit down and eat. Maybe you've gone away in order to return to a world outside the world. Something weird just happened here. Marceline thought that she would sit in your place at the table. Alexa objected. "I won't sit at this table as long as Marceline is sitting in Mama's place."

"Don't carry on like that, Alexa," Papa threatened.

It made no difference. Alexa said: "I'd rather die."

Dear Mama, does this surprise you at all? Alexa is ready to die rather than see another woman take your place. So Marceline isn't a nurse, a governess, a housekeeper or a maid, Marceline is a woman. It was me who came up with a solution. Since the table is round, we just had to shift the chairs twenty degrees clockwise so that there was no one in your place. It's a good thing the table is round. I'd never noticed that we used to sit at the table as if it were square. Alexa can glare at me in silence all she wants, she can glare and mutter that we don't need Marceline, that it's money thrown out the window. Did anyone on the train recognize you? Oh Mama, it felt to me as if all the travellers were dead. It started badly and I can sense that it's going to finish badly too.

Dear Mama, Nathe thinks to herself, I thanked Marceline for cooking everything and for waiting for Papa and me without getting impatient. Alexa whispered that was precisely what Marceline was paid for: to cook and to not get impatient. It's always Alexa who reduces to nothingness my efforts to make life pleasant for everyone, she's the one who checkmates me, who disorganizes me, who stops my crust of impassivity from thickening, and she's the one who's always filling my ears with depressing nervous laughter about Marceline's stoutness. Tonight Marceline is twenty-two, she wears Afro-type extensions and thick mascara. She blinks. She looks at us as if we could start to like her. Why not simplify things for her once and for all?

Dear Mama, Nathe continues in her head, Alexa warned Papa that the soup was scalding. I explained to Marceline that Papa hates burning his tongue on the soup, that when he burned his tongue he threw his spoon at the ceiling and got up from the table and left the house, slamming the door as hard as he could. "Nathe always has to caricature us," said Alexa. Marceline took a spoonful of soup. Alexa pretended not to notice, and since Papa didn't react, she told Marceline that usually, according to family custom, it's the father who takes the first spoonful of soup. Marceline burst out laughing and her laughter made her laugh so much that she started crying.

There were caramelized apples for dessert. We could hear spoons scraping plates so they wouldn't waste any caramel, and Marceline laughed again. "Papa," said Alexa, "could you tell Nathe not to talk out loud before she goes to sleep, either that or close her bedroom door?"

"Not tonight, I beg you," said Papa, "just for tonight can't you be something other than dog and cat?"

"Bitch and kitty maybe?" said Alexa.

I held my last mouthful of burned sugar in my mouth for a long time.

At this point in time, 22:04 according to the digital clock on the dresser across from Nathe's bed, the train is chugging, chugging and whistling as it approaches towns, triggering the pain of exiles and insomniacs. It switches on and off the warning signals at level crossings. If the train hits a bear, the bear won't die and will come back to get his revenge. Never will Nathe be able to recapitulate everything that's happened if she is forced to close her bedroom door. She promised her mother that she would recapitulate everything that happens while she's in the clinic, so that her mother will know everything that has happened and so that, when she comes home, she won't forget anything that has happened to her during her brief stay in Borigine. As soon as Nathe shuts her bedroom door, it's not living things that appear, but things that are very dead. When she shuts that door, it's as if she herself were gradually becoming some dead matter that weighs such a huge enormous amount that the greatest will can't make her raise her arms or legs. The sheets on her bed seem to be made of concrete, the air that she breathes thickens in her chest. There's nothing to be done against that material whose weight cannot appear on any scale, and that made her conclude that it's an invisible matter and therefore the invisible also has weight, but the instrument that would allow it to be measured hasn't been invented yet. So no thank you, Nathe will leave her door open as agreed upon with her mother and Marceline.

From her bed, Nathe called to Alexa, oh, no more than a breath that escaped from between her lips. Then turned her back on the door so that if Alexa does turn up, she'll be positive that she imagined Nathe calling her. Waiting always makes Nathe hypersensitive to the slightest vibration of things. Nathe becomes the air that brushes against the walls and windows of the house, that stirs the last dead leaves still clinging to the branches of the trees. Nathe drifts in the fleeting glimmers and the fluttering shadows. Especially when she's not waiting for any response, any event or person, when she is breathing inside some state of waiting that has no name, no address, no face, Nathe has the sensation that she is part of the black tone that inspired her to create the being outside the universe. There's nothing that can pick up that loud emission, or broadcast it or reproduce it, yet it seems to Nathe that she is becoming that sound. Until an image intervenes and reminds Nathe of her state of waiting. We don't know from where these images are projected—like the one this evening: the dawning of a golden island on the surface of a violet sea.

Alexa finally turned up and slipped silently into bed. She'd kept her bra on under the big T-shirt she preferred over all the pyjamas in the world and all the nightgowns in the universe. But there's nothing inside it, Nathe thought, and my sister is such a snob that I won't even talk to her. Alexa would say something eventually. She couldn't help it. Alexa asked Nathe if she knew what their mother's sickness was called.

"Nobody knows, not even the biggest snobs," said Nathe.

Alexa laughed and said jokingly that Nathe was nearly as blind as Blanche, their great-grandmother who had amaurosis.

"We've never gone to see her," said Nathe.

"She's the one who's never come here," said Alexa.

"Grandma won't let her," said Nathe.

"If I didn't have proof that you're a girl, there are times when I'd think you're a boy. Know why?" asked Alexa.

Nathe replied that she might actually be a boy, why not? Maybe she would turn into one, after all.

"After what?" asked Alexa.

The minutes were dropping on the digital clock, increasing the distance that made Nathe and Alexa strangers to one another until neither one remembered being assembled from the same genetic baggage, as Alexa often put it, surprised that two individuals so different from one another could have been created from the same baggage. Alexa said that she could see their mother on the train and that she thought their mother could see them in their bed. Nathe told her: "Stop. The invisible doesn't see us, we're the ones who see it."

The bed was getting hotter and hotter because of the heat given off by Alexa. Nathe began to suffocate.

"You stop too, stop suffocating," said Alexa, "stop being violent, I'm talking to you about Mama's sickness, do you want me to explain it?"

Nathe began to struggle with the dead matter that was creeping over her arms and legs.

Alexa was scared. She called out: "Papa! Papa! Nathe's having
a suffocation attack!"

Their father came running, marking time at the bottom of the
stairs. He asked if he should come up. Both Nathe and Alexa
shouted: "No, no! Don't come up!"

Nathe got out of bed and leaned over the stairs. "No, it's okay
now, I'm not suffocating anymore."

Alexa waited until their father was gone from the foot of the
stairs to accuse Nathe of violence. "You did it on purpose, you
don't want to know what's wrong with Mama, you want to play
ostrich."

Alexa went back to her bedroom. The temperature dropped
between the sheets of Nathe's bed. I prefer that, I don't want a
girl who's in heat and in a bra in my bed, thought Nathe.

Around midnight her father was going to find himself all alone
in the big double bed. Maybe he would discover an icy revolver
pressed to the back of his neck. "Good night, Monsieur Saint-
Arnaud," Nathe said aloud. And laughed. She'd never thought
of calling her father by his family name. She started again. "Good
day, Monsieur Saint-Arnaud, Merry Christmas, Monsieur Saint-
Arnaud, Nathe Saint-Arnaud bids you good night."

Hundreds of little sounds of every shape, which hadn't existed
a second before, suddenly emerged from each nook and cranny
in the bedroom and leaped up to Nathe's bedside. She clapped her
hands hard. *Clap!* The sounds stopped. In the time it took Nathe
to catch her breath, they started up again. Oh no, things would
be different when Nathe was an orchestra conductor. She would
whack the podium with her baton and all the instruments would
stop breathing, working, screeching, moaning: silence! And that
was it, Nathe would have all the time she needed to get her breath

back, then presto! she would raise her baton, hold it up, suspended. Every form of every sound that had emerged from the musical instruments of all time would be mute, locked in the troposphere. I'll control them with an iron rod, Nathe promises herself. I'll teach all those instruments how to hold their breath indefinitely, in a state of apnea, the way I've already taught my violin to do as soon as Madame Boismenu's back is turned.

Nothing and no one knew that Nathe was going to become a conductor. The first time Nathe Saint-Arnaud drove up to the house in Carouges in the new limousine fit for an internationally renowned conductor and specialist in musical instrument apnea, Mme Émilie Saint-Arnaud would be delighted. "Delighted," she would say, applauding. "I am delighted!" Nathe would invite her to get into her limousine. Alas, thought Nathe, by then my mother will already be old, she won't want to get into any limousine. Then again, maybe her mother was already old. Old and sick? But then, thought Nathe, I may already be too old myself to embark on such a destiny. Everything starts to be impossible very early. As of the moment when we cannot be simultaneously a man and a woman, there's no going back.

Ah, Nathe moaned, already I can no longer scrutinize my image in my own grave when just a short time ago I could spend hours imagining my bones impeccably cleansed of their flesh and laid out in order on the satin, my cavity-free teeth that scholars would analyze centuries later with technical innovations that enabled them to make the teeth of the dead speak, everything's happening too quickly and I haven't even decided on a colour for the limousine. Under no circumstances will it be black, Nathe promised herself, under no circumstances white, because blacks and whites determine how long a sound lasts. I'm going to give up whites and blacks. My limousine will be silent and immortal, Nathe decreed during the night. "Stop being violent," Alexa whispered inside Nathe's head. "Stop being a snob," Nathe answered inside Nathe's head.

Alexa thinks straight, thought Nathe, Nathe is a bloodthirsty monster and excessively violent. Why does Nathe grind her teeth in her sleep if it's not because her jaws are trying to crush that violence? Sometimes Nathe crushes the horsehair in her bow against the strings of her violin to distort the sounds, to hear them plead and moan under the torture of her violence. And when she plays dodge ball, she's actually playing deadly ball, she likes to kill, likes to shout, "Dead!" Often, she imagines her whole family, herself included, being blown up by a car bomb and Alexa's brain going up in flames in the night. When she thinks that she could have been born in a remote village in Algeria and expect to have her throat cut and to be torn limb from limb in the night, when her nerves are strained, waiting for the sound of footsteps gliding across the dry earth, sometimes she has to hit herself to avoid committing the crime that would put an end to all those horrors. Because she sometimes has thoughts that make her omnipotent, and they're the furthest thing from good thoughts that pass through her, oh no, they're thoughts of weapons of mass destruction that massively destroy all the dandelions and with them, alas, all the fields, all the forests, all the animals, and finally all of humankind with all its violence, her own included.

When Nathe was young, thought Nathe, she believed that her mother's and father's navels were the scars of a cord that had connected them first to Alexa and then to her. She didn't know that her mother's navel was the scar left after the cord of her own mother, Grandma Fabienne, was cut, and her father's the scar left after the cord was cut between him and a woman who is dead and unknown. Alexa decreed that it's absolutely impossible that Nathe can remember what she thought when she was little, because Alexa herself couldn't remember a thing, and in eighty percent of cases memories are invented stories. More of Alexa's made-up statistics. As usual, Alexa makes up statistics to intimidate us.

Alexa is convinced that Nathe invents memories of this and that to play to the gallery. "Nathe was born to amuse the gallery," Alexa decreed, with the disdain of a gifted child swelling her upper lip. Alexa speaks only in decrees. Luckily, Papa knows how to intervene from behind his newspaper, with his feet crossed on the leather pouffe from Morocco. "I can remember a little Alexa who thought that islands floated on the water."

"That's absolutely wrong," replies Alexa. "What you ought to remember is a little Thomas who thought that his mother couldn't see him if he couldn't see her. Oh, sorry, Papa, I forgot that you didn't have a mother."

In spite of everything, Alexa has a kind heart. Don't hold it against her. Alexa was born with the suspicion that a human life is very short, no matter how long a person might live. She wants to acquire as much knowledge as possible before she dies. She couldn't come to the station because she had her Chinese lesson. Starting when she was nine, Alexa wanted to learn the rudiments of one foreign language every year. This year she's starting her sixth—not counting French and English. She opens a new vocabulary file for each of the language rudiments that she studies. She doesn't want to become a United Nations interpreter. She doesn't want to become a diplomat. She doesn't want to become a foreign correspondent.

"If I were learning a foreign language," Nathe explained to Alexa in a voice full of regret and sadness, "it would be ancient Egyptian, but ancient Egyptian is just a dead language abroad."

"Lots of languages are dead," said Alexa in a voice overflowing with pity to show that she wasn't fooled by the show that Nathe was putting on for her, "but don't worry. Lots of leaves are dead, and flowers, and old people, and babies, and flies, and lice, and spiders, lots of ladybugs in every corner, lots of hairs are dead, even golden ones like mine, even not so golden ones like yours, they die in every corner."

When Alexa mimics Nathe with the intention of consoling her because her IQ is no higher than that of the average bear, she's exasperating. Nathe wasn't the least bit worried about the death of ancient Egyptian, she simply didn't want her father and mother to hope she'd follow in Alexa's footsteps. Even so, discovering that the language spoken nowadays by the Saint-Arnaud family will one day be added to the list of dead languages undermined Nathe's resolution not to walk in her sister's footsteps. Because of all the dead things that are weighing on her and paralyzing her in the darkest part of the night when the earth has its back turned, Nathe can identify some that are already mummified inside her, for instance the desire to suck at her mother's breast. That, of course, she'd had. And that, she no longer has. So it's mummified, a mummy, that's how Nathe sees things, and she has the right to complain about it.

Tears start to flow from Nathe's eyes. She was too exhausted to get up, turn on a light, watch the tears flow in the little mirror that hangs behind the closet door; too exhausted to fall asleep either. She imagined then that she was finally giving in to the urge to burrow into her mother's mink. In that warm nest, woven with impalpable threads of perfume, her tears would stop flowing. If someone from outside the world had come to her now, had come to be silent with her, she could have confided in them.

Catherine and François Piano. They say things like "tough luck" and "situation outcome." Alexa says those are regionalisms. Idiotisms actually, says Mama. Alexa purses her lips. It looks like the zipper of a crocodile purse with all the animal's teeth lined up inside. Catherine Piano gave Nathe a copy of *The Anatomy Colouring Book* intended for medical students. The book is in the drawer of the seven-drawer chest that Catherine has set aside for her. The authors suggest colouring the course of the nerves yellow. Nathe used lime green because it's the colour that sets her teeth on edge more than any other. Ulysses' parents, afraid of losing him in the crowd, often dressed him in phosphorescent lime green. They called Ulysses Ulysses and right afterwards they started to be afraid of losing him. He was wearing lime green on the posters.

Nathe has always spent a long time studying the faces of missing children on posters. It was only sometime later, when she woke up in the middle of a dream and realized that one of the missing children had appeared to her in the dream and was now standing beside her bed in the night and that it might have been the child who'd pulled her from her sleep, that she discovered she was looking for them without being aware of it. Nathe sometimes dreams that she herself is a missing child. Sometimes she lies on her belly and, while waiting for her future, becomes a missing child. Her kidnappers have locked her inside a passenger cabin on a freighter that's sailing towards the Gulf, towards the ocean. Every passenger authorized to enter the cabin where Nathe is being held is looking for a missing child to adopt. Nathe feels that she's ready to be adopted. Alexa says that not all that long ago, children, both boys and girls, were displayed at the market like animals and sold to the highest bidder. Their mouths were held open to check on the condition of their gums, they were prodded all over to be sure their bones were solid and in the right place. It was the words "the highest bidder" that shattered Nathe. She asked her mother if she had any memories of being a captive. Has she ever dreamed that she was a captive? Her mother looked up the word *émissole* in the dictionary. It is the name of a shark. When she looked up, her mother had forgotten everything, both Nathe's question and the word *émissole*.

Usually when she lies on her stomach, Nathe falls asleep before she has been sold to the highest bidder. She can't see the face of the highest bidder when it suddenly appears in the night, but the thought that he's close to reaching her scalds her blood. "The highest bidder" then becomes "the most bitter." The bitterness is a delight that goes up and down the course of Nathe's nerves.

In November 2001, Nathe and Ulysses formed the best research team in their class. They'd met the Pianos during a study of immigrant businesspeople in the Faubourg. Their main advantage was that they experienced the same terror at entering unknown places. They both knew Daphné Leduc, who had discovered a hanged man in the closet of an apartment where her father had asked her to drop off the mail while the tenant was away. Daphné's hair had turned white while she was running away, trying in vain to imagine how to get her eyes out of her head. She hadn't left home for weeks, and as soon as she tried to stick her nose outside, everyone had stared at her. Nathe would have stared at her too if she hadn't been in the habit of staring at herself in mirrors until another face appeared that would make hers go. Nathe and Ulysses also knew Robert Plomb, who'd returned from a vacation in Brittany to visit his mother and found his father's corpse sitting in front of the TV, which was still turned on. Robert Plomb had bought a black band that he wore on his head, and he stared at people before they could stare at him. He would spit on the ground and eventually disappear, wearing the red leather jacket his father had died in.

It was because of those events and many others, which hadn't happened to them but which haunted them anyway, that when Nathe and Ulysses finally made up their minds to enter dark and unknown places—to them, unknown places were always dark— they talked very loud, nearly shouting, thinking that their voices, which preceded them, would protect them from horrific apparitions. The day they stepped inside the Piano pet shop, hollering their hellos and their names, Catherine Piano came down a few steps of the spiral staircase and leaned over in the direction of the noise.

"Hello," she said in a voice that was slow, calm and gentle, "hello, children, my name is Catherine Piano. What can I do for you?" She motioned to the children to follow her. "Come on up."

They obeyed, tiptoeing between the aquariums and cages to the waxed stairs. They emerged on the floor above, in the centre of a big room with books piled chaotically from floor to ceiling. Catherine cleared two chairs, cane-bottomed like the one in Alexa's room, and took a seat in a little armchair made of lacquered wicker, behind the narrow, dark wooden table. She stretched her arms above the table, finally setting her hands on it, palms down. "Now then, tell me your names."

Ulysses was the first to shake himself out of his dream and tell her: "Ulysses Godbout and Nathe Saint-Arnaud. We're doing a study in human geography on immigrant businesspeople in the Faubourg."

He waited to ask the first question until Nathe had taken out the notebook in which she would write the answers, but Nathe had just realized that she hadn't cleaned or cut her nails and she didn't want Catherine Piano's eyes to light on her dirty fingernails. She decided to lie. She'd forgotten the notebook. But she promised to memorize word for word every one of her answers and to transcribe them that very day. Ulysses frowned and asked Nathe to look harder. Catherine waited, smiling.

"Place of birth," Ulysses read.

"Oh no!" Catherine sang in her deep and gentle voice, "we aren't going to play Canada Customs or RCMP, Ulysses! Never mind your little list, let's get to know one another."

Beads of sweat stood out on Ulysses' brow and inside Nathe's clenched fists. Ulysses folded his paper and started to breathe again. "Before that, we'd like to know where you were born and how you came to the Faubourg."

When they left the pet shop, Ulysses and Nathe ran to school to write up their report. Ulysses couldn't get over the fact that Catherine had treated him as an adult, and he mentally repeated what she'd said so that her words wouldn't be erased. Ulysses' eyes, thought Nathe, have never shone as brightly as they did that day, the Wednesday when we met Catherine and François Piano. François looks after the fish and the birds on the main floor, while Catherine runs the used bookstore in the big room upstairs. She teaches French to immigrants, she founded a reading club. They live above the bookstore. Catherine was born in Senegal, François in Brazil, to French parents. They had met in Vancouver, on their way home from Nepal, where they'd lived for more than a year without ever meeting. Their baggage had got lost between Tokyo and Anchorage, or between Anchorage and Vancouver, Nathe couldn't remember exactly where the baggage had got lost. The last question had been about how they'd adapted to the Faubourg: had they had trouble adapting? Catherine and François had exchanged a questioning look, then François explained that as a businessman he'd taken a while to adapt to the way people repeated the same greeting—Bonjour— when they were meeting you or leaving you. "What about the two of you, have you ever been outside the Faubourg? I mean, long enough to feel what distance is like?" François added.

"Excuse us, but we absolutely have to leave now," Ulysses replied, after a pleading look at Nathe.

"But we'll come back," Nathe promised, "we'll come back to see the fish."

Nathe counted the days. Ten days to resist going back to sit across from Catherine Piano, not Pia-no, but Pi-a-no, softly and softness, mute and soft pedal, thirty years old, seventeen older than Nathe, who ran to the store for the first time at noon, slowed down, speeded up, gave up. The second time, she tried to spot a customer through the aquariums in the window. If a customer had gone in, she would have squeezed in behind him. No one came. The third time, when she was about to push the door open, she heard Catherine's voice singing behind her: "It's little Nathe! Hello, Nathe! Will you come up for a minute?" Now Catherine was speaking to her as an equal.

Nathe went back more and more often. Catherine offered her the big *Anatomy Colouring Book* and showed her to the drawer in the tall chest with seven drawers that was reserved for it—the Wednesday drawer—but it didn't mean that Nathe would have to come only on Wednesdays. Nathe wanted at all costs to keep her visits to the Pianos secret. Ulysses was the only one who knew. But more and more, Nathe was missing the bus that brought her home from the Faubourg to Carouges and she'd run out of reasons to justify her tardiness.

"You make everything complicated," said Catherine. "Look, I'll phone your parents myself, I'll tell them that you come to the bookstore for lunch. Or would you rather come after your violin lesson? Your father could pick you up between six and seven, you'd have done your homework, learned your lessons, you'd even have had time to feed the birds and fish."

"I'll talk to my parents myself," Nathe said. And she did.

"We don't know them," her mother protested.

"You and Papa can go to the pet shop and go upstairs to the bookstore, they're always there," Nathe pleaded.

And that is what happened, and after her violin lesson Nathe rushed to the Pianos'.

I was asleep, Nathe discovered, I went to sleep and my leg dropped out of the bed. I tried to move it back between the sheets, but I couldn't, it's too heavy and I'm scared. I'm scared that my leg has broken away from me and hung itself. I need some letters so I can hang the man. If I can concentrate on fear, Nathe promised herself, experience fear when it's there, I'll understand that fear behaves like ice on the river and that I have to follow the movement of the fear, whose reason isn't outside of me, whose cause sinks its roots into the invisible, with no proof that any instrument can measure. If I could go back in time, I would change events that have already happened. If I could throw them into the mirror, I would. If I'd been able to film them with Alexa's camcorder, the events wouldn't have taken root inside me, they'd have taken root in the camcorder, which I would throw off the bridge into the St. Lawrence today.

That's wrong, I'm not insensitive, Catherine! I'm not insensitive! But you're right, I am insensitive to the spruce-woman who bursts into bathrooms, who pushes me towards the exit, who grabs my bag to take out what she's stuffed inside; I'm insensitive to my father who gets on his high horse, who burns his tongue on the soup; I'm insensitive to the sight of an invisible revolver pressed against the back of my father's neck; to the sight of Alexa stuffing her bra with future. I'm as insensitive as if Nathe herself had become insensitive to me that evening, that night, and all the days that followed.

What am I talking about? Nathe asked the luminous dial of her alarm clock on the chest of drawers. What am I talking about?

I, Nathe, became insensitive to Nathe the night I slept at the Pianos' because my father was stuck in his office on account of the storm, that terrible storm I'd seen hovering over the Laurentians in Madame Boismenu's music room. And when I left my class, I recognized the white wind that comes before the worst storms. I was excited by it, by that sharp, naked wind that drove me into the pet shop. We closed everything. We went up to the Pianos' floor above the bookstore. It was the first time I'd been there. François phoned to say that the road from Beaupré was already shut down, that he was going to stay with friends in Beaupré. The snow started to hurl itself against the windows like a lunatic.

"Are you afraid?" Catherine asked. I wasn't afraid of anything. Catherine put on some soft music, a woman's voice that was soothing the world in Italian. We ate bread and cheese while we watched the snow and listened to it lash the windows. The power went off. Catherine lit a candle and we could hear the gusts of wind whipping the window and whistling through the Faubourg. It was the kitchen. It wasn't their bedroom.

Then Catherine brought her face closer to the candle, then she moved it away; she put her hands around my face and brought it closer to hers, she opened my lips to taste, and the more she tasted the more she wanted to taste, and she guided my hand onto her so that I would slip my hand onto her, onto her neck, onto her face, and onto her. No one, ever. Never had anyone told me, not my mother, not Alexa, that something, someday, would tighten inside me like that and break inside me, something that isn't nerves, that isn't muscles, that isn't blood, but maybe water, my water, the water I'm made of, that it would tighten, burst, break into millions of shivers of water, and that I would let lips, hands, fingers, the whole body of madness begin to taste me, devour me. Because Catherine Piano had gone mad. Everything started to swerve towards the windows and everything was threatening to send us into the void along with the battered and terrified walls of buildings.

Then Ulysses' face appeared through a black swarm of biting snow, and in that snow Ulysses was dead. It was there, at that instant, that insensitivity numbed me, froze me, dried me on the spot, and I let Catherine taste me as if I had died with Ulysses. The more she tasted me, the more death drove back far inside me the possibility of stopping her hands, her mouth, her body that pressed and rubbed itself against me and hollowed out its place in me.

So, today I scream no! No! I am not insensitive, that's wrong. I'm only caught in this trap that has closed over me, and I haven't even been able to struggle. I know, I'm to blame, but it was too late, I was helpless against that madness, it was as if I'd already encountered it in another life but hadn't been able to recognize it in time. And I'm to blame because I didn't give up going back there every night, and every night she found a way to make me go up the stairs. I'm to blame because even today, nearly a year later, I have no idea what it was that drove me to her place. And every night before I went to sleep, I vomited. And I had constant attacks of suffocation. As soon as I lay down on my bed, nausea overcame me and made me run.

"What's the matter with you, Nathe?"

"Nothing's the matter, Mama, I just have to pee."

"But it sounds as if you're vomiting, are you vomiting, Nathe?"

"No, Mama, of course not, it's over, you can see that there's nothing wrong with me. Please, Mama, leave me alone!"

I wish that you'd leave me alone. I wish that Catherine Piano would leave me alone. How can I stop going there? As soon as I started wanting not to go there and hung around the Faubourg after my violin lesson, Catherine would demand explanations. I was cold. I didn't want to take my coat off, not at school, not at my violin lessons, not at home. Catherine would wait for me at the door of Madame Boismenu's building. And my father: "You're shivering again . . . Don't they heat that bookstore of theirs? They don't heat, the French. Tell them this isn't France. And stop chattering your teeth, it's annoying." He turned up the heat in the car. It was suffocating. I complained that the air was unbreathable. Ah, I always had to slip my hands inside Catherine's sweaters. No night was long enough for me to think things over once and for all.

Yes, I'm to blame, I admit it, it's true that I had dreams about adoption. It's true that my dreams about adoption awakened the fire that was sleeping in its nest inside me and that sometimes started to race between my skin and the sheets. I admit it, the face of the highest bidder who approached me in the cabin of the freighter where I was a captive and that I couldn't recognize made my blood boil. I shout: "I didn't want to!" But when I shout, all the words skip, explode into thousands of splinters of broken letters, and they fall, inanimate and lifeless, to the bottom of the huge Scrabble bag that my head has turned into. To hell with you. You piece of shit. You piece of filth. I am to blame. They're coming down in insults, and it's on my head and on my soul that they are coming back down, and no one can see them, will see them, will see me.

I didn't go to anyone else's house. I stopped inviting Dorothée, Mélissa, Lara, Étienne, Marc, Sylvia to mine. They chit-chat together. I don't chit-chat. At school my grades are better than ever, but I can't explain why. Madame Boismenu told my parents that I was turning into a real musician, that I was doing really good work. I wasn't working at all. I mashed my bow full of rosin onto the strings of my violin. I could spend hours scraping the open strings.

"Don't touch me ever again," I finally told Catherine when all the snow in the Faubourg had melted. She moved towards me even though I'd told her not to. "I'm going to scream, I'll tell François everything!"

She started to laugh, hugging herself. "François! You're going to tell François everything! My heart! What are you going to tell him?"

"That."

"Wait till you've had your period before you talk to him, you'll be more convincing."

I don't get it. I didn't have my period, I'd never had my period, no more than Alexa has breasts, I didn't understand a thing, but I was scared. Catherine took advantage of it to phone Carouges. She invited herself to the Saint-Arnauds' house. Seduced them. Persuaded them to turn Nathe over to them at Les Éboulements for the summer. Nathe says no. Her parents don't understand.

Alexa: "It won't cost anything and since Mama isn't working now, you ought to go."

"You're so stupid, Alexa, you and your runaway IQ, with everything you know, you know nothing, absolutely nothing!" says Nathe.

"Mama, why is Nathe so belligerent with me?"

"I don't know, sweetheart, Nathe's the only one who can tell you."

But Nathe doesn't answer anymore.

"I swear on my mother's head that unless you ask me to, I won't touch you once all summer," said Catherine. "I'm cured."

Nathe thought that she'd love to see the look on the mother on whose head Catherine had just sworn. They had to drive through the village of Les Éboulements, go one more kilometre until they spotted the roof ridge of the house built on a rocky plateau between the river and the road, turn onto ruts barely visible in the high grass that keeps the earth from sliding down the hillside. It was an old grey frame house, with window frames and crossbars painted white. When you went inside, a powerful smell of linseed oil assailed your nostrils.

Nathe got out and in a flash had spotted the steep footpath the water had hollowed out through the cedars and aspens, which ran all the way down to the river. She calculated the distance to the nearest neighbours, they were far away, you could cry out and no one would hear you. She spotted the red strawberries that she'd been crushing with her feet. She crouched down to pick some. She filled her hand. Then, she didn't know why, she started mashing them in her fist, weeping and dribbling in silence. She explained to herself in bed that night, "It was because I knew that if I ran and offered them to her, she'd think she could start again."

Nathe finally understood the reason for her tears. Never again could she offer Catherine anything. No movement must ever start from her towards Catherine, not even a smile. She must refuse her everything in order to refuse herself. And something else: she was afraid of getting her period and not being able to hide it. She'd taken some tampons from her mother's box and some from Alexa's, but she didn't know exactly what she was supposed to do. And she had a hunch that if Catherine found out about her period, it would be exactly as if she'd found out about her tears. And when she found out about Nathe's tears, Catherine would go crazy again.

To Nathe's great relief, the house was soon filled with friends of François and Catherine. Some stayed for a few days. They pitched their tent at the end of the property, near the juneberry trees. As well, Catherine was offering a watercolour class and her students, retired people, came twice a week to set up their easels and paints in the grass, where Nathe agreed to pose for them, wearing Catherine's straw hats and seemingly deep in a daydream that was actually suspicion and high surveillance. Catherine didn't pester Nathe, who behaved herself and did her holiday homework, math, then went down to the wild deserted shore at the foot of the cliff. Nathe was calmer now that she realized that to get to Carouges she just had to follow the railway tracks along the river. Some mornings, fog patches that washed up at the foot of the cliff swelled, let themselves be slowly lifted up by the heat of the rocks and sand, floated to the crowns of trees, gradually went inside the grey house through its open windows, and climbed up the pale grasses all the way to the road, arriving there in shreds. Because she had to hide from Catherine the keen contentment that transported her in spite of herself at the view and at the sound of the little plane that seemed to slow down and brush against the tops of the aspens, and at the sight of the lights that were more and more plentiful and shimmering, Nathe got headaches that wiped out the day and thrust her into the dark.

The raspberries ripened. Nathe scratched her arms and legs in the bushes when she went to pick the biggest, reddest ones, crushing them in her hands then flinging them into the sea. She listened to the rumble of the freighters that plied the St. Lawrence. She let herself become drowsy from the heat that made the rails expand. She went back up to the house empty-handed, cleansed of the raspberries' blood and without the fragrant wild roses that she'd gathered and then torn to shreds and tossed into the sea.

What was ridiculous was knowing that she was dull and awkward and being bored to tears at the table by people who thought she was too thin and insisted that she eat everything on her plate. Those people were called Catherine and François Piano.

Why did it take months for Nathe to remember the recipe for a natural death that Ulysses had given her? She had not stopped recapitulating, but she never recapitulated what had happened in the hospital with Ulysses after seeing him in the gust of wind at Catherine's place, or what had gone on, or what had been repeated at Catherine's place. Was it because her soul was connected a little too closely to dread?

When she discovered that she had her period, Nathe remembered Ulysses' recipe. She counted a thousand railway ties and at the thousandth, in the centre of an inextricable tangle of brambles, she dug a little ditch to discard her tampons. When she looked up, she spied through the blossoms of clover and the spikelets of wild millet the plant Ulysses had told her about—devil's tobacco. It was stiff and covered with greyish hairs, had bluish green leaves and a white flower veined in red. Nathe started to harvest its seeds. She now had two reasons to come here, a thousand ties away along a path, following the river water to the sea. "On the left bank," Catherine would have said in her low and lilting voice that mocked everything and that all the students in her watercolour class adored.

It was on a Friday that Nathe had discovered the devil's tobacco next to the railway tracks. Easy to remember because every Friday night, François came from the Faubourg for the weekend. He closed up the shop around four o'clock, arrived at Les Éboulements with a supply of fresh baguettes, wine, sausages, pâtés and cheese. He embraced Catherine and Nathe. Friends were following him. It was just the same on the Friday when Nathe had remembered. François kissed her, turned to Catherine, asked her what had happened to Nathe. Nathe seemed taller, stronger, even more threatening than she'd been five days earlier. Catherine and François burst out laughing, started to show Nathe how to prepare the mussels intended for that evening. First you had to beard them. That meant getting rid of their byssus, "byssus with a *y*, a word you won't hear often in your Nathe life, make the most of it, Nathe dear."

The friends arrived, talked about the war, always the same one, talked about Islam, then about old-age pensions, the mentality of the people in the Faubourg and, finally, brokers and plastic surgery. Nathe had washed the lettuce, whipped the cream for the raspberries, Nathe washed the dishes, Nathe played at being the maid, the servant, and she enjoyed it because it allowed her to be alert to the furious galloping of the wild horses up and down the bank of the river that stopped to sniff Nathe's blood in the bushes. François said again that Nathe had changed, that she'd become threatening as only a woman can. Nathe avoided being alone with Catherine, but Catherine cornered her: "Have you got your period?"

"No, I haven't got my period," said Nathe, keeping her eyes on the glass she was drying.

"You're too calm, what's the matter?"

"Hate is chilling me," said Nathe, staring at her defiantly. In her hands, the glass appeared to be a weapon, ready to kill. What's wrong with me is hate.

Catherine hesitated. She leaned against the door of the fridge and moaned: "I love you so much, Nathe dear, won't you come once, just once, into my bed?" She pulled Nathe to her and pressed her lips onto her mouth. Nathe pushed her away brutally.

Suddenly François appeared in the room. When Nathe saw the inscrutable smile he levelled at her, she was flooded with shame. She would run away. She would run away along the railway. She would go back to Carouges, to the house in Carouges where her mother was probably playing Scrabble while Alexa, at the Orford camp for gifted children, was perhaps learning how to master the game of Go. Nathe would run away, but not before she'd completed her seed harvest. Yes, that's what it was, shame. Nathe howled inside herself to scare off that shame and drive it away. Nathe howled inside herself so that shame would not be the beginning of her destiny.

The next day at dawn, Nathe walked down the footpath to the shore. The sun rose in the middle of the river. Nathe counted the ties. When she got to the raspberries, she wanted to change.

"What are you up to, Nathe, on your knees in the raspberry bushes?" François. Nathe choked back a cry. Why hadn't she seen or heard or smelled him coming? Oh, she wasn't afraid of him. Why would she be afraid of him? Because of the inscrutable smile the night before that had provoked the burning sensation of shame? Maybe. But just behind him, Nathe could make out the red-veined white flower that would put an end to all shame.

"I'm praying, just praying," said Nathe.

"Praying! Who for?"

"I'm praying, that's all."

Nathe freed herself from the raspberries. François sat on a rail and grabbed her hand. "Look at yourself! You mustn't let yourself get scratched like that! At least tell me who you're praying for."

"I'm praying for the Angolans who don't have hands to pray with and for the Algerians who never know when they're going to get their throats cut, that's who I'm praying for."

"Don't shout like that, Nathe, there's nothing shameful about praying," said François quietly. "And there's nothing shameful about becoming a woman, you know." Both Pianos have soft voices. François kept Nathe's hand in his. "I'd like you to teach me how to pray. I'd really like to pray with you."

Nathe didn't like in the least the turn that things were taking and she wanted to go home.

"Wait, stay awhile. Do you know how beautiful you are?"

———————

I had to yank my hand out of François's. I had to run, I had to go down to the shore and run. I had to twist my ankle and fall. And François's eyes had to move back very far inside him, like the eyes of a wild animal, like those of a wolf about to pounce. François had to pounce and grab hold of me. I let the ice carry me away and wash me up on the shore of my life. "Go away."

He had to start moaning that he couldn't take it anymore, that he'd waited so long and what had I done to him? I'd cast a spell. "You won't say anything, I trust you, you know that Catherine mustn't see us together, I'll go up first, I love you so much I know you'll understand me."

He moved away, dancing along the railway ties on his moccasined feet. I washed in the icy water of the river. I collected more devil's tobacco seeds. You only need thirty to kill an adult, I already had enough for four. To kill four. To kill four adults. The sky suddenly turned dark. One of the best moments in life, if you don't want to die, is located between the flash of lightning and the peal of thunder. The visible event happens long before the audible one. That delay between the visible and the audible is never exactly the same, and there is no constancy in the relationship between them. It would be impossible for me to tune my violin during the storm because it's unthinkable to put any order at that moment into the relations between the sounds. The storm burst and the lightning fell straight into the river. Nathe stayed sitting on the rails because she thought that metal attracted lightning. She pictured herself burnt to a crisp on the rails and her courage came back. Finally, her mind took off and rose up above the troposphere where she created that being outside herself to whom it was impossible to speak because it was outside and because it had neither eyes nor ears nor sex.

Catherine was worried sick. She insisted on tucking in dear little Nathe after she'd given her a scalding herbal tea. "Go away!" howled Nathe. François came running. Catherine and François exchanged a look of hatred.

———————

Nathe couldn't bring herself to do it, to drop the tiny seeds of devil's tobacco into the evening tisane or the morning coffee. She watched the Pianos breathe, she thought to herself that they wouldn't be breathing anymore. They lay down on mattresses to wait for shooting stars, she thought to herself that they'd never see them again. They sang, too. She liked their voices so much. And laughter, she loved their laughter. Words: she liked the words they taught her because they were real, like the byssus of mussels or the chalazae of eggs. Salad: she liked the escarole that they liked. The blue of the sky, and the pink, orange, mauve, lavender, magenta, lime green, sage, chartreuse that they liked. Trees too, they liked trees and birds and fish. They liked everything in the world, and Nathe was a fragment of the world that they loved. What to do? Nathe did nothing. She'd have had to crush the deadly seeds and drop them into her own bowl as well as theirs.

They returned to the Faubourg. Nathe went back to the shop, climbed upstairs, Catherine held her in her arms, kissed her face, opened her lips. Nathe didn't stop her. François drove her to the other side of the river, kissed her face, opened her lips. Nathe didn't stop him. The day of her mother's departure arrived. She walked out of her violin lesson, crossed the street, went up to the Pianos'. She made the coffee herself. Served it. But her father rang the doorbell. Time to go to the station.

Fugitives

Nathe would know tomorrow if the Pianos had died a natural death. She managed to get her dead leg under the covers, wondered vaguely why her mother had taken along a mink that she'd hadn't worn since the dawn of time, any more than her diamond ring, in fact, and fell asleep. Soon it would be dawn.

BORIGINE

W HEN SHE REALIZED that the gentle, familiar murmur enveloping her came from other passengers'
telephone conversations, Émilie congratulated herself for refusing the cellphone that Thomas had urged her to take
and for making him swear that under no circumstances would
he try to contact her in Borigine. Once the train had crossed the
bridge and reached its cruising speed, Émilie closed her eyes and
tried to follow the rhythmic pattern created by the rumble of the
train and the joints of the rails. One to five, twice; one to five and a
quarter, three times; one to three, once; pause, inhale, hold the
breath, let it go, exhale slowly. She counted up to thirteen, thirteen years, the age of Nathe. At the end of the exhalation, Émilie
tightened her diaphragm, then released it as she'd learned to do
when she was a dancer, then let her ring slip off her finger and into
her purse.

She could admit everything. She wasn't going to Borigine, she
would never go to Borigine, she had cancelled Borigine, she was
deserting: what an act! She could barely make out when the performance, her performance, had started. She pushed down deep
inside herself the face of François Piano. He had nothing to do
with the act that she'd created for herself. She would think about

him when she was even farther from Carouges, when Nathe's and Alexa's antennae were down for the night.

Ever since the night when Danielle Simard had told her about Thomas's affair with a girl the same age as his own daughters, "closer to Nathe's age than Alexa's," what a great act she'd made up for herself! The big news Danielle had heard from Claudine Patry, who'd heard it from her husband, Jean Patry, who'd heard it from a colleague of Thomas's, each confidant, male or female, having sworn to take that secret to the grave. On the night of September 11, 2001, Émilie had agreed to go with Thomas to the Patrys'—the Simards were already there and the Towners would arrive a little later—because Thomas had been obnoxious with Alexa. Émilie feared that Thomas would be even more insufferable with Alexa as the wave of panic that had swept the United States in the aftermath of 9/11 was gaining ground, crossing the borders into Quebec and the city of Quebec itself and then Carouges, a suburb of Quebec, threatening even the tenuous equilibrium of the Saint-Arnaud family, especially since one of its members—in this case Alexa, the eldest, an exceptionally gifted girl who at the time was living through a little hormonal drama that was impeding the growth of her breasts—was stubbornly taking a stand against any coalition, the coalition of Good or the coalition of Evil.

"Closer to Nathe's age than Alexa's," as Danielle Simard, who was in the habit of never looking at anything but the neck and chin of whomever she was talking to, so that they were convinced they were the ones who didn't come up to her short stature, had repeated three times to Émilie as she turned over the pork chops and the lamb shanks on the gas barbecue on the Patrys' deck, by the light of anti-mosquito torches and citronella lamps. Fascinating, what her fake fingernails put her through just so she could hold on to a fork, an activity that set off the course of her body's entire nervous system and made erotic even her pronunciation: "Closer to Nathe's age than Alexa's."

The Patrys, Émilie recapitulates, have a deck and a barbecue, the Simards have a terrace, a barbecue and a pool, and the Towners have a spa and a barbecue, while the Saint-Arnauds have a garden where the smoke from a barbecue, the chlorine fumes from a spa or pool, will never mingle in the shadows of the apple trees, tamaracks and lilacs, or of the cedar hedge, as long as Émilie Saint-Arnaud—I mean myself—is alive there. It's that big *myself* that digs its heels in, stubbornly refusing barbecue, spa, above-ground pool and background music—I nearly forgot the background music, Émilie giggled—that Émilie Saint-Arnaud—again that big *myself*—wants to get rid of. She doesn't want to know herself anymore. She wants the din of snowmobiles, Sea-Doos, lawn mowers, chainsaws, leaf blowers and skateboards to ring out for her someday like a national anthem that will have her in tears whenever she hears it and at the same time will confirm her status of the well-adapted immigrant from the interior. Someday, Émilie promised herself, I want to walk with a mauve drink in my hand onto the imported Brazilian flagstones of my neighbours' patios, toenails glossy with bright red polish, and to dance as if I've always known poolside choreography by heart and, I would add, without knowing that I know it. Awareness of my acts makes me keep tabs on them and deprives me of the full pleasure of those acts. My thinking, Émilie mused, has become a kind of thinking outside my acts. More and more, my thinking has lost touch with my acts as the scrutiny of my acts has increased, making them seem stranger and stranger to me. I want to be done with the immigrant identity that stops me from being at one with the universal magma of acts.

Some night at midnight when the moon is full I want both to desire and to let myself glide naked and in a state of grace into the

Towners' spa, under the excited gaze of the Patrys and the Towners, to be given a massage of the sacrum without clenching my jaws. I want to be truly dazzled by the flames of candles that smell of mango and passion fruit. I want to be an impassioned person, avid and insatiable. I never want, thought Émilie ironically, to be obliged to hide a jar of Metamucil or oat bran in the back of a cupboard, or to hang around for one more second gazing at the master of instant oatmeal, Mister Quaker, while I watch lumps form in the pan. Alas, achieving that ideal would mean rooting out the surveillance posts that have proliferated in my brain ever since I suffered a series of unexplained and inexplicable fainting spells. Never could an affair of Thomas's, or ten or twenty affairs, set off such a break between my life, my thoughts and my deeds, it's pointless to go over that again. At no time did it occur to me to confide to Mister Quaker about that affair, when he was hounding me to find out more about the state of my conjugal relations. In Quaker's mouth, "conjugal relations" always makes me think of "oral hygiene."

———————

When Émilie told her therapist after a few scathing sessions that she'd christened him "Mister Quaker," he hadn't caught the allusion. She'd suggested he check out the cereal section of the grocery store, where he could easily find the portrait of Mister Quaker, master of a useful habit that, to put it bluntly, facilitates bowel movements. Thanks to her skill at giving random answers to American tests adapted to the context of Carouges by a team of experts from the Hôpital-Dieu, Émilie had earned herself twenty hours of fully refundable therapy with Mister Quaker. The notion of randomness, according to Émilie's use of the word, meant shaking up the tiles for a game of Scrabble, then drawing one letter from the plastic bag that would point to the answer to be invented when an elaborate response was called for. In an objective test, it was enough to play the game of no *i*'s, no *o*'s. If the question contains neither an *o* nor an *i* in its formulation, the answer was yes. One or more of either, no.

When her therapy began, with tests replaced by an interactive relationship, Émilie changed her method. She borrowed their story from the heroes of *General Hospital*, an American soap that her sick leave, authorized by the Hôpital-Dieu team of neurologists, had introduced her to, whose daily episodes she had followed while fearing that Thomas or Alexa would catch her *in flagrante*. "What? You're watching . . . *that!* Mama!" Alexa would have howled. Her dread of Alexa's amazement made Émilie feel guilty and doubled her excitement at finally letting herself be slowly caught up in the descending spiral where reality clearly becomes the script you haven't decided on but have finally agreed to. Little by little, Émilie had started to believe, yes, and she clearly recalled being conscious that she had started to believe, and that she told herself at the time that it operated exactly like faith. It was a slow contagion that only her diligence at the daily appointment made possible. She also recalled telling herself that it was in the same way that she'd believed in the world of Aiguebelle as a child and then stopped believing in it; that she'd believed in dance and then stopped believing in it; that she'd believed in her life in Carouges and was now ceasing to believe in it. After three months of diligence, she would see everywhere—in the street, at the bank, a restaurant, the grocery store—she would see suddenly materialize one of the characters from *General Hospital*, to bestow on the world a transparency and stability that she hadn't experienced since Aiguebelle.

Never, absolutely never would Émilie have confided to anyone what she devoted an hour to every day, not really understanding why, given that the drop in her mental energy was all the same accompanied by the tremendous discovery that reality was a question of diligence. She would have died of shame. Shame of what? Émilie didn't know what she would have been ashamed of had Alexa or Thomas caught her falling asleep without a thought for them but shedding tears over the tragedies in *General Hospital* as if they were her own. Still, it bothered her: ashamed of what? She would have liked to ask the question, not publicly but privately, of all the men or women like her who isolated themselves for their daily date with *General Hospital* and who panicked at the thought of missing it. If Stéphanie had still been of this world, Émilie would quite simply never have discovered *General Hospital*. But Stéphanie was no longer of this world and *General Hospital*, that stable and punctual other world, once a day relieved the anxiety that was eating away at Émilie as she realized that from now on her destiny was nothing but submission to the fact that her own acts, including the desertion of those acts, which is to say her fainting spells, were indeed the fruit of her own efforts at scriptwriting.

Still, he was a nice man, the therapist, and unlike Émilie he hadn't taken ballet lessons from early childhood until adolescence, and modern dance from adolescence till adulthood. His body had stayed diapered and swaddled on his mother's back. He hadn't had an older sister to drag him from the library to the dune at Petit-Pilat with a pile of books to devour and legs and bum sunk into the sand. Mister Quaker's mind, Émilie had judged from the very first session, was as shrivelled and dried out as the flower buds whose growth and opening had been brought to a halt by a late frost or a premature journey in a refrigerated truck. For Émilie, Mister Quaker had tossed a salad composed mainly of self-esteem—which Émilie had understood was a common variety of cabbage—and seeds of personal growth. Of course, if Émilie refused to co-operate by picking at her food, if she continued to see herself as omnipotent, her fainting spells weren't about to stop. Mister Quaker wanted Émilie to assess her resistance to healing on a scale of one to ten. Was she aware of that resistance? Resistance, co-operation—what was he getting at? Was he recruiting for some army or sect? Quaker wasn't quick on his skates. He hated allusions. He hated leaps into the history of the world, he never zapped his own *idée fixe* and he could only tune to one station at a time. During the session on her heightened coefficient of resistance, Émilie hadn't insisted because she'd just thought of *desertion*. Her fainting spells were desertions. She was a deserter. Or a desertress? Quaker had grumbled that he wasn't paid to deal with words like that.

In spite of her allergy to interactive methods, Émilie decided to put an end to her role-playing and she informed Quaker of her wish: "I'd like you to help me put an end to my acting. Let me explain: those fainting spells of mine have no origin except the acting that was set off by a false move, you see, as if you'd made a false move that turned on your windshield wipers and at the same time locked the lever that would let you stop them."

"If you absolutely insist on treating me like an idiot, I'll see to it that your therapy is quite simply stopped," replied Quaker, surprising Émilie, who had finally decided, after eight sessions of bad faith, to ask quite sincerely for a little professional help. Émilie had apologized profusely. She'd never intended to wound Mister Quaker. It was a misunderstanding caused—perhaps but without a doubt—by cultural differences. Poor Mister Quaker! He always had to row against the current of the pointless activities he called scooping up clouds. Thomas, maybe because he often gave in to random thoughts, would have called it nitpicking. Quaker: "You must feel. Don't think, feel. Try to be aware of moments when you feel that it's your deepest self that is the motor of your actions."

Émilie still made an absurd effort to become aware of something without thinking about it, then she gave up. "I'm trying to find those actions you talk about. What actions? My actions?

Eating? Drinking? Washing? Sleeping? Lining up columns of figures? Balancing receipts and expenditures? Do those actions need my deepest self if they're to be accomplished? Blinking? Breathing? How deeply?" And she thought: "Fuck you, Quaker, you and your irrigated colon, fuck you, asshole."

Her head was filling with filthy words and insults that didn't show on her face or in her actions, just as, in the days of ballet lessons, before the days of modern dance, she danced with the grace and smoothness of swans, emblem of toilet paper, letting nothing show of the cruelty of swans that can kill a dazzled child who believes they're gentle. Émilie got so far as to think that the waves of insults giving way in her like a breakup and creeping into her head were the sign of a "deeper self" that was extremely violent, a violence that wanted the extermination of . . . of whom, of what? She couldn't have said, but that violence was diffracted through her connections with telephonic and electronic robots that she insulted enthusiastically, and with her so-called nearest and dearest, with Alexa, with Nathe, with Thomas. Since Émilie was hoping to find some truth—or should she say *some mechanism?*—that would help her emerge from her role-playing, she was prepared to admit that there was something inside her that was nothing but savagery, war and barbarism—three words that summed up her genesis and that of humankind.

Poor, poor Nathe, who saw her sweet and tender mother's deepest self as the silent heart of a swan sailing calmly across smooth, still water with her babies between her lovingly folded wings. Poor Nathe, who thought that her mother was on her way to Borigine. Émilie regretted her irony, regretted that she'd lied to Nathe, to Alexa, to Thomas, to everyone. Oddly enough, that regret was soft and affectionate. It did more than make her sad, it moved her too.

Émilie went back to counting the movements of the train along the tracks. "So you switched from dance to accounting. I'd like to understand how that happened," Mister Quaker had said pleasantly, so pleasantly that Émilie had wondered if he'd turned on a hidden tape recorder under his armchair. He didn't know that dancers are continually counting, counting steps, counting beats, counting and counting the bars; he didn't know that musicians also count, count sounds, noises, slides, shocks, they try to penetrate the rhythmic structure of every sound phenomenon; he knew nothing about how sounds are reflected through physical membranes, he didn't know that the body's organs are wrapped in membranes to which sounds are transmitted, didn't know that while his voice thrilled his fiancée, it gave his patient cramps. So much for *process*, so much for *development*, so much for the *path*. She had stopped dancing because her body—if it is with one's body that one dances—had become deaf, as deaf as Stéphanie's mind and body at the end. Or was it she, Émilie, and not her body, who'd become deaf? Was she the one who could no longer hear her own body dancing? She couldn't even determine whether she'd become deaf one day or if she'd been born deaf. Her obsession with dancing could have been a development in congenital deafness, who knew? They don't tell us anything. They know everything, but no one is ever informed.

For instance, Émilie thinks to herself, I know that several times someone saw Thomas with a young girl the age of Alexa or Nathe. I was told. I know all about it. And yet I'm not informed and I have no intention of becoming informed. Another thing: what is the deep self that was shaken up by the images of the collapse of the twin towers in New York a year ago? What is the self from which emerged a kind of trance that ended in my mouth with a triumphant cry: "At last!" What conflict had just been resolved in the eyes of my deeper self, so far away, so foreign, for whom I sought to develop such great esteem? I haven't stopped looking, stretching out those solitary games of Scrabble—what an ice jam the collapse of those towers had broken up in me. If Nathe hadn't been sick that day, I would have started to dance and sing, but I stifled that incomprehensible moment of personal frenzy to get in tune with the general horror and fury. That same evening, when Danielle Simard told me about Thomas's supposed affair, I had to hide another quirk—my insensitivity to hearsay and malicious gossip. That Thomas can do what he feels like, I didn't tell Danielle. I said nothing. I looked at her as if I'd become the superstar fish in an IMAX aquarium, opening and closing its mouth, letting out a rosary of three-dimensional air bubbles. Danielle will have been able to tell her husband, who'll have told the Patrys, that the shock had left me speechless, transfixed in front of the pork chops and lamb shanks. I can hear her now: "Wasn't it crucial to let Émilie know so she could warn Thomas that tomorrow morning he could be arrested for sexual abuse of a minor?"

As for me, I say that savages aren't naked, only nudists are naked, and I won't budge from that position, declared Émilie for herself. For who else? She turned towards the window. The reflection of her face looked a hundred years old. If her brother, Antoine, saw her in such a state of dilapidation he'd drive her straight to the hospital. She put on some lipstick. It only accentuated her pallor. She rubbed it off. And having wiped the stuff off her lips, she thought about Carole Monty, because Carole Monty always wiped the lipstick from her sister Stéphanie's lips when Stéphanie came in from her nocturnal expeditions. It was the first thing Carole did when Stéphanie came in via the college fire escape early in the morning. She rubbed the lipstick off Stéphanie's lips as if they were her own. Carole Monty had got hold of Stéphanie, of Stéphanie's body and soul, she'd made a double for herself out of Stéphanie. To hell with her.

Émilie struggled against the gush of Monty images, but the reel of film where she could see Carole Monty wiping lipstick off Stéphanie's lips had started to move in the projector. If you only needed, thought Émilie, to know once and for all what it is that memory files away, what it is that sets off the projector and launches the projection of scenes you'd like to be rid of forever no matter what, if you just had to know the mechanism in order to prevent it from starting at will or to order it to start or stop at will, you wouldn't have to use diving gear to plunge in search of some supposed deep self. Understanding the mechanisms of memory is unproductive because that understanding will never reach the age of the overall memory of the world events that every person inherits like an inaccessible maelstrom implanted and nurtured in each one's cells. And neither will such activities—cloud-scooping, nitpicking—ever be able to help Alexa, among others, to get rid of the supposed memory of her own birth when she was drowned in broken-hearted tears. No one can know better than I do to what point Alexa's birth was an exception in the history of births, to what extent only softness, silence, light and peace greeted her birth. What to say to Alexa? Why wouldn't Alexa have inherited a memory of other tragic births, as births actually are in thousands of places on the planet, let's say in Sudan, let's say in Rwanda, let's say in the Algerian countryside, let's say everywhere that populations are dying of hunger, of fear, of AIDS, dying of death and executions, dying, quite simply dying?

If she wanted, Émilie could also rid herself of the Monty and Co. reel, she could relax, distance herself and watch it unwind the way she often did during the night, when she was aware within a dream that she was dreaming. In the same way she often did in life, when she was aware that she was living. When she danced, that she was dancing. When she watched TV, that she was watching TV. But never when she was doing bookkeeping that she was bookkeeping. And always, during her sessions with Mister Quaker, that she was finding a way to put an end to what she called her role-playing. It was enough, Émilie resolved, to move to the very back of my mind's screening room, to bind myself to my seat even if, unlike Ulysses, I don't have a whole crew to help me consolidate the knots and speed up the unwinding of the Monty and Co. reel.

We are in Aiguebelle. Summer 1976.

Stéphanie has just turned fifteen, Émilie thirteen, Antoine eight. All their friends have already left the city for the family cottage where they will spend the summer. The Dumonts don't have a cottage because they prefer to take trips. They save their money for trips. Lakeshores crowded with people whose "hairy legs" (Stéphanie) they wish they hadn't seen, they don't like.

"We're snobs and proud of it," says Stéphanie.

"What's a snob?" asks a worried Antoine.

"It means that Mama and Papa and us don't have the same tastes as other people," explains Stéphanie patiently.

Later, Antoine sings softly: "We're the snobbity-snobs, we're the snobbity-snobs!" Papa slaps him. Why does Papa slap him? To teach him that a snob doesn't know that he's a snob. He is, and that's that. He couldn't say that he is. Antoine never learns what you mustn't repeat to the parents. So he gets slapped. Logical.

Until the day when they will set out on their trip—to Virginia this year—planned for July 16, the three Dumont children spend part of the morning either on the violin (Stéphanie and Antoine) or dancing (Émilie). For Antoine, a little math before noon. They spend their afternoons on bikes, their evenings catching fireflies. They always have books in the baskets of their bikes, and each has a jar with holes in the lid for bumblebees. They occupy the dune at Petit-Pilat from where you can see trains coming and going.

They draw maps in the sand. Map of the galaxy. Map of the earth, the continents, North America, the Great Lakes, the St. Lawrence River; maps of smaller rivers, map of Aiguebelle, map of the roads that leave from Aiguebelle the way that dendrites extend from nerve cells; map of the town of Aiguebelle crossed through by the Muddy River and a map of the Black Blood hill; and finally, this is where they are, the three Dumonts, sunk in the sand at Petit-Pilat, chewing licorice—red because they don't like black. There they are under their sun hats, absorbed in their books. When a crow or a tern flies across the sun, Antoine says: "Tern or crow?"

Stéphanie and Émilie reply in unison: "Tern if it's white, crow if it's black."

Antoine: "But the shadow's always black anyway!"

"Anyway!" reply the two sisters, as if they were saying "Amen!" without taking their noses out of their books.

So Antoine said, "Tern or crow?" and it was Carole Monty whom no one had heard arrive.

The three Dumonts looked up and shaded their eyes with one hand so they wouldn't be dazzled. At first they thought they were seeing an old woman who looked as if she had a halo of white hair fluttering in the air. They thought it might be their grandmother Blanche, who'd surprised them by coming from Victoria to see them, wearing white pyjamas with big pockets in which she stuffed her hands. Then they saw that she was barefoot, they saw her bike at the top of the dune, they saw the fringes and beads sparkling on her flowing shirt, and they realized that it was some girl or other who was passing by.

She said, "Hello!" They didn't like people who call out "Hello!" to just anyone. She said, "Don't even think of answering, that would hurt my feelings." She started to laugh because she thought she was so brilliant. The three Dumonts had plunged back into their books, but they weren't reading, they were barely breathing, they were refusing to share their dune with anyone. "My name is Carole," said the girl. She went up to Stéphanie's bike. "What's in the jar?" Under their hats the three Dumonts didn't miss a single move the girl made. "I got here on the train from Quebec yesterday at noon," said the girl, who didn't seem intimidated by the barricade of the three Dumont heads. She took her hands out of her pockets and sat down beside Stéphanie. She rolled up the hem of her pant legs to her thighs, as if she thought she was at the beach, and she started to act like the teacher of a slightly moronic class. She spoke only to Stéphanie, in a sing-song voice that emerged from lips which looked slightly mauve, and her blonde, nearly white hair, and her ring, a cat's eye, that she wore on her index finger. "Let me explain. You know the Monty garage, you know where it is, with the gold-coloured garlands and the shiny red icicles around the cars for sale? It belongs to my grandfather and my uncle. I'm going to work there till August doing bookkeeping with my grandmother Monty. If you think I'm doing that because my parents are poor, you're mistaken, they're rich, but they're sick of watching over me. They've decided to turn me over to my grandparents. What does your father do?"

Antoine committed his first mistake by replying: "He does things with instruments."

"Oh, he's a musician, I love musicians," Carole Monty concluded, snapping her fingers and wiggling her hips to a tune that only she could hear.

Antoine's second mistake: "We're snobs," he announced, trying to meet Stéphanie's gaze. When he couldn't, he burst out laughing. And since he was laughing all by himself, he couldn't stop. And since no slap came to punish him, he laughed until he cried, rolling in the sand.

"Is he your brother?" Carole asked Stéphanie. She gestured vaguely at Stéphanie's hair, decided not to touch it, took the book out of her hands, read the title and the author's name, *The Odyssey of Homer*, handed it back. "I've read every book by Roald Dahl," she said.

Antoine had got over his fit of laughing. He committed his third mistake: "No, he isn't a musician, he's an ear doctor! He puts *doctor's* instruments in people's ears."

"Oh please, Antoine!" sighed Stéphanie, exasperated.

And that was it! Too late, Carole had heard her voice and Carole realized that she could make short work of Stéphanie. She lowered her voice to ask if she was familiar with Pink Floyd. The words "Pink Floyd" came out sounding like ancient Greek. Pink Floyd isn't ancient Greek, you know. And Carole's voice narrowed down, as if it were trying to find a way through the fence. "Have you ever made love? You have to do it as early as possible. It calms you down. Have you ever smoked? I'll show you how." She took a ratty-looking cigarette out of the pocket of her saint's jacket, lit it, shielding the lighter flame with her hand to protect it, inhaled deeply, held the smoke in her lungs, and offered the cigarette to Stéphanie. She took the joint—it was a joint, the smoke from the joint was travelling down towards the wild roses at the bottom of the dune—and slowly mashed it in the sand before diving back into her book.

"I get it," said the Monty girl, laughing with her voice that had become hot and burning and taking back the extinguished joint. "You can't do it in front of your brother and the other one, like, your sister maybe, or your cousin? My parents have never minded smoking in front of me, but now they wish I didn't, and they ship me off to my grandparents because they don't think there's any grass in Aiguebelle. Okay, have it your way. I'm Carole Monty and I'll be at the Monty garage six days a week. If you want to see me alone, without the others, that's the place. Actually, I can't stand children. Bye." She climbed up the dune, stepping backwards in her own footsteps. At the top of the dune, she put her shoes back on, hopped on her bike, and shouted "Ciao!" as if she were on intimate terms with a Venetian gondolier.

Antoine and Émilie watched her disappear in the direction of the locust trees. "Bye bye, frog legs, bye bye, toad spit," hissed Antoine, unscrewing the lid of his jar to send his bumblebees in pursuit of Carole. Stéphanie was still glued to her book.

"Stéphanie?" Émilie called to shake off the sensation of paralysis that had taken over her legs. Stéphanie didn't react.

It went on. Antoine tossed his jar and it rolled all the way into the rose bushes at the bottom of the dune. He put his shoes back on, then he in turn called Stéphanie. "Stéphanie?" The light formed an icy spiral under Émilie's forehead. "I want to go home," said Antoine.

"Go by yourself," snapped Stéphanie.

"Mama says you aren't supposed to leave me all alone," said Antoine.

"Mama doesn't want, Mama's afraid, Mama this, Mama that, put your hat on! Why did you take off your hat?" asked Stéphanie with a harshness that neither Antoine nor Émilie had ever heard before except in the voice of their father.

Antoine bit his lips and told her bravely: "How do you know I haven't got my hat on, you aren't even looking at me?" But he whimpered that he had a stomach ache.

Stéphanie stared vacantly in Émilie's direction. "You take him."

Émilie pulled her legs out of the sand, which had got heavy, did as she was told and started dragging Antoine and the bikes to the road. Stéphanie would never know anything about Émilie's struggle to the death against the desire to check, by turning around just before the curve that would hide the dune from her, to see if Stéphanie went back to reading or had already gone to join Carole Monty. Émilie lost that battle and turned around. Carole Monty was bent over Stéphanie. Carole Monty sat down beside her. They were so close to one another that Émilie could braid their hair together—Stéphanie's maple syrup blonde and Monty's blonde that was nearly the white of a white butter sauce. Once again the icy spiral behind her forehead blackened the sky. Poor Antoine, he had a terrible stomach ache. Émilie pedalled as hard as she could and cried: "What got into you to have such a stomach ache, what got into you, talking to that girl, what got into you, taking off your sun hat, what got into you, throwing away your bumblebees when they were practically ripe?"

Antoine cried out in turn: "Bumblebees don't get ripe, that's just a story! I can't stand those girls' stories you tell! I don't want to hear one ever again."

That night, Émilie and Antoine looked gloomily at the fireflies blinking in the grass. Antoine declared that he hated fireflies and always would and threw up his supper on the lawn.

Nothing was ever the same again. Stéphanie was always slipping away, using Émilie and Antoine to cover her dates with Carole. A few days later, at the table one night, Stéphanie declared that she didn't want to go to Virginia, that she was too old to go on trips with the family, that she was ashamed of travelling with the family at her age, that she was sick of having to babysit Émilie and Antoine, that she wanted to stay in Aiguebelle where she'd already found a job as a presser in Madame Demers's shop.

"So now you're a presser! That's enough, I don't want to hear another word, you're coming with us," said their father.

"Stéphanie was right to remind us that she isn't a little girl now," their mother pleaded.

Their father started to snicker, repeating word for word what their mother had just said, before he grabbed the breadbasket and sent the *biscottes* flying to the ceiling, shrieking: "Never! Or if I don't count for anything in this house, figure it out yourself, I'm leaving!"

No one hears the front door slam, shaking the house. No one sees Émilie waiting in vain for Stéphanie to slip into her bed and tell her everything. No one sees Antoine let himself die if he really loses the only person who can defend him against typhoons, earthquakes and crocodiles. The family takes a cheerless trip to Virginia. All things considered, Émilie thinks, the Monty reel doesn't show much, doesn't tell much, doesn't reveal a thing to anyone who hasn't experienced Monty's arrival. Nothing could show the enormity of the sadness that Émilie and Antoine overcome by pacing the beaches at dawn in the hope they'll find one of those shells that are filled with the roar of the sea to give to Stéphanie. Whatever they do—whether they pretend to disappear forever in the waves or sacrifice both claws of their lobster, whether they fool around or are absorbed in reading books that don't have anything to say to them now—nothing can shake their sister's black mood, nothing will ever take their sister back to the time before that moment when the indelible shadow of Carole Monty masked the sun at Aiguebelle. To reassure Antoine, Émilie tells him that Carole Monty could never be Stéphanie's real sister. "Besides, you know perfectly well that Stéphanie's leaving for boarding school in September. So in September we'll all lose Stéphanie at the same time—Papa, Mama, you, me and Monty."

Stéphanie had promised to write, she never wrote. She came home at Christmas, she tried to slip into Émilie's bed and tell her about boarding school, but Émilie turned to face the wall. "Do I disgust you or what?" Stéphanie exclaimed.

"No, but you smell different now and it turns my stomach."

"You're jealous, I can see that, you're just jealous."

"Why would I be jealous?"

"Carole, that's why."

"Carole who?" cried Émilie softly. "She dropped out of my life ages ago!"

"Since you don't know, I have to tell you, Carole and I are together at boarding school."

Émilie would be going to boarding school too after the summer holidays. She tried in vain to persuade her parents that Montreal would be better for studying dance. With a heavy heart she boarded the train with Stéphanie in September 1977, without having held Antoine in her arms. Antoine was at his violin lesson. Before the train had crossed the limits of Aiguebelle, Stéphanie had taken out her lipstick, lit a cigarette and transformed herself into a rebel who was stamping her feet with impatience and excitement. At last she would be able to introduce Émilie to the battle she'd begun to wage and would go on waging till the end against the opposing forces that tried to stop people from fulfilling their destiny.

"Émilie, I'm not going to beat around the bush. You'll be shocked and it's best if it's me and not Carole who shocks you. At school there are two clans. The OZ, or occupied zone clan, like Mama, don't panic, and the FZ, or free zone clan, don't get all worked up. Carole and I are the heads of the FZ. We've decided we're tired of being scared, don't panic, breathe through your nose. Not the kind of fear you think you know, not the irrational, childish fear that someday Papa will kill Antoine: he'll never do that, you know as well as I do. Not the fear that Mama will never come out of her coma: she was born in a coma and she'll die in a coma, she's OZ from birth, it's in her genes. Not the fear of thunder or ghosts or wolves. Another kind of fear, a new kind, one that has a hold on you all the time.

"You'll just need this one night on the train to choose your clan. In two hours it will be dark. The train will stop at Terre-Grise and men will board our car. Are you ready to not be scared? Are you ready to prepare yourself to never be scared again? I already know, you'll smell of fear, Émilie, of fear rising in you like a raging sea let loose by a typhoon that will flood your brain; and that fear will really have nothing to do with who those men are who are going to see us and sniff us the way every normal man in the world sniffs the women he sees. Fear is already in your nerves, in your cells, just waiting for a sign before it erupts inside you and takes you over, body and soul, and sweeps you along in its breakup. That's what will strangle you, not the men who're going to board the train at Terre-Grise. If you can't disconnect from the fear that wants to erupt in you at the slightest provocation, you'll never become somebody, you'll always be the embryo you've never stopped being, most of all and even in your tutu and toe shoes. You'll never be anything but inert matter, blind matter that fear will shift at will in the direction it chooses. You'll never be able to start anything that you can finish and sign your name to, you'll be an OZ forever, a zone occupied by fear.

"You have to start right away. Start by telling me how you feel about knowing that soon some men from Terre-Grise are going to board the train, that they're going to sit right there, ahead of us and behind us, that they'll be sniffing us—you and me, you and me and not the two nuns disguised as lay people buried in the prayers in their missals. And you'll see the case of beer they'll set down at their feet. Describe for me what you feel just thinking about it. You're shrugging nervously. Maybe you'd rather be alone? Maybe you'd prefer it if I sat a little farther away, if no one knows I'm your sister? Go on, answer me, choose: do you want me next to you or do you want me to move?"

Émilie felt that the thousands of steel-wool connections in her brain would blow unless she could find out how to get away from Stéphanie. "I don't want anything, I don't want either one, I don't want fear and I don't want the men from Terre-Grise, I don't want to go back to Aiguebelle and I don't want to go to school or get off this train. I don't want anything," she told Stéphanie in a faint voice, so faint that she could barely hear herself.

"See! You see! The mere thought of fear has just killed your love of life, Émilie, your love of life! You're afraid of some vague and murky and slimy idea that's replacing your life, when you get right down to it you're afraid of being raped, Émilie. You know that one of those men could decide to rape us, or two of them or all of them, they could decide to do it, to rape us, decide to shove their stiff cocks into your virginal cunt, or into your virginal guts, or into your mouth or your hands or onto your budding little virginal tits; that they'll twist themselves and empty themselves into your holes; that's what you're afraid of, that's what's got you glued to your seat; and you promise you'll behave till the end of time if you can avoid that rape and another one tomorrow; you'll behave yourself forever because you don't want to suffer pain, to be crushed, disfigured, lacerated, cut up, strangled; you don't want to suffocate, you don't want your dead body thrown onto the railway tracks between Aiguebelle and Quebec, you don't want. You're prepared to not breathe for the eight hours this trip will take and for the eight years that will follow, you're prepared to become a goddamn OZ who'll die without ever breathing freely the air of this world, never feeling at home in the world, never having any destiny except for avoiding what she imagines to be the worst— namely a rape, to have survived a rape, do you know what I'm talking about? Carole and I have decided that we won't let fear have a hold on us and we've founded our own clan. Come on, Émilie! You can breathe, breathe; that's right, breathe deeply, get some oxygen into your neurons, here are the men from Terre-Grise boarding the train, you're afraid, you smell of fear, you're shaking, don't panic, you'll see, everything's going to be fine."

The truth was that Émilie had stopped being afraid since the men from Terre-Grise had boarded the train and settled into their car because they all looked very nice, they'd taken their showers, they'd combed their hair, they were most likely going back to their wives and children after spending the summer battling forest fires. They are, thought Émilie, the brave men who stopped the fires, they're probably worn out, they'll have a drink and go to sleep. Émilie was absolutely not afraid of the brave men from Terre-Grise because they all looked like good papas who would have adopted any lost orphan, wrapped her in blankets and taken her to their wives like a bouquet of wildflowers: look, darling, we're going to adopt this little girl even though she's already a little grown up and even though she dances all the time in a way we don't dance around here. Because Émilie would have gladly danced for the men from Terre-Grise who'd just boarded the train, she would have gladly danced to thank them for their bravery. In fact, Émilie hadn't felt any fear ever since the men boarded the train because Stéphanie seemed to have calmed down.

"Pick one," said Stéphanie.

Émilie thought about Antoine, who was going to be by himself in Aiguebelle. "You aren't Carole Monty and I'm not Stéphanie Dumont," said Émilie. "You don't scare me with your stories about clans in some war film or sex film, war or sex, espionage, war or sex, I'll never be on Monty's side."

"Jealous," said Stéphanie warmly, putting her arm around Émilie's neck. "You know perfectly well that Carole could never be my blood sister." Then hard again: "Out of those men, pick the one you'd like to hate for the rest of your life. Now listen. I'm going to change cars, I'll leave you alone. It's very simple. Instead of gathering dust in fear, make your fear pay off. You're really cute, it will work. Understand? While you think about the money you're piling up, and I can already tell you that you'll pile up a lot as a result of a transaction that you'll agree to that will change your fear to gold, you'll see, you'll feel amazingly free."

"You're crazy," Émilie replied. "It's you I'm afraid of."

"Suit yourself, but I'm telling you, they're filthy rich, it's up to you to make the most of the situation," said Stéphanie. She moved to another car.

The train was travelling through the night and the reel of film had burned. There was nothing more to see. The Monty reel had jammed in Émilie's projector. Now Émilie asks Ulysses' crew to release her from her seat at the back of the screening room. But Ulysses' crew doesn't exist, Émilie, and you're alone in the screening room of your brain. I wonder, Émilie asks herself as she tries to find some warmth by nestling in her mink, I wonder how it happened. For thousands of years matter didn't even have an eye for looking outside. Matter had to work for thousands of years to invent an eye for itself. I don't remember the first time my eyes saw outside. I don't remember the moment when I realized that my eyes could see. But I do remember the moment when my eyes stopped seeing, when my eyes reverted to blind matter because what they saw caused unbearable pain. I am remembering that for the first time tonight, in the Montreal train. I'm not going to Borigine. I'm going to Montreal. And I remember. Papa hitting Antoine, Antoine stretched out on the floor in the garage. I see Papa's shoes and he's kicking Antoine. I hear Papa yelling: "Take this! Take it!" He dragged Antoine to the garage, pounding him with his fists, "Catch," and Antoine fell down. I can see that my father's going to kill my brother. I can see that, that he's going to kill him. And then I don't see anything else. Never. It never existed until tonight, and even tonight, in this train, it doesn't exist, it has no witnesses. I can only hear the toneless voice of Stéphanie who wants to find a way out of the nightmare. "Mama! Your husband is killing your child! Are you going to make a move? Mama! Fabienne! Can you see your husband killing your child!" The body, thinks Émilie to herself, what a strange organ. Deaf. Then suddenly falls sick, faints, catches the ball, catches disease, catches fear of the ball and of disease. Doctor, I've come down with fear. I've come down with the fear of Carole Monty and my sister Stéphanie, those twins.

When we got off the train, Stéphanie showed me the bills, some fifties and a hundred, a triumph. I told her: "If you get caught, you'll have dirtied your name, our name."

Stéphanie sneered. "The business about the name being dirtied is the fear that Mama and Papa, the OZs, are wallowing in. They call it their honour, their pride, fuck them. Do they think we take our names with us when we die? I don't give a shit about words. I'm going to live through it all—words, fries, hot dogs, grease, their triple burgers, everything that oozes; I'm going to swallow it with my tongue, you see, Émilie, and you, you'll have nothing but fear between your teeth and the sound of grinding to feed you while you wait for the crime that each person might have committed, that each person has dreamed of committing, that each person suspends inside himself at night for fear of having committed. Not me, though, never. Oh, I'll hang myself, but I won't be suspended during an investigation that will last a lifetime. You, though, I can already see that you'll actually get a doctorate so you can stay in the occupied zone, where you feel that your holes are safe. And once you've got that, along with the congratulations of the jury, you'll do a post-doc to avoid freeing yourself from fear, and you'll go home framed like your diploma, still afraid of being raped, strangled, left to bleed to death in the alley. I know I'm right, so as far as the Dumont name is concerned, you'll pass it on."

"Every word that comes out of your mouth comes from that Monty girl's book," cried Émilie.

———————

At boarding school it was Carole who ran the business, who found the clients, covered up for the nocturnal outings, who waited at the door to the fire escape, who kissed Stéphanie—she, the pimpette. Neither one of them spoke to me, I was in the OZ clan. Until the day when Stéphanie needed me to take part of her earnings away from Carole. I laid down one condition: Stéphanie wouldn't know the hiding place that I'd invent, would not have access to it for a period of time that I'd decide on. Since I was an OZ stuffed with scruples, Stéphanie could trust me.

What Stéphanie didn't know was that, on the train, I'd chosen from the men who'd got on at Terre-Grise the one by whom I'd have liked to be adopted. And he was the one who came to sit in the seat vacated by Stéphanie. He was the one who told me that he had the impression I was terrified, who asked if he could help me. He was surprised that we hadn't taken a berth since we had to spend the night on this train. "My sister didn't want it to cost our parents too much." I didn't ask him to adopt me. He adopted me. It was to him that I entrusted Stéphanie's money, to Thomas, Thomas Saint-Arnaud, a political science student who'd gone to battle the forest fires around Terre-Grise. Stéphanie's money is still in the same bank account today, in my name. Her daughter will inherit it when she comes of age. Stéphanie Dumont's daughter is Nathe Saint-Arnaud. Poor Nathe, poor Nathe who doesn't know anything, who doesn't know. Neither Thomas nor I has ever worked up the courage to tell her the truth about her birth.

Émilie saw that the train was crossing the river. It was about to pull into the station. Now she didn't have enough time to understand that the collapse of the twin towers had finally made it possible to divulge the secret about Nathe's birth, and that once again she had slipped away by fainting in every corner and by totally losing her head over François Piano. There, she was giving herself permission to think about François. She was far enough away from Carouges that she could say the name of François.

She pushed open the door of the shop, squeezed her way inside, slipped soundlessly between the cages. "Do I hear a fish swimming and trying to find the way into his aquarium?" said François in his gentle, captivating voice. "Come." He took her hand. "Shall we go up?"

They went up, above Catherine Piano's bookstore, which was closed for the summer. "Tell me everything."

Émilie said: "When I was a child I had a sister and we were always clinging to one another."

"Clinging how?"

"Just clinging."

"Just clinging! You must have been afraid of something."

"There was a war on, you see, it wasn't over, it was still being fought, so we thought we'd be raped and cut into pieces unless we clung together. Are you positive that Catherine won't come home without warning?"

"Come here now, come."

François. And again: François. He was going to join her in Montreal. They would have Stéphanie's, sorry, Antoine's apartment to themselves and no one, they would be no one to anyone. Catherine and Nathe would look after the fish and the birds, Nathe would do her homework, Alexa would learn Chinese, Marceline would do the shopping and cooking, Thomas would work at the ministry, *General Hospital* would still be broadcast, suicide bombings would go on, the leaves would keep falling from the trees, the leaders of the Axis of Evil would depart in a caravan with their doctors. Trains, planes, buses and cars would travel in every direction, depart, keep going, come back, but as for them, they would stop, look at one another, press themselves against one another, tell one another everything. Wasn't it ridiculous that Mister Quaker had asked her the same thing—"Tell me everything"—when he wasn't in love with her or she with him, when that request is the most upsetting and the most erotic of all requests? How hungry François was for Émilie's childhood and adolescence! It was precisely that part of Émilie's life that drove him crazy with love, the time when Émilie and Stéphanie clung together to escape from the terror of war, of rape, of being cut into pieces, of death.

"Tell me your deepest secrets, secrets you've never told anyone," said François.

Émilie replied: "I'll have to make them up."

"All right, make them up," said François.

"I should have been a boy," said Émilie, "and I was a girl and Antoine is the boy, poor Antoine."

"Why *poor*?"

"Just because," said Émilie.

That *just because* filled François with tenderness. He enfolded Émilie in his arms, he fed her with a spoon, he did up the buttons on her blouse. "And you and Stéphanie never clung to Antoine against the war?"

"Me, yes, a few times, twice maybe, but Antoine had been raped during the war, so he couldn't cling like the others."

"I don't understand, explain what you mean," François whispered. He filled Émilie's ear with his breathing and kisses.

"I don't know, I don't understand either, all I know is that he was raped during the war and that my father hadn't forgiven him."

"What was your father?"

"A doctor. A bad man and a doctor."

"It's incredible, sometimes, you know, you're even smaller than a little girl, I adore you."

They hadn't yet made love together. In fact, Émilie didn't dream of making love with François. Or rather, she would have liked what she did with him to be called making love.

ANTOINE, SEPTEMBER 13

NTOINE FOUND A PARKING SPACE beside the cathedral, from where he could simultaneously keep an eye on people leaving the train station and follow the traffic in and out of the Queen Elizabeth Hotel, if the hotel was still called the Queen Elizabeth and not the Maracaïbo or the Zen Palace, who knew? Hotels, squares, forums and airports, just like cities, towns and villages, are constantly having their names changed and then changed back to what they'd been before. Nine-twelve p.m. So the train was late. So Émilie didn't have a cellphone. If she did, she'd have let him know.

The Volvo was spotless. Antoine had stopped at the car wash on Resther Street earlier that day. He'd asked for "The Works," at twenty dollars. He'd sat in the glassed-in space designed for customers. His discovery that there were no French newspapers or magazines on the low table and that he didn't recognize any of the car washers had exasperated him. The new car washers were a lot younger than those in the past. They didn't wear high rubber boots or checkered shirts. They communicated with one another only with brief gestures that must be universal but that Antoine couldn't decode. And then the round metal box attached to the cement column on which was written in red felt pen *Pension Fund,* where he liked to drop his tip in big two-dollar coins, had disappeared. Ulysses, because he persisted in working, could have got a job as a car washer instead of a gas station attendant. It would have been less risky.

To chase away the thought that Ulysses was bound to be discovered if he stayed at the gas station, Antoine had gone outside to wait. He'd walked up the street as far as the Laurier station, where he'd bought a box of Clorets that he'd emptied in no time. He sucked the sugar off the flat little tablets and chewed them for barely ten seconds before swallowing them. Great. Fine. Perfect. His anxiety over the fact that Ulysses might get caught had been dealt with. Antoine slipped the empty box into the inside pocket of his windbreaker.

All the letters he'd slipped into that same inside windbreaker pocket and failed to put in the mailbox day after day, so that the contents of those letters finally seemed outdated if not senseless and which he'd ended up putting into the blue recycling box along with all the circulars, came to mind. Letters to Amina, mainly, because she didn't have an Internet connection when she was still living in Montreal. After the abortion. Before she had a new hymen made, before she went back to Morocco. The abortion—Amina preferred to say termination—had been performed on rue St-Hubert, not all that far from the car wash. In fact he'd had the Volvo washed while Amina was having the abortion. In fact he had bought the Volvo for Amina. Let's say that he'd bought it on the day Amina told him she was pregnant by him. It hadn't changed her decision, but when she left the clinic she'd felt like going to an isolated mountain or the shore of an isolated lake, to cry. They'd been crying while they drove and Antoine had decided to keep the Volvo. Immediately after that, Ulysses had dropped from the sky "courtesy of Nathe," to be adopted.

But he'd been thinking about letters, and there'd been at least one more, to the ENT (Ear, Nose and Throat) man. Come on, more than one letter to the good doctor, let's say a dozen different versions of the same letter on the pharmacy letterhead, folded in two in stamped envelopes and slipped into the left inside pocket of the windbreaker, then crumpled and tossed into the blue box along with the newspapers, a dozen letters announcing the news: "Dear Papa, I'm writing after all these years because I finally have proof that I'm not sterile. And by the way, I've bought myself a Volvo with headlight-wipers. Would you pass on these pieces of news to Mama? Thanks."

After he left the car wash, Antoine had tried to find a florist, but as he couldn't locate a parking space he wished he hadn't moved the Volvo and wondered if it would even be appropriate to give Émilie flowers. He could have walked downtown to enjoy the mildness of the air. He could have brought Émilie home by taxi. But he'd kept driving as if he hadn't given up on finding flowers. He'd pictured himself walking down the corridor from the station to Place Ville-Marie, where at least he could have bought a ready-made bouquet, but he remembered how ugly ready-mades are and decided not to. He could have chosen a single flower, a bird of paradise maybe, or a half-dozen or a dozen white roses. White or vanilla, if vanilla was a colour as well as an aroma. They say "champagne." "Champagne roses," that's what they say nowadays. Maybe he could have unearthed a gift, but why should he have to unearth a gift? Anyway, how could he hope to unearth a gift in mid-September from under the piles of pumpkins and the stacks of hideous masks and costumes in garish Halloween colours? Maybe he could have bought a carnival mask, one of those Italian imports made in China and trimmed with beads and feathers, but that wouldn't be appropriate for Émilie if she was sick. Was she sick? Who could predict how Émilie would interpret the gift of a carnival mask? Antoine thought it best to refrain from triggering Émilie's obsession with interpretation and at the same time his own anxiety about Émilie's interpretations.

He turned on the radio and scanned the airwaves in search of a friendly voice. It was best to avoid letting oneself be waylaid by words like "obsession with interpretation." I know all too well how those words operate, thought Antoine. In no time at all they bind you, and the more you resist, the tighter the bonds. He didn't find a friendly voice on any radio station to back him up in his determination not to let Émilie disorganize him—because Émilie had a gift for screwing things up in any organization.

He switched off the radio and got out of the car. Mid-September already, but so delightfully mild that he could have spent the whole night not waiting for anything, not waiting at all. Antoine just stood there on the sidewalk, between buildings, ears strained for the murmur of the city in which he eventually made out the slow undulation of a *basso continuo*, and more and more clearly the rustling of the dried leaves piled up at the foot of the fence surrounding the cathedral lawn. He wasn't thinking about anything. Rather, it was the act of thinking itself that was thinking for him, that had led him to find out why Émilie had given up dance after she'd moved heaven and earth to become a star of contemporary dance. A Greyhound bus pulled up, blocking his view of the station exit. Émilie, Antoine explained to himself, didn't hear the sound score of the world in which she danced, nor did she hear the sound of the instrument that was her own body within that score. She could only see her instrument. She didn't hear it. That deafness to the harmonics produced by her own body made her rush and bump into the walls of the enclosures where she danced. It was the repeated shock of her body against the walls of music that, for her, replaced the acoustic image of her body of which she was deprived.

Strictly hypothetical, of course, thought Antoine, but when the driver of the Greyhound finally turned off his engine, a new hypothesis, this one even more convincing, came to mind. Émilie had stopped dancing quite simply because dancing had become useless to her as soon as she'd escaped from the family authority, when she stopped being a Dumont and became a Saint-Arnaud. Meaning that Émilie had only danced as a Dumont. In other words, the dance stage would block access to her private life. People thought that Émilie wanted to put her body on display, but it wasn't that. The display was a kind of locked showcase in which Émilie took shelter from the Dumonts' break-ins. The proof? Never again did she have the slightest need to display her body on any stage once she belonged to the name of Saint-Arnaud. Antoine promised himself that he'd talk to Émilie about it if he couldn't think of anything else to say to her.

He didn't notice Émilie until he was saying that to himself just as she turned up. He hurried to take her suitcase. She offered her cheek, he did the same, they hesitated, Antoine gave in, held out his other cheek, they kissed. Émilie didn't look as unwell as she'd led him to believe on the phone. Antoine stowed the suitcase in the trunk. Émilie tossed in the mink.

"I had no way to let you know, I'm sorry, I was worried to the bone," said Émilie.

"What about a cellphone? Have you ever thought about getting one? Don't you want one at least when you're moving around?" asked Antoine.

"I never move around," said Émilie, laughing. She fastened her seat belt. "I'm glad, I'm really glad you're here. Tell me, did you have your car disinfected in my honour?" She rolled down the window to let in some air.

Antoine repeated to himself, "worried to the bone." None of the three Dumonts had ever been able to talk like everyone else. Even in Aiguebelle, when they thought they spoke like everyone else, everyone else asked them to talk like everyone else, chided them for not talking like everyone else. It was only when he was speaking English that Antoine was at peace. Often he spoke English in order to get some peace, to avoid being chided for not having the Aiguebelle accent, and when he came to Montreal he spoke English because he couldn't acquire the Montreal accent, and finally he spoke English as often as possible so he'd feel that he talked like everyone else. Worried to the bone: why not? Émilie still had the same blunt way of tackling a subject and cutting short effusions. Within a fraction of a second, thought Antoine, no sooner has Émilie taken three steps in my direction, disoriented me with the words "worried to the bone" and then got to me with the word "disinfected," than the man I know I've become was demolished.

Antoine decided that he wasn't exaggerating. Of course, the citizen who had just been demolished by Émilie's voice had, ever since Amina left, spent a good part of his nights in his pharmacy playing war games online under the moniker Skippy, with citizens who played online every night using the moniker of their choice, but it is by their days and not their nights that men are judged. Antoine wasn't going to let himself be had. He was not going to become, in a flash, an old-style man, an embryonic man, actually, panicked by his heartbeats, racked with cramps that made his stomach churn, looking in vain for the sign to the men's room down the packed corridors of a hospital emergency room, not knowing and worrying about whether he had on matching shoes and socks, a comical and ridiculous man, a man incapable of detachment, incapable of hindsight, feckless, a man caught in a trap and pleading, spineless, a nightmare. And I'm not exaggerating, Antoine tells himself, but he had no idea who it was, inside him, who accused him of exaggerating. Antoine had always defended himself against that anonymous accuser who attacked him from inside. He no longer defended himself. It's impossible, he thought, absolutely impossible to think without exaggeration of the place one occupies in space.

"You're giving me the grand tour, over the mountain," Émilie noted.

How could he be sure that it wasn't him, Antoine, who was interpreting his sister's tone? And why was he among the men who always end up in short pants, in their high chairs, when someone talks to them in a certain tone?

"He thought," Antoine replied, "that you'd enjoy seeing Montreal at night from the lookout. He thinks that every person would like to have a view of the entire city where he or she is going to spend the night."

Émilie shivered and rolled up her window. She moved her seat back and straightened it a notch. "Don't start now, I beg you." She opened the glove compartment but closed it right away. "I beg you," she said again. She added that it was quite enough that Nathe spoke of herself in the third person, enough of Nathe's dual personality and overall views. "Nathe is in the process of creating God, if you can imagine such an invention."

Maybe Antoine should have reacted with a knowing laugh, but instead he noted that the boulevard's girders seemed to be narrower and longer. Émilie suggested that he find himself an ophthalmologist. Antoine finally admitted to himself that he desperately regretted agreeing to lend his apartment to Émilie the dancer. The fact that the apartment had belonged to Stéphanie first had distorted and forced his decision. Basically it was Stéphanie's indelible debt towards Émilie the dancer that had misled him. That debt, he had endorsed without realizing it. Too late. He couldn't imagine where the spineless individual who'd taken his place behind the wheel of the car would find the strength to stop fooling around and back out. There was nothing to stop him from dropping off the dancer at a hotel, any hotel at all, assuring her that he would pay the bill, except that if he decided to do that he wouldn't be able to give her his reasons, reasons that weren't really reasons. My reasons for wanting to drop the dancer, Antoine thought to himself, are nothing but a mixture of anxieties and infantile fury that won't subside until her visit is over—a brief stay, she said, but without explaining exactly what "a brief stay" meant. I should have understood, Antoine raged, and reacted right away after her call when, no sooner had I recovered from my surprise at being among the hundred or so people whose number the ex-dancer possessed and had chosen to help her, I started to scrutinize every square centimetre of every cupboard, closet, shelf and shelf unit, to sort and bury in the cedar chest inherited from old Blanche the slightest trace of Stéphanie. Instead of understanding and reacting, I was caught up in a frenzy to erase every sign and vestige. More always materialized, despite the horrendous but obligatory garage sale imposed by Stéphanie. And like some lunatic I kept up my hunt for remains, reproaching myself for not getting rid of the clutter as soon as I bought the apartment.

I'll have to clarify matters. That I didn't inherit Stéphanie's apartment but bought it from her doesn't seem to be clearly established in Émilie the dancer's mind. It's absolutely certain that I'll never be sufficiently lucid about myself to understand why I was so determined to buy that apartment and why, as soon as the papers were signed, I didn't clear the bathroom shelves of the gentle cleansing milk, primordial intensive night cream, tubes of long-lasting lipstick and bottles of witch hazel, and throw out the shells, pebbles, stones, sachets of black, grey, ochre, pink, white, and yellow sand, and mother-of-pearl buttons, and dildos, including one of carved ivory and another in ebony, stunning, from a drawer in the chest. Dump it all into green garbage bags with no concern for the person who would take it away for burying; why didn't I do that thirteen years ago? Not until Émilie asked me to put her up did I discover the clutter that Amina never seemed to notice, Ulysses even less. But once these leftovers were piled into the chest and the chest padlocked, I could have, *should* have realized what an aberration it was to have agreed to take in the dancer and called her back and begged her to give up on the idea of taking shelter here during her brief stay.

I am sorry, thought Antoine, that I call my sister Émilie a former dancer. I'm sorry that I hammer out the word *dancer* as if it were the worst insult, even though I'm still a fan of the kind of dancing Émilie practised before she gave up practising it to become a chartered accountant. As much as Émilie's obsession poisoned my life, so contemporary dance exhilarates me. Antoine hesitated. He was not exaggerating, but did he have to be so solemn, and was it really exhilaration? He forced himself to restrain the flow of his thoughts, he meditated. Cold exhilaration. Icy exhilaration. He doubted now the alleged exhilaration afforded him by contemporary dance performances. Was it Émilie's presence in the Volvo, Émilie in Amina's place and, after Amina's departure, in Ulysses' place, that was making him doubt? More specifically, was it Émilie's private odour, filtering through her clothes, reminding him vaguely of the childhood he'd been part of, that had led to his discovery that the fascination which had him glued to his seat at a contemporary dance performance was only his way of fuelling an enduring resentment that was totally pointless and consequently shameful?

The theory of an enduring resentment was of no interest, except that at the very moment when he was saying this to himself it became glaringly obvious that thinking so was bullshit, since he'd spent years feeding it. You don't feed your ducks, your geese, your hens, your pigs and your goats unnecessarily. Therefore, not his jealousy or his cravings or his resentments either. But which ones? He had, he acknowledged, at the outset of his life envied Émilie for being prey to an obsession that had a tyrannical hold on the entire universe (Aiguebelle). At the time, he felt that only an obsession equal to his sister's could have freed the entire universe (Aiguebelle) from the tyranny of dance. "If you'd wanted to, you would have become a great violinist, you'd have made a name for yourself in the entire world (Aiguebelle) as a great violinist," Stéphanie had said with a hint of reproach on the days that she'd devoted to the inventory of her life. If he'd wanted! Easy for her to say! It was against the resistance of the ENT man that Stéphanie had been able to have Antoine enrolled with her in Madame Bissonneau's class. The ENT man didn't want a queer son. Though Antoine watched himself so that the violin wouldn't turn him into a queer son, he didn't know what exactly to watch. And so he watched Madame Bissonneau's big boobs. In particular, watched so that they didn't brush against him when she corrected his posture or the position of his violin and bow. "I was too afraid of Madame Bissonneau's big boobs."

"And what were those big boobs going to do to you?"

"I don't know, I didn't want to become a queer son."

As her death came closer, Stéphanie would forget what she'd been talking about. "What were we talking about? I wanted to see Nathe so badly, why won't Émilie come with Nathe?" And then: "Antoine, tell me about your last concert again."

And Antoine talked about his last concert to distract Stéphanie when she was thinking about Nathe at the end, when she was delirious, accusing Émilie of stealing Nathe from her. "My last concert," said Antoine, "was one Christmas when I dreamed about the battery-operated helicopter I was going to get, I could already see myself making it fly between the sand and the sky at Petit-Pilat."

"Where Carole Monty appeared in the universe," said Stéphanie.

Antoine was filled with despair. So there would never be another name for Aiguebelle but "the universe" and no project in the universe for a Dumont except to be the greatest pharmacist in the universe. It was futile to protest and denounce what was grotesque about the megalomania they'd inherited as a defect. "I come onstage and I count my steps to the proscenium," Antoine began, "I anchor my feet to the ground at the very centre of the spotlight."

"You were absolutely adorable," Stéphanie interrupted him. "I think back and I cry from nostalgia even though I'm too young to cry from nostalgia. It's true, Antoine, isn't it, that I'm too young to cry when I call up some memory?"

"Once the violin is wedged under my chin," Antoine went on, his head tilted slightly, "I see the four strings coming out of my left ear, then rolled onto the four pegs at the end of the neck. I can see my right hand extended by the bow but, how can I put it, it's inside my head that I see myself, I don't see myself in the auditorium at all, or in the circle of the spotlight, I see my curved wrist move up towards the bridge, I remember that I fear and detest the measure to be played on the open *A* string. The bow has to go up and down the open *A* string. Be careful that the horsehair doesn't touch the bridge. Every time, that measure breaks my heart, makes me fall into the pit of the open string."

"Do you hear 'broken string' at least?" said Stéphanie, laughing through her tears. "Tell me that today you understand that, at that precise moment in your childhood, you were afraid of a broken string, and what is that broken string you were afraid of? You won't die before you've found the answer to that question, right, Antoine?"

"All I can say is that Antoine was split in two to escape the giddiness brought on by the passage about the open string. I can't say that *I* was split in two, you understand, I can only say that *it* was split in two or that *Antoine* was split in two. It's something between him and his double, which suddenly looks like the ENT man, though it isn't Papa's face, I mean yes, it is, but with that gasping, damp and made-up face, old too, and a flash of hatred strikes him down by shredding all the sounds."

"Who strikes down who?"

"I don't know, him or the double, but it's always me. A halluci-
nation maybe. Those four strings that emerged from my skull and
were going to wrap themselves around the four pegs of a violin
have broken. The bow gets away from me and lands at the foot of
the front row. When the bow leaves the light of the spot, Antoine
is no longer divided in two, it's Antoine, it's me."

"You're eight years old, you have perfect pitch, you have the
instinct, the musicality, you've got the memory, and there you
go, it's over, it's lost. For too long I thought that gifts couldn't be
lost. But they're as elusive as fireflies. You sent them after Carole,
remember?"

"No," said Antoine, "they can't have been fireflies, I would
remember."

He never went back to Madame Bissonneau's classes. He taped
his hockey stick and took it from rink to rink. He chased black
pucks, lost one here and there in the deep, blue snow. He let himself fall into the snow, upsadaisy. He learned that he'd been signed
on as goalie for a hockey team without understanding why or how
the black pucks that flew up, that soared above the ice, came to
nest in his glove. "WITH NO EFFORT HE COULD GRAB AN ARROW
IN MID-FLIGHT." ANTOINE DUMONT, SON OF DOCTOR DUMONT,
REMEMBER THAT NAME, in big letters in the sports sections. The
doctor sets fire to the newspaper, throws the lit torch into the fireplace and walks out, slamming the door.

"And that was it for your career as a goalie, right?"

That was it. All that remained was to slump in front of the
TV, to sink twenty thousand leagues under the sea while envying
Stéphanie and Émilie for already being far from Aiguebelle, for
already living their lives. Twenty thousand leagues under the sea
was the refuge from where Antoine was still threatening the universe with imagining an obsession that would bring all the others

to an end. Until the day when he discovered that by smoking a joint here and there, in lanes and in back of sheds, he could hear again the vibrating strings that were an extension of his nerves. The sounds he heard sent him very high above Aiguebelle and guided him through the northern lights to a mirror suspended in space.

"You were dreaming, you little sweetie," Stéphanie had whispered. "It's so beautiful, and was that you, the handsome young man who watched you lovingly as you entered the mirror?"

The ENT man evoked the spectre of reform school while he crumbled soda biscuits into his soup. That was just before the disaster. "How he hates you!" thinks Antoine. "Who's that?" thinks Antoine. "Your father: how he hates you," thinks Antoine. "I'm not so sure," thinks Antoine. "To be hated you have to represent, I don't know, at least the embryo of a threat." At the very moment when he would have been prepared to confide these thoughts to Stéphanie, Stéphanie entered into the storm of her death throes.

"Ever since I told you that Nathe was in the process of creating God, you haven't said one word, I wonder if you've even taken a breath, have you got apnea or what?" Émilie was growing impatient.

They were nearing the lookout. There was one parking space left, very tight, squeezed between two big silver grey Pathfinders. Émilie refused to get out, she remembered every detail of this city, this view, she loathed the lingering smell of rut that came down from the paths on the mountain and turned her stomach. Anyway, those paths have been meeting places for homosexuals for a good twenty years now, and the lookout is for tourists. What did Antoine want to prove to her? Why was he hanging around? What exactly was he afraid of? Why didn't he say anything? "Come on," she said, "answer me: if you were told that you had just one year left to live, what would you do?"

Why this cross-examination? Couldn't she be quiet for two minutes, just long enough for them to see a little more clearly what it was that was trying and refusing to be connected again between them? But that was unfair, she'd been quiet for at least seven minutes. But then he wasn't unfair, either, because her silence was merely the expectation of a response, therefore stressful, therefore violent. "I would look at the twinkling city lights from the top of the mountain," said Antoine.

He got out of the car. A year to live, that wasn't something that floored him. It had taken Stéphanie four months, and those four months had lasted an eternity. He thought that he would need only ten days. Ten days would be more than enough, Antoine told himself. He filled his lungs with the mild and muggy air that was spreading a light mist over the city. He got closer to a small swarm of Asians who were searching the night with their binoculars and going into raptures. When they became aware of Antoine, they rushed to pile into a Caravan that started right away. If I were genuinely crazy, Antoine realized, I wouldn't understand that the flight of those tourists wasn't caused by my appearance, and the coincidence of my appearance and the packed agenda of some Asian tourists would have switched on my madness. If that crosses my mind, Antoine also understood as he chewed at the right side of his tongue, it's because I have been crazy, crazy enough to think that I was the true object of the ENT man's hatred. Ten days to live: I'd want them in November, he mused, I'd get the Volvo tuned up by the Armenian at the garage on the corner of Van Horne where Ulysses works. While I waited for the car to be ready, I'd drop in on the notary and leave everything to Ulysses. Then I'd phone Jérémie to tell him about his new title—Ulysses' guardian. He would say: "Are you crazy?" Jérémie always thinks that I'm going crazy. I would say: "If anything happens to me." I would reclaim my car from the Armenian. I'd pack the trunk with groceries, get onto the Laurentian Autoroute, drive through the

La Vérendrye park, the inland seas, and I'd speed northwest all the way to Louvicourt.

Antoine pictured himself loading groceries onto the rowboat. The river seemed as peaceful as a sated snake, but it was bare and on guard, like a wild goose that had waited too long before going south, that had lagged behind, its gaunt face hollowed by night and long eyes deepened by the kohl of bulrushes. Putt, putt, we'd have filled the gas tank and gone back up the river and docked on its anonymous island before sunset. The water would be low. The water is low. Antoine wonders what the squatters will have spared. It would surprise him if they'd been able to lift and carry the cast iron stove down to the dock. The only thing Antoine really wants is that the squatters haven't set fire to the chalet, or shit on the walls, or broken all the windows. He's not asking for much, sure that there'll be at least one broken window and maybe some blood on a mattress. One thing is certain, the door won't have been smashed with an axe, because he hadn't locked it—precisely so that squatters would feel they were expected and welcome. Ten days, but one has already gone by. He'll make a fire in the cast iron stove if there's any wood left. If not, he'll go back on the river, putt, putt, all the way to the beaver dam. He'll take some dry wood right out of their lodges. The next day, rain will start to fall, colder and colder, and finally snow will fall into the water, the water will be more and more cold and glossy, smooth black lacquer confusing the issue with manes of thick, slow water weeds, I'm getting carried away, thought Antoine. After ten days the water will be seized by cold. Slowly, lovingly, he repeated to himself that the water will have been seized, and that gave him a demented urge to be seized as well.

He tried to meet Émilie's eyes through the windshield. With her head thrown back on the headrest, Émilie was dozing or pretending to, filled with herself like a ripe fruit bursting with its colour, its taste, its juice. The body that she'd tormented day and night from the time when she'd taken her first steps—which had been nothing but dance steps—until she turned twenty-two; the body that she'd trained and shaped without let-up, that she spied on and that spied on her as if they were two bodies in one; mirrored walls; the continual gliding of ballet slippers; the pounding of pointes, the creaking and loud protests, falls and blisters, warm-up of muscles and adjustment of fabrics; fasting and diets at the ages of eight, nine, thirteen; this body that had imposed on the universe—that is, on Aiguebelle—its categorical decrees, you might have thought it had been left behind on the seat of a car, silent, not applauded by anyone, not kept carefully in a case of oil and tulle. Antoine was touched. He should have bought flowers. He should have bought the finest wine. He should have got a present. He bent over the windshield and lifted a wiper so he could brush off the seed pods that were stuck there. Émilie opened her eyes and smiled, giving him a friendly wave. Antoine thought to himself that neither he nor Émilie knew the origin of the hostility they were trying to mask.

"I've made my choice. If someone tells me that I've only got ten days left, you see, I'll spend them on my island," said Antoine softly.

"You won't believe this: I came here because I'd love it if you would lend me your island for a few days," said Émilie.

Antoine scowled. "You aren't going to tell me that you've just got ten days left!"

"Of course not! I'd just like to behave as if I've only got ten days left," said Émilie.

"You can't possibly go there alone."

"I won't be alone. I'll be with someone," said Émilie. "Do you insist on knowing his name? His name is François Piano."

Antoine choked, coughed, nearly scraped the Pathfinder in backing up, then abruptly started up again, heading for the boulevard to go back down the mountain. Ulysses hadn't told Antoine much, but there were four individuals to whom you were never to give Ulysses' whereabouts: his parents, Jax-Yuck, and François Piano. Antoine had been really inspired when he asked Jérémie to take in Ulysses for a few days, just for the time of Émilie's brief stay.

They were nearly there. They climbed up to the third floor, to the much-talked-about apartment where Émilie had never set foot after spending a month there waiting for Stéphanie to give birth. There was no mystery: Stéphanie was pregnant by Thomas and that was that. Nothing terrible: no one knew about it save the three Dumont siblings, Stéphanie, Émilie, Antoine, and Christine Musse, who was neither doctor, nurse nor midwife but all three at once, hence a mother and a friend of Antoine's. That's all, there was nothing more to say. It wasn't cause for a party. It happens all the time, goes on happening in every life, in every era. In every life, there are plenty of coincidences. That a woman finds out late in her pregnancy that she's suffering from a terminal cancer, all right, maybe that doesn't happen often. But Stéphanie had begged Émilie to adopt her half-daughter, yes, that was it, her half-daughter, what can I say? She'd got down on her knees to beg forgiveness: "I swear that's all it is, I only did it because I was so curious, Émilie, I wanted to know the man who adopted you so long ago, I swear, we only got together so he'd give me back the money I'd entrusted to you, I swear, I'd finally freed myself of Carole Monty, I swear, I was never going to work for her again or have sex with her, I swear, it was just to convince Thomas that he could just as well have adopted me instead of you, Émilie, you always did exactly what I asked you to do, until the day Thomas adopted you on that train and I wanted him to adopt me too, just for one night. But he didn't adopt me at all, Émilie! You haven't said anything! Say something!"

"We aren't at the theatre," said Émilie finally, half-heartedly, "you want more theatrics, but I don't feel at all theatrical, I'm not offended or jealous or envious or wounded, nothing, I don't even see the action and I can't imagine the lines, to tell you the truth, I don't even see any reality when you talk."

"But I really am dying!" Stéphanie protested. "You don't understand!"

"No, I don't understand, I'm sorry," said Émilie sadly, "and I have the feeling that you died a very long time ago, long before today."

"You're so cruel! You've never understood, you're still mad at me and you're still ready to murder Carole Monty, you're worse than Mama! And to think that it's you who'll be bringing up my child."

"Ask Carole then, if you think she'd be a better mother." Stéphanie dissolved into tears. Émilie held her and rocked her. "Do you remember . . ." she began.

And Stéphanie agreed to listen to Émilie's account of the gilded childhood of the three Dumont orphans that every sound, every smell, every shape splashed with pleasure and joy. The caribou is crazy about? Reindeer moss! The moose is crazy about? Water lily rhizomes! The skunk is crazy about? Sarsaparilla! Crack! The beaver cuts down? Aspens! She talked about sand and buttercups; about the porcelain head like a newborn baby's that had been Blanche's doll in 1920; about wild roses, blackbirds, about the scent of buds; she talked about tunnels in the snow and the bare thighs of majorettes; she talked about celery, Kellogg's corn flakes, puffed rice that goes soggy in the bowl if you don't eat it when you're supposed to, about Mister Quaker's hat on the oatmeal box; about Antoine's eyes when they opened onto the universe; about lemon and lemon candies; about the trip to La Malbaie, the ghost ship in the mist on the river when the big mother whale had rubbed against the hull of their boat; about the thunderbolt that had shot through the house; and about Madame Bissonneau's breasts. In the silence that followed the mention of breasts, Émilie began to sing softly "Anicouni."

"I know that you're doing it for the baby," Stéphanie wept, "you're only doing it for the baby, not for me. Dear God, Émilie, will I hold out till the end? I want to so badly, I wish I could call Mama."

"You're the Mama, come here, easy now, look in the mirror, the Mama you see there is you."

Stéphanie looked at herself in the mirror and fled the woman she saw there, going back to Émilie's arms. "I sacrificed everything for you and you don't even remember! I was your shelter, your lightning rod, your nanny; the same for Antoine, and now you watch me dying as if I had the plague! I can see you, your eyes dripping forgiveness, at Mama's bedside when she is dying. Ah! I hope when her time comes that you're already dead and that nobody's with her, nobody! I'm going to call and tell her."

Émilie and Antoine watched her dial the number in Aiguebelle. But she gave up. She dragged herself over to Émilie, clung to her, rubbed against her, breathed her, asked her to adopt her, suckled her. But as soon as she had suckled her, she pushed her away with all the rebellion she had left and accused her of betraying her since the moment of her birth. She huddled and spoke to the daughter she was carrying. She had christened her Nathe. Nathe would be born to avenge her. Nathe would carry out the revenge, Nathe would find out whom to kill to make the universe livable again.

Émilie went in first, caught her breath, and exclaimed: "No! I don't believe it! They're still there!" So what! All right, yes! They're still on the walls in the entrance, old press clippings that Stéphanie had had blown up and laminated. And frankly, who gives a damn? In close-up, for someone who has already met him, it's easy to identify the man who's trying to avoid the photographers' lenses. It's the ENT man, Dr. Dumont. According to the paper, he had sexually abused one of his female patients, a minor, Ms. X. The forty-seven-year-old father of three was arrested at his home, it says. In one of the photos you can recognize the silhouette of a young boy in the doorway of a house buried behind clumps of bushes. It's Antoine. You can't make out his face. The caption informs us: "One of the three children of the alleged abuser, indifferent indifferent witness to his father's arrest." The repetition of "indifferent," a typographical error, had been underlined in red by Stéphanie before the clipping was laminated. Just before the living room arch, another clipping, inordinately blown up, no photo this time: DOCTOR DUMONT CLEARED.

Antoine rolled Émilie's suitcase to the bedroom door, following with his eyes the marks it left in the brand new, almond green carpet that he'd chosen with Amina to celebrate her new artificial hymen. Émilie took off her socks, sank her feet into the thick wool, slowly crossed the room to the French window, opened it and stepped out on the balcony. Back inside, she said, "They've cut down the maple." She heaved a long sigh of relief. "Everything's changed, it's wonderful, Antoine, fantastic, there's nothing left!" She meant that once she was out of the corridor there was no trace of Stéphanie.

The phone rang. Antoine asked Émilie if it might be for her. Émilie seemed surprised. She stammered that she wasn't expecting a call tonight. Antoine finally picked up the receiver. The caller had hung up. Antoine could have used Émilie's indecision as an excuse for getting a little worked up. He had absolutely no desire to get involved in something that didn't concern him, but dammit, did she want him to answer the phone or didn't she? He was careful not to. He wanted to leave. A giant invisible spider was spinning its web at record speed in the air he was breathing. Now let's get this straight. Neither he nor Émilie was that spider. Nor was the ghost of Stéphanie. There was no ghost of Stéphanie. Why think about a ghost of Stéphanie instead of talking about her non-existence now? Because it was a matter of non-existence, exactly as for Amina's "embryo." Hurry up, Antoine, don't try to understand, get moving! Antoine hurried. "There you go, Émilie: a comfortable bed, fresh sheets, clean towels—everything you need in the fridge, listen, it's late, I'll be on my way. I'll leave you the car keys, the papers are in the glove compartment. You've got my cell number, I wrote down the number where I'll be tonight, don't hesitate to call me if—"

"Where are you going? You aren't going to leave just like that, you can't, you can't leave like that, Antoine, you can't! If you can't stand to spend a night or two in the same apartment as me, listen, I'll go to a hotel, what's going on, I can't understand what's going on here!"

Courage, thinks Antoine, where family is concerned, always involves taking to your heels. But after looking at his watch and noting that Ulysses would be at the service station for at least another hour, he asked Émilie if she wanted something to drink. What? Scotch, a tisane, champagne?

"Champagne," Émilie murmured, and followed Antoine into the kitchen. She perched on one of the two stools. "You keep champagne in your fridge? Where did you pick up that habit? Not in our family, that's for sure, not in our family, unless Blanche . . . Yes, it could very well come from old Blanche. After all, Dumonts aren't the only ones in the family," she muttered while she watched

Antoine take out two champagne glasses, remove the wire cage, then the capsule. The cork hit the ceiling. Émilie didn't feel the ice jam give way, but she was submerged in sobs.

"Here, Milie, sit down, lie down, here, I'll spread your mink over your legs, it is mink, isn't it? Here, take a sip, drink, I'll hold it, take a good round sip. It is round, isn't it? Yes, it's round in the mouth! It's good champagne, Milie, go on, drink."

"The glass is like the ones in Aiguebelle," Émilie noted through her tears.

"It's a glass *from* Aiguebelle, I swiped a couple." Antoine moistened his fingertip in his champagne and ran it around the edge of his glass until it sang. Émilie listened as the sound intensified, plugged her ears. Antoine held out the glass and asked Milie-Milie what medication she was on. Émilie choked a little, coughed, and swore that she wasn't on anything, that she only collected prescriptions. She could show him her wad of prescriptions if he wanted. She'd only taken the antidepressants for a while, well, a few months, well, nearly all year, but nothing else. She drained her glass in one gulp and asked for more. Take it easy, thought Antoine, you'll start in on the "Do you remember. . . ?" and I'll have to say again that I don't remember anything except today, except the empty box of Clorets that I'm about to put in the garbage while I think of it.

Émilie straightened up, pushed away the mink, ensconced herself in the cushions and declared that her fainting spells were only acting.

"That's all?" exclaimed Antoine.

"That's all," said Émilie, "but it's a disaster. Could you open a window?"

"The French window is wide open," said Antoine.

"Why a family, why a brother, what is a brother, tell me, a pharmacist brother, that's what I always say, that I've got a pharmacist brother, my witch-doctor brother . . ."

"The greatest pharmacist in the universe," said Antoine, hoping that Émilie would join him in recalling the family's delusions of grandeur.

"You're silly. I warned François, watch out, François, I told him, I have a witch-doctor brother who could supply me with a little navy blue pill that would give me the power to make you disappear. François Pi-a-no, in three-quarter time: pi-a-no. Like on a score. He has a shop, but like you he isn't a shopkeeper. He has a bird and fish shop. He's a dreamer. Now that you've torn that Clorets box to shreds, are you going to swallow them?"

"Do you want me to tell you, Émilie—" Antoine started.

"No, I don't want you to tell me. I want to tell you something."

"That's just it, the problem is that I don't want to hear and I'll tell you why: I don't want to take Stéphanie's place, I don't want you to force me to take it, and I don't want your place either, understand? And I don't want my own place either. That's why I'm not going to stay here tonight. I wouldn't be able to sleep."

Émilie had picked up two cushions and was holding them over her ears. She declared, enunciating much too carefully, that Antoine was totally mistaken. If there was one person in this room who didn't give a damn about the past, it was her. She wanted to talk about the island, she wanted him to explain how exactly to get there, she'd never been so totally in the present as she was now, Antoine had to stop taking her for Stéphanie. It was Stéphanie who had stayed in Aiguebelle in her own mind, Stéphanie who'd taken both of them for the garbage can where she could dump her insatiable grudges, and it was precisely at the moment when she, Émilie, had finally refused to be that garbage can that Stéphanie had started with the suicide threats.

Antoine interrupted Émilie. Stéphanie had never threatened suicide. No one had ever heard the word *suicide* in Stéphanie's mouth. "Death. You can say trolling death. Trolling death. But I'll say it again," insisted Antoine, "talking about Stéphanie is out of the question."

Émilie started to press the cushions against her ears again. "I can't hear a thing."

"You can hear everything," replied Antoine. But he calmed down as he put on his windbreaker and tried to fit the zipper's teeth into the slider, unsuccessfully at first, then successfully, even doing up the snap fasteners. He said nothing more. He kissed Émilie and stroked her head. He pulled the door open quietly, closed it again without a sound, and slowly went down the stairs.

Slowly. The steps, he goes down silently, his hand gliding along the oak banister. How did it happen that a banister is called a *banister*, and does the word *banister* come from the same family as the verb *banish*? He doesn't know the answer and what use would it be if he did know? It's an unanswerable question that he uses to distance himself, to move away, to free himself of the slight remorse that he feels, a remorse that is also useless.

Dear Amina, wrote Antoine in his head, I miss you, soon it will be time for you to get up over there in Morocco. It's midnight here, I'm crossing Outremont Avenue, I'll take it to Park Avenue, then down to Édouard-Charles where Jérémie lives. I'm going to spend a few days at his place, you remember Jérémie, you're the same age, you were actually born on the same day, you hesitated slightly between him and me, but in the end you preferred the older one and that was me. Me, you preferred me. I'll never forget that. Otherwise all is well here, Ulysses hasn't decided yet whether to go back to his parents and I haven't adopted him, either. Obviously he sends you a big kiss, unless he's washing a windshield at the service station. It will be Halloween soon and right after that, Christmas and the New Year, farewell, Antoine.

There, it was faster than the Internet, faster and a thousand times more efficient because he wasn't expecting a reply, because he wasn't subjecting himself to stress and the duty to reply. Antoine quickened his pace. He was anxious to get to Jérémie's place. Under the bell for Apartment 3 someone had written "Jelly" with a yellow felt pen. It was related not to Jérémie's name but to that of a previous tenant. People who ring Jérémie's bell—people who deliver pizza, chicken, sushi—tend to call Jérémie *Jelly*, and Jérémie is more and more being called Jelly. Ulysses, for instance, swears by Jelly because Jelly created a website for people who want to turn their fantasies of rebellion into concrete actions.

Antoine went charging down to the basement, where Jérémie was waiting for him, sitting on the floor surrounded by piles of CDs, with the phone between his legs. He muttered something without raising his head and turned on the answering machine. "Jelly? It's Ulysses. My parents have turned up. I had no choice, either I went with them or the cops would take me. Tell Antoine not to worry, I said I'd slept on the street. They didn't believe me, but they won't find out anything else. Tell him I've got the plan carved inside my skull, okay? Okay, Jelly? I'm crazy about both of you, watch out, they're going to cut—"

Without a word, Antoine began to pile up the CDs that were cluttering the sofa where he would sleep. The cases slipped out of his hands. He couldn't catch them. He was in the grip of a mixture of fury and distress. The phone call that he'd taken his time to answer because Émilie couldn't make up her mind to tell him if she was expecting one or not had probably been from Ulysses.

And the anxiety he'd dispelled while he was waiting at the car wash was a hunch. Jérémie was moaning that he couldn't forgive himself for not being particularly worried when Ulysses, on the way home last night, had told him about his concern at being recognized. "Don't worry," Jérémie had told him, "people around here can't tell the difference between one Chinese person and another, any more than between one sparrow and another."

"I'm not Chinese," Ulysses had protested.

"So what's the plan?" said Jérémie.

"The plan?" said Antoine.

"Don't jerk me around: the map that's carved inside his skull."

"Oh, never mind," said Antoine. He pinched the bridge of his nose as if he felt the first signs of a headache.

"You aren't going to start crying. What's the plan?" said Jérémie.

"My island," said Antoine, "how to get there."

"Let's sleep on it," said Jérémie.

Antoine had to get some sleep or he didn't know what he might come up against. When Ulysses had come into the universe six months earlier, his head swaddled in a lime-green cap, eyes burning with fever, saying that Nathe had promised that no one at this address would ask any questions, Antoine had been cautious. He had warned Ulysses. He didn't want any trouble. He didn't run a shelter for wild animals injured in accidents, and certainly not for children wanting to be adopted. Perched on the kitchen stool, Ulysses was silent. "You have no idea what the life of a child being tracked down means," Antoine had said, to persuade him to give up on running away. "You say that you're fifteen, but I'd say you're no more than twelve, even if the Chinese look younger for longer than we do."

Ulysses had protested. He was neither Chinese nor wanting to be adopted, once was enough.

"Oh, no? You aren't Chinese?"

"I'm Québécois, can't you hear me talk?" Ulysses had said. "And I'll have a Canadian passport."

"Ah," Antoine had warned him, "it won't be a simple matter for you to get a passport. It will take a long time. You'll have to figure something out inside our borders if you insist on being a fugitive."

Ulysses had replied that the country was big and that there were no borders in the north. He could head up north. Saying that, he didn't laugh, which had provoked a snicker from Antoine. "With a forty-ouncer of stolen gin maybe, is that how you'd head up north?"

Ulysses had buried his face in his hands. Antoine thought he was crying. He asked what he could do. As it was time to eat, Ulysses replied without looking up that he knew how to make omelettes and to open cans, but he could also fast for seven days in a row and not feel hungry.

"And then? Nothing else? You know what would be good, it would be good if you could look me in the eyes for once," Antoine had said. "If you could hold your head up and look me squarely in the eyes. Can you do that?"

Laughing, Ulysses had raised his head and Antoine realized that he wasn't crying at all. On the contrary, he felt more like kidding around. "I could also make myself disappear as soon as I've decided to do that, which I haven't yet."

Antoine felt won over. He'd remained strict. "All right, you can spend the night here. First, though, we'll go out for mussels with Amina."

"Amina, this is Ulysses, he's a fugitive. He doesn't want to go back to his parents. The very opposite of you." That was three days after the abortion, a three-day period when Amina had sobbed non-stop because she was entirely responsible for having chosen abortion, entirely responsible and entirely in agreement, she said, with that choice, but she was grappling with inner demons that she wasn't able to muzzle and that Ulysses' appearance drove away. Soon, Amina blamed Antoine for not wanting to get involved. In her opinion he ought to adopt Ulysses, ought to begin the necessary process. Ulysses might be fifteen years old, as he claimed— she didn't believe him, she would have liked to see his birth certificate—but leaving him on the street meant condemning him irreparably. If she hadn't been on the point of leaving, she would have adopted him without hesitation and quite legally. Antoine had to get involved. He ought to enrol him in a school and all the rest. Could Antoine explain to Amina why, since Ulysses' arrival, he'd become heavy and passive, heavy and slow and mentally retarded?

"Yadayadayada," Antoine murmured.

Amina: "Well, I wouldn't have wanted a father like you for my child."

Antoine closed himself off, the better to ruminate. He was grappling with feelings in which hate, rage and shame were mixed with desire, love, helplessness. If he hadn't run away at fifteen, it was because he knew at the time that neither his father nor his mother would lift a finger to look for him. Antoine was jealous of Ulysses' courage, but he discovered that his jealousy included all the people who had known Ulysses before him. He wished that he had brought Ulysses into the world and that he belonged to him. His mistrust of himself intensified. One cannot, he admonished himself, be useful to the person one would have liked to be unless one has renounced once and for all having been that person. Antoine was far from convinced that he'd done that. There was nothing about him of the fanatic who moans that someone should have seen him as the intelligent, reserved, curious, sensitive, wise child that his parents every second desired madly. There remained in him, though, some hazardous material that was ready to explode. Firecrackers that lit up now and then to denounce the injustices he'd suffered. He had never taken a tranquilizer like the ones he sold to men of all ages, even the age of his father the ENT man, who ran aground at the dispensary counter with their prescriptions, hoping to see the end of their fits of rage, their cold sweats, their wall-to-wall anxiety. Antoine wasn't there yet. But he was sometimes annoyed by stupidity. Those annoyances got away from him, were transformed into irritations and then, very quickly, into an urge to kill. Moreover, he told himself, once he'd calmed down, the child we bring into the world or adopt doesn't belong to us. It's because my father thought that I was his that he could afford to treat me as he'd never treated anyone else.

Ulysses spent his days exploring the town. Amina arranged to meet him downtown, at the Pain Doré, where they would order a sandwich and then make the rounds of the museums and galleries. Ulysses wasn't afraid of being recognized. Amina's self-confidence took away any apprehensions. He broke into a smile, then a laugh. Finally he took off his cap. When she saw the scars, Amina understood that he had mutilated himself. She was silent.

One day Ulysses asked Amina if she was afraid of one thing in the world, of one disaster—war, rape, starvation, slavery—was she afraid of one thing? He was convinced that Amina was shielded from fear. Amina told him that her only fear was that he, Ulysses, would start to mutilate himself again. She added that she knew perfectly well she shouldn't confide that fear to him or ask him to stop doing it. That it was up to him to invent within himself someone to whom he would promise not to do it anymore. That she hoped, if he was tempted to begin again, he would think about the Inuit carvings they had seen together, where the bodies blinded by night advance and breathe in the night—if it is possible to be blinded by the night. They laughed together and went to join Antoine.

At Dorval on the day of Amina's departure, Ulysses had assigned himself the role of monkey, yes, a leaping monkey, a silent, leaping monkey that transformed the farewells into a celebration of gratitude and joy. On the way home in the car, though, for the first time he asked why. Why did Amina have to disappear totally into the word *Morocco*? "Because she is convinced that it is more normal to become a mother in Morocco than in America. Amina said that in her country, mothers take care of one another, that they don't find themselves isolated in small individual cages as they are here, that children there have a childhood, whereas here, in her eyes, children are responsible from birth for filling the desert of their mother's solitude, I can't explain it any better than that."

"When I have a passport, I'll go there," Ulysses had concluded.

Antoine had thanked Amina inwardly for this promise which indicated that Ulysses had chosen to live.

ALEXA, SEPTEMBER 14

V IRGINIE, who does Catherine's facials, had lived in Ethiopia during the 1970s. And then one day her dentist, a German who'd settled there after World War II, disappeared. There was a search. His body was found floating in a swamp teeming with crocodiles, eeew. The crocodiles hadn't touched him. People there said it proved that even the crocodiles wouldn't touch a piece of old Nazi scum. Get it, dimwit?

A person can't know everything, I didn't know that private commandos had tracked down Nazis hiding out in Ethiopia, Mexico, Argentina and even in Canada, and dealt with them. "Patiently," said François, "little by little, and over the years, the Nazis were wiped out."

"They were?" I said to François. "Then why are there still so many around? There's a whole slew of them on the Net and in the Faubourg."

"They've reproduced, all species reproduce," said François.

He was wrong. Species vanished every day. I printed up a list for him. François laughed. I grabbed his car keys and we raced through the parking lot at the shrine to Saint Anne, I got there first, I started the car and he jumped onto the hood. I drove around the parking lot in circles. It could have ended badly, but we had fun. No one knows that I've learned to drive. I could drive for hours and hours without being bored to death inside my head. As soon as I have a car I'll drive for hours and hours, I won't be like my mother, I'll never abandon my car and take the train. You just don't do that.

I like stories that travel all over the world and come to me crumpled and warped. That's what is missing in this house. Here, we've only got suppressed stories. "Don't tell this story to Nathe or Papa," said Mama.

"Why?"

"It's pointless, may his soul rest in peace, even if the crocodiles don't want his corpse," said Mama. "The soul isn't the corpse, what do we know?"

I don't agree. With stories, you have to let them run around. I like all stories. There are some running around about Catherine and François Piano. Maybe they're not French at all. Maybe they're not married at all. Maybe they love children and have agreed to love children. I don't even remember being a child. If it weren't for photos, we wouldn't have any proof that adults were once children. Without photos, there is no proof that one's own parents began their lives as children. One had to believe them. One had to have been told. One had to believe that those who'd seen it, told. When I look at my own childhood photos, I don't know if they make any sense. I don't think so. I watch, I listen to my mother say that it's me, I'm glad for her, she seems to think that it's really fantastic that it's me: Look, Alexa, it's you! Me? I forget my life as it passes. Already, I don't remember my childhood.

Today, September 14, 2002, everything is present, concentrated, the outlines are clear. I remember perfectly well that yesterday my mother left for Borigine, I remember that Marceline is going to live here for the whole time that my mother is away, it gets on my nerves, and in seventeen years I won't remember anything about this morning, it will be erased, absent, nowhere. Just as it was before the countdown started. It makes me anxious. The only thing that soothes my anxiety is stories, stories that haven't ended. There now, I wonder what exactly the old Nazi dentist remembered when the commando showed him his photo. I asked François if he thought that, while he was filling cavities and doing root canals, the Nazi dentist remembered that he'd been a Nazi. "Yes," said François, "he knew it at every moment. Especially when he drew or shot the bolt to open or close his door, and every time the phone rang, and also when he slipped between the freshly washed and ironed sheets." François didn't convince me, but I like it when he tells me things. I hate photos. I'd rather be told things. When I'm very old I'll tell Nathe that when she was thirteen the blue-black colour of her pupils would overflow into her eyes in such a weird way that people always thought she had on makeup. When Nathe was thirteen, the blue-black of her pupils started to overflow and stretch the almond shape of her eyelids. In a little while I'll have forgotten the sentence that just existed in my head, that is already disintegrating, that is falling into oblivion. In one year's time I'll have forgotten that I don't like having Marceline in this house where stories are supressed. There aren't a thousand reasons that justify Marceline's presence. We're perfectly capable, Papa, Nathe and I, we can organize ourselves without my mother for as long as we have to. If my mother died, would we keep Marceline? That's the only question, and the answer is no.

While she was following the course of her thoughts, Alexa stroked her wrists and arms with her fingertips. She didn't open her eyes. The near-ghostly presence of a second Alexa whom she surprised just as she was emerging from sleep, touching her very gently, was delicate and fleeting. To keep that presence she mustn't pull on the thread of her thoughts. She should let the thread unwind by itself, because as soon as her consciousness obeyed some outside curiosity—to know what time it was, for instance—the second Alexa vanished. That morning, it was the roaring engine of a small plane in the sky above Carouges that made her vanish. Her father's voice pulled her out of her daydream for good. Her father called to them, to her and Nathe. What were they doing up there, it was past nine o'clock, they had to be at the pool for their swimming lesson at ten, or had he got the day wrong? It was Saturday, right? Alexa emerged from her room, noticed that Nathe's head was buried under her pillow. Nothing was moving. She called. A lifeless and exhausted voice crept out from under the pillow: "Tell Papa I've got a temperature of at least thirty-eight and I'm not going to the pool."

"She drives me crazy with her fevers, one of these days I'm going to skin her alive," Alexa told her father while she wolfed down her cereal. "And no, you don't have to drive me there or pick me up, I'll take my bike, don't start making programs and plans because Mama's not here." She sped off to the pool. Phew! That was a close call! Let him read his papers in peace. Five minutes shut away inside the car with her father and it would have taken her all morning to recover from the onslaught of ringing ears, wobbly legs and cold sweats. With all that, Alexa hadn't found the time to buy herself a new swimsuit. She didn't like the orange one anymore. She had vowed that she'd never wear orange again and here she was, about to do just that because of François, who was always turning schedules upside down. Only yesterday she'd missed her Chinese class because of him and she'd stood around like some silly goose, if geese stand around, in the garden of the bishop's palace. The way a silly goose would walk the street, right? In any case, she was going to give up Chinese and all those languages that all she did was forget, in the end, forget, right?

What had come over her, to study all those languages just when the entire universe had turned to English—English and that was it? She was going to drop everything.

———————

She dove one last time in the orange swimsuit. Then she took forever to soap herself in the shower, rubbing her body with the loofah to get rid of the smell of chlorine. She massaged herself, rinsed herself, tried to sort herself out. Her breasts suited her perfectly, despite the fact that her mother would have preferred it if they'd been a little bigger, and what business was it of hers? Alexa was absolutely not becoming the woman her mother dreamed of. Now her mother wasn't there at all. Or Nathe, for that matter. Nathe and my mother, Alexa thought to herself, they cling to the illusion that I experience my intellectual abilities like an oil deposit buried in the folds of my brain. They're stupid, God they're stupid! Alexa felt nothing at all. What was she responsible for? She hadn't done anything, she was only guilty of getting perfect grades. After all, she wasn't the one who set the scales that decided if a grade is perfect.

Alexa was drying her hair and regarding herself between the two mirrors. If she concentrated her gaze on a point that was slightly out of line with her reflection, if she could neutralize her usual way of seeing her reflection, she could catch a glimpse of herself from outside, the way others saw her. By keeping her eyes off-centre, Alexa was becoming an unknown woman whom she did her best to notice, then forgot as soon as she'd met her, the way she forgot the people she met in carnival crowds, whom she tried to remember before she fell asleep and of whom there remained in her memory only disparate fragments that she was unable to put together. And she told herself that was how she herself existed in the memory of others: as fragments. That game in which she glimpsed herself fleetingly from the outside freed her from her frustration at not having access to her own appearance. She felt less visible then, not so easy to locate, relieved of her identity, as if she'd been transported into the heart of a crowd that she became part of, stripped of the reference points that designated her as Alexa Saint-Arnaud who was taking her oversize brain for a bike ride.

And here's what that oversize brain does with the orange swimsuit: throws it into a trash can while she vows that she's going to learn Inuktitut. And then she'll take off on her own, by car, for the Far North, along with two malamutes, a male and a female. For the moment, since Nathe was sick and her father was reading his papers, since Marceline did the housework, laundry, ironing and grocery shopping, since François had left for Les Éboulements with Catherine, she didn't have to justify her actions to anyone. She was going to take chemin Ste-Foy to the Faubourg. She would just ride past the shop. Maybe even step inside for a look at the fish and birds, if it was open. She would see who replaced the Pianos when they were away. And if François had changed his plans again and was in the shop, she would suffer a panic attack for the thousandth time: "You must never, never, do you hear me, never turn up at the shop without warning, do you understand, dimwit?"

The dimwit understood perfectly well and became a little snoop as she approached the Faubourg, and the scenarios that had crossed her mind when she was standing around in the garden of the bishop's palace the day before gradually assumed the shape of an overall doubt that for the moment gave her the courage to pedal like a madwoman. Alexa didn't need François, but she was sensitive, first to his need for her and secondly to the fact that he had no reason to think she was brilliant, because his understanding of the world satisfied him fully. Not like Alexa's father, who thought he was obliged to suffer because he couldn't on his own muster all the knowledge in the universe. That suffering, Alexa wasn't fooled, was a genuine and pathological rivalry with the overall intelligence of the universe, as if there were some global trend that her father could and should have got hold of, had life not been so unfair to him by having him born into the wrong family, in the wrong country, at the wrong time. He was expecting, then, that Alexa would avenge him for that unfairness—she who had been born in the right place, into the right family and, what's more, in a university town. And of course, thought Alexa, my father didn't say clearly that he expected me to avenge him. But all he does is yearn for an event that won't let him down. The only time I saw my father free of his disappointment was when the twin towers collapsed on TV. Otherwise, he feeds on just the disappointment that events inspire in him. He only reads so he'll be disappointed by what he reads. He surrounds himself with books, magazines and newspapers that annoy him and let him down, he only turns on the TV so he can feel more keenly the disappointment that allows him to snicker in silence. So there are times when I walk into a classroom and start to snicker even before the class begins because nothing will ever triumph over my father's disappointment. My father says that there's no other world except the one we're in. Very well. Okay. But then I wonder how he explains his disappointment. If he's disappointed, doesn't it prove that he imagines another world?

I don't argue with him. I only argue with François. Arguing with François is like driving in a car for hours without boredom starting to screech between my ribs and in my knees. It was for the third reason that Alexa had a weakness for François. Nothing disappointed him. And she had to add, since she was drafting a kind of appraisal of François without wanting to, that the whiff of lying and betrayal that emanated from François—an acid smell that obscured his lavender toilet water—captivated her more than all the knowledge packed inside her computer. Alexa was dying to discover the nature of that lie and that betrayal.

Her bike was badly adjusted, the front wheel pulled towards the left. Already, at the pool, Alexa had been bothered by the poor distribution of her weight that made it feel as if her right leg was longer and heavier than the left. Delusion in perception, that was all, but aggravating when you want to slice through the water along a perfectly straight imaginary line, or to let go of the handlebars and enjoy your own stability.

Catherine couldn't have stayed in the shop in weather like this, but if Alexa came across her, she would tell her she'd come to let her know that Nathe had a fever. Alexa had only seen Catherine once, when she came to plead her decision to take Nathe to Les Éboulements for the summer, but that was enough for Alexa to understand to what degree the woman had become Nathe's ideal. Anyone would have realized at once why Nathe was trying to speak in a deep voice, to pronounce words as if they might break at any moment, to lift objects as if they were sacred, as if they could lose their shape if they were handled roughly. It was incredibly stressful to move around like that, as if everything were suddenly going to vanish, to breathe as if the air were a rare and breakable commodity. Catherine hadn't created the universe, after all, yet it was as if the universe emanated from her alone and was subject to her influence. Alexa preferred not to run into her at all.

The shop door was open. Alexa hesitated briefly, grimaced and went in. Not seeing anyone, she opted to take her time and wander around the aquariums, memorizing the names of the fish. She hadn't the slightest interest in fish in captivity. She hated all captivities, all cages, so the fish's names slipped across her eyes and she couldn't hold on to them. Catherine appeared on the stairs.

"Is anyone there? Alexa! What a surprise! Hi, Alexa, to what do we owe the pleasure?"

No way for Alexa to recognize Catherine's voice from its high-pitched and irritated tone. She made an effort. "Hi Catherine, I was in the neighbourhood, I dropped in to let you know that Nathe is sick, her temperature's thirty-eight." Grotesque! She'd tried to seem natural, but her struggle against succumbing to the hypnotic effect of Catherine's appearance had made her stammer, practically howl. Had she howled? No, surely not, but she felt as if she had yelped, not spoken. She had completely forgotten the power and the force that Catherine gave off, and the light, and the beauty. She was so beautiful! And her perfect look! How could you be touched by it without your toes gripping your socks to keep you from falling into the void that was swaying before you?

Catherine asked her to come up. Alexa moved back to support herself on the frame of the front door and wiped her forehead. She couldn't think of any reason to refuse, she certainly had no reason to accept. Catherine had joined her and was looking at the street. "I'm supposed to be at Les Éboulements." The impulse to take off right away froze in Alexa's legs. "If you have a message for François, François is in the hospital," said Catherine, pulling shut the door to cut off the noise from the street.

Choose your words carefully, Alexa advised herself, choose, measure, wait—otherwise something will get away from you, will say that it must be silenced. She thought about the word *sympathy*, about the word *condolences*, but she was powerless to place them in an expression. "Do you have a sick friend? Nothing serious, I hope." Again, that torture of the ridiculous that started up while Catherine was weaving between the aquariums, apparently listening for some signal that Alexa couldn't identify.

"You and I could open all the cages and let the birds fly away to Mexico. We could empty the aquariums and cook up a feast of angelfish for Nathe. A feast that would bring down her fever. What do you think?" She inspected the aquariums, flicking her nails against them in a way that Alexa found chilling.

"I'm sorry," she managed to mumble, "is it something very serious?"

Catherine rubbed some invisible lotion into her hands, and that massage added to the silence a threat and obscured the daylight. "François is out of danger. He nearly died."

Alexa's heart thumped, then stopped beating altogether. She felt it drop into her stomach. A cramp made her moan.

"What is it?" asked Catherine wearily.

"Nothing serious," said Alexa, "but I'd like to use the bathroom."

"On one condition, that you come upstairs," said Catherine.

Alexa lifted the latch. Her legs gave way under her. She pressed her hands against her throat to muffle another cry. She managed to vomit silently. The cramp let go, came back. She vomited again. Shivered. Looked at herself in the little mirror above the sink and suppressed a laugh. So! Now she was as hysterical as Nathe! What a joke! She splashed cold water on her face and neck, then ran warm water over her hands. She clenched her fists and took a deep breath. A triumphant pleasure at being alive and at feeling her lungs fill. As soon as she was out of this hornets' nest she would forget everything, she'd run and buy the swimsuit of her dreams, blue-grey with a touch of emerald. The news that François had nearly died had no consistency, didn't strike a chord in her dimwit's head, which she bravely raised to leave the bathroom.

Catherine offered her some of the hot coffee she'd just made. Alexa thanked her, she never drank coffee.

"Do you know about plants, Alexa?"

"No, I don't, I don't know anything and I absolutely have to go home now, excuse me."

"You won't say anything to Nathe," said Catherine, "I mean that you saw me or that François is in the hospital or that you came here."

Alexa hesitated. "Is that an order?" she asked finally.

"If you want," murmured Catherine. She did not get up to show Alexa out.

———————

Alexa persisted in pedalling in fifth gear despite the weakness in her legs. The blue-grey swimsuit with a touch of emerald had taken over and completely filled her mind. She went along chemin St-Louis to the shopping mall. It wasn't until she was locking her bike that she noticed the university hospital just across the street, on the other side of the boulevard. Though the blue bathing suit had become an obsession, it let her see the university hospital where François was hovering between life and death in the ICU. Maybe he was waiting desperately for Alexa to visit before he expired, or to give him the strength to not expire.

Alexa walked across the boulevard to the hospital entrance. She inquired. Yes, there was a François Piano in the ICU. He could have one visitor at a time. When he saw her, François scowled and gestured to her to leave. "I want to know what you had. I'm not leaving," said Alexa.

"It's nothing, a minor heart problem," said François.

"A cardiac problem," Alexa corrected him.

François insisted: "Heart. I said heart problem." It was hard for him to talk. He wiped the corners of his lips and shielded his eyes. Even the half-light in the room dazzled him. "Go away! Catherine will be here soon, I don't want her—"

"She doesn't know anything," Alexa interrupted him, "I saw her a while ago."

"I beg you, go away, now, I don't want anyone to see you here," François commanded. He looked away.

Alexa got back on the road to the shopping mall. She was travelling at a measured pace, as if she were trying to escape and was going to be successful. She was nearly at the exit, she must not run under any circumstances or the escape would fail. Her senses were trying to play tricks on her. Though she knew it was daytime, her brain wasn't obeying and was floundering around in the middle of the night. François was dying. No, François was not dying, she'd just seen him, he was alive. And yet he was dying and she was running away. Every move she made she must perform in a concerted way, yes, she had to confer with herself to find the shop through the obstructions and debris from the explosion. She hadn't done anything. She wasn't guilty of anything, of other people's heart problems in particular. There was no blood on her hands, yet she was committing the offence of running away.

She dived into the crowd of shoppers and found respite there. François was dying inside her and she was going to pick out a new swimsuit, blue-green with a touch of mauve. She'd made up her mind, she no longer wanted the blue-grey with a touch of emerald. She refused the salesgirl's help. Under the fluorescent lights in the fitting room, she was frighteningly ugly. It was the death of François that was disfiguring her. She shook her head, smacked her chest and belly, she opened wide her mouth and saw the silent cries emerge from it and fog up the mirror. She adjusted the swimsuit over her breasts. It was fine. It was exactly the swimsuit she wanted.

She found her bike and got back on the road to Carouges. It was an ordinary Saturday on the road to Carouges. The sky had clouded over. The light was no longer glittering on the handlebars. Once she'd passed the bridge over the Rouge River, Alexa started to climb the long hill that ended up on the cape. Between the houses, the grey water of the St. Lawrence flowed towards the Atlantic. Never would the water run up to the Great Lakes. Never would the leaves that were breaking loose from the trees go back up to the branches. Never would Alexa see François again. François was dying, he was dying right here, she was burying him in this crack in the sidewalk.

She kept pushing her bike ahead of her. When she got to the top of the hill, she turned around and didn't feel anything. It was over. The atrocious anxiety that had crushed her heart in a vise back at the shop meant that Alexa had quite unwittingly attached herself to François. Even if he was the one who'd approached her on the ferry to Lévis, she went on thinking that she had decided everything on the Saturday before 9/11, which had turned everyone, even her parents, into a stunned and rudderless mob. That Saturday before the fall of the twin towers, Vanessa couldn't follow the others into the pool and had suddenly gone straight to the bottom without putting up any resistance. Right away, Alexa had gone to rescue her. She had been unsettled when she sensed that Vanessa seemed unable to help herself come up to the surface. The teacher had thought that Vanessa had her period and had given her permission to go home. Alexa had offered to walk her to the bus stop, and that was where Vanessa told her that she had to go to her mother's place in Lévis every Saturday after the pool and that she didn't want to go there anymore, but that the judge had decided she had to go until she turned eighteen; she couldn't do it, he might as well have said forever. Vanessa was furious about everything she knew about her parents and the judge and that cow of a social worker who forced her to lead a dog's life, going from kennel to kennel. She didn't want either one, neither her father nor her mother, nor her father's new girlfriend nor her mother's new boyfriend, she spat on them, she wanted to stop carting her universe in her backpack with her wet swimsuit, her hairbrush, toothbrush, books and everything she left behind when she travelled from the south shore to the north shore, she wanted her room in Carouges and that was that, why did people come of age so late, weren't you of age when you got your first period?

Alexa had taken the bus with her and had gone with her to the ferry and then, since Vanessa didn't calm down, she'd taken the ferry with her. The St. Lawrence was choppy and the two girls had talked about the existence of God while sharing a diet Coke. They both had the same trouble with God, their parents weren't religious because their grandparents had forbidden it because their great-grandparents had been. Be that as it may, when they were seven Alexa and Vanessa had both wanted to take the catechism class like some other girls in their class. Though their parents had donned kid gloves to reason with them, they'd ended up yelling that it was crap, the girls had held firm and they'd believed in God and been baptized despite their parents' stunned looks, and the two girls were in stitches when they talked about it. Some months ago, though, Vanessa had stopped believing in God. Since she had got her period, actually, she'd stopped believing in God. "God does not exist," she said again to Alexa on the deck of the ferry. They'd finished the diet Coke around those remarks while being careful not to let them fall into the ears of other passengers. Alexa would have loved it if Vanessa had burst out laughing when she realized what was fantastic and comical about their exchange, as seen from outside the couple they formed on this ferry, on this river, on that day, that year. She'd have had to practise long before that day the method that allows you to see yourself from the outside, even fleetingly, like a total stranger. In any case, whispering the word *God*, even to say that she no longer believed, seemed to reassure Vanessa and calm her, seemed to turn her rage into determination. Alexa had refrained from arguing, she'd been content to link arms with Vanessa, mindful of the quivering of her voice and lips.

Vanessa had told her that she hated the name Vanessa, a loser's name. Alexa had brought up Ulysses' disappearance. Did Vanessa remember Ulysses? She remembered Ulysses very well, he was Nathe's friend, but she wasn't a boy, able to sleep in the ditch in the summer, in cars in the winter, girls didn't have any luck. Alexa hadn't pushed it. If Vanessa thought that being a fugitive was not a way to get out of something because she was a girl, it was too late; she would never get out of the prison that had been erected inside her head.

The two girls had embraced before they parted, and once she'd left the wharf Vanessa did not turn around. When François approached Alexa, the ferry was already in the middle of the river. François had asked Alexa, as if he'd always known her, what she was doing on the deck all by herself and what she was thinking about. She'd replied that she was praying. She'd said that to show off, to defy this angelic-looking stranger. François had said that he would like to pray with her, because no one had ever taught him how. Alexa told him that it wasn't something you learn. You start to pray in the same way you started to breathe, when you were afraid for someone and couldn't do anything. It was something you did just like that. A way of hoping and wishing that nothing more serious would happen. François told her that she could confide in him, if she wanted to tell him what and whom she was afraid of. Alexa hadn't said anything because she'd felt her heart get excited and her hands go damp, but she began to laugh like a little bell and to be annoyed with herself because she'd let herself get carried away by that laughter, as if it were a kite. She concentrated on the docking procedure to get her laughter under control. Then she realized that this man could teach her what she wanted to learn about love.

She gave herself some time to think it over, until Monday in fact, she remembered clearly because it was on Monday that she'd found out, along with all the other pupils, from the school psychologist, that Vanessa had hanged herself at her mother's place. And it was right after learning that and after thinking that the school psychologist didn't have to slather on so much lipstick to give them the news and to assure them that she absolutely understood what the class was feeling and then explain what it was important to feel and not to feel, not to feel guilty or responsible among other bullshit, and never would that painted face have imagined that one of the girls in the class could feel a sense of triumph or relief or desire or jealousy, and what to think and what not to think, and why cry and why not to cry, that she'd gone to meet François as arranged and that she'd decided to obey François as she would have obeyed a dance teacher, which often made her giggle and was tremendously good for her. She went to meet him the way she went to her ordinary classes, and, as with her ordinary classes, she got the highest grade.

When François sped along the highway to take her back to school or to the bus stop on time, Alexa tried to count the yellow lines as the car swallowed them up. She was convinced that she herself controlled not just the wheel and the engine of the car, but also whatever resisted and tugged a little, in her body and in her moods, through her initiation. And it was not until today, after she'd behaved like an idiot in front of Catherine, that she realized she hadn't been aware of it, but she'd become attached to François. When she'd vomited her anxiety back at Catherine's place, her attachment to François had stopped at the same time. She felt liberated. Catherine could drink her freshly ground coffee in peace. Alexa had her whole life ahead of her. She was young. She had no time to waste as she set out to discover the nature of lying and the betrayal of the angels. Because François was an angel, and the fact that he was cheating on Catherine hadn't dimmed his halo. Alexa admitted that, even on his hospital bed, François's halo hadn't stopped shining. Which could explain why her own mother was in love with him. Still, it was mind-boggling: her own mother! "Your mother is in love with me." François himself had revealed it to her, pleading with her to be more cautious than ever, to be sure not to let out anything that could make her mother think they were seeing each other. "She came to visit me, she pressed herself against me." As soon as the words were out, as soon as they struck Alexa's eardrums, those words had been smashed to pieces. Alexa never thought about them again. And now they'd been stirred into action: "Your mother gives herself to me, it's a nuisance. I'm telling you so you'll be even more vigilant about sheltering our love from others. Like your father and his girlfriend."

"My father *what*?"

"Your father goes out with a girl your age, you must have known that!"

But that was over now. François was dead and Alexa was not in control of his life. He alone was in control of his love life. The lifeless white sky overturned in her eyes. She touched her cheeks and forehead to brush away a feeling of nudity. She would have gladly rolled in the wild rose bushes and the nettles to increase her skin's resistance and fortify the envelope that kept her from vanishing into thin air. Time had not been measured as a quantity for her. Countdowns are only good for rocket takeoffs, not for people's lives. To no one, she thought to herself, has time been given as a sum to be spent. Time is created by each one of us, and death is the end of that ability to create time. When she asked François to give her more of his time, and when she was waiting for him to give it to her, she stopped creating the time for which the onus was on her and no one else to create. Alexa tried to figure out where such a thought could have come from, one that seemed to her to have passed through thousands of other thoughts before coming to her on that day, at that hour, on the north shore of the St. Lawrence River.

She thought about old Blanche. She would go to see her in Aiguebelle before she died. Don't die, Blanche, she prayed, don't die before I get there. The glints and the shimmering of her affair with François would be erased. Alexa remembered then, but from very far back, as if her story was already unbelievably old, that her tears excited François. He would draw her to him to console her the way one consoles a child, but then he would take her harshly instead of soothing away whatever was causing her tears. Until then Alexa had only cried because crying was part of the role that she was playing in order to be introduced to love. When she spied the roof of the house among the spruce and maples, tears poured from her eyes. She slowed down. She blamed the tears on the second Alexa. She must have been asleep on her feet without noticing, because she, Alexa, had so far never really cried. She would go home and make her way directly to Nathe's room, she would lie down beside her and tell her what Catherine had forbidden her to tell. Sure that she was going to do it. It was urgent to break all the oaths that bound her to anybody. Even to herself.

It was her father who greeted her, rather coldly: "Explain yourself."

Alexa explained. She'd gone to the Place Laurier mall to buy a swimsuit. She pulled the suit out of her bag. "Proof."

Nathe's laughter rang out through the house. "She's been laughing with Marceline for hours," said her father. "I don't know what they're talking about."

"I'm not surprised," said Alexa. "Nathe has a weakness for fat women."

"Alexa," said Thomas, "I'd like to take you out for dinner tonight."

"We can't leave Nathe all alone!" Alexa protested too quickly. She felt herself blush. She apologized.

"Look, Alexa," said her father, "I want to talk with you quietly about certain things where Nathe won't hear us. She'll be thrilled to be alone here with Marceline."

"Okay, if you want," said Alexa, resigned. On her way upstairs she sighed and shrugged. She went into Nathe's room. Marceline had brought up a platter of fruit, cookies and yoghurt which she'd set on the bed for the sick girl, who was glowing now, a genuine miraculous cure by Saint Anne.

"Marceline and I are fomenting a revolution," said Nathe, "and we're going to recruit you." Alexa held out the thermometer so Nathe could take her temperature. "It's over, my fever's gone," said Nathe.

"We'll see about that. Open up!"

Nathe grumbled that Alexa couldn't stop playing mother. Marceline slipped out. Alexa set the platter on the floor, fluffed up the pillows, asked Nathe to make a little room for her. Nathe gave her the bigger part of the bed. Alexa lay on her back, noisily expelled the air from her lungs, inhaled deeply and again exhaled, silently.

"Aren't you going to ask me anything?" said Alexa.

"I don't ask anybody anything when I'm chewing a thermometer."

"You don't want some news about Catherine?"

"Meaning?" said Nathe.

"Don't you like her anymore?" said Alexa.

"Meaning?"

"I went to the shop. She told me that François nearly died. I went to the hospital and I saw him there, in the ICU. He's completely recovered."

"Ah," said Nathe.

"He had a heart attack," said Alexa.

"Ah," said Nathe, "that's too bad."

"Catherine didn't want me to tell you," said Alexa.

"Ah," said Nathe.

"She didn't seem to be in very good shape."

"Ah," said Nathe, and showed Alexa that the thermometer read exactly thirty-seven.

Alexa turned onto her side and took Nathe's hand. "What is it that's too bad, dear Nathe?"

"Too bad she didn't die, too bad he didn't die, that's what," said Nathe, making an effort not to choke up. "Now everything has to start over."

"Explain," Alexa urged her gently, "explain what you mean."

"I'd like to get out of this place, not know anything or anybody, be some other person than the one I am, with other ears, another memory," said Nathe. "I close my eyes and I climb up very high above the river and I pray that someone will carry me away up there, forever."

"You pray?"

"I pray because I'm scared," said Nathe.

"Yes," said Alexa.

"You say *yes*," said Nathe, "but what do you know?"

Alexa thought it over. Of course she could tell her the whole story, but since *everything* never exists once and for all, and since *everything* was constantly being created, changing places, scattering, even when you said *everything* you still weren't saying anything about what has been created unbeknownst to you at the very moment you were saying it. She thought to herself that she always complicated everything. That it wasn't so very complicated. All she wanted was to hear herself say, outside herself, very calmly, some definitive words that would make things definitive because of the fact that they would be said outside.

"I was his mistress," said Alexa simply, but the word *mistress* made her a stranger to herself and her words resonated as if

François were truly dead, as if he'd truly been deleted from her hard disk.

"Whose mistress?" asked Nathe as she shook the thermometer to make the mercury go down.

"François's," said Alexa.

"Ah," said Nathe, "François's. Poor you."

Alexa smiled, Nathe smiled back. Alexa asked: "Why *poor* me?"

"Because I don't like his smell," said Nathe.

The two sisters embraced and stayed entwined in the dimness of the room.

"Forever and after," said Nathe, "you won't say a thing."

"You didn't tell me anything that I could give away," said Alexa.

"Ah," said Nathe, "I thought—oh well, I'll tell you. Ulysses is back, he isn't allowed to leave the Faubourg." Then Nathe told Alexa that she didn't like it when girls stayed in her bed too long.

"What about Marceline?" Alexa teased, gently extricating herself from their embrace.

Nathe gazed at Alexa's profile. "If I were a man I'd love you too, and I'd understand why you don't love me," said Nathe. She started to cry. She was inconsolable and she couldn't stand Alexa's presence anymore.

Alexa went down into the garden. Her father was already raking up the leaves. Couldn't he leave them alone for a while, couldn't he leave them in peace after they'd fallen? And what should she wear for going out with him?

"Put on whatever makes you happy," her father said. "I'll be proud of you no matter what you wear."

"In other words he couldn't care less," translated Alexa, who hated those boilerplate remarks, "which explains why what he told me was so trite." She swaddled herself in the brightly coloured sweater that was too big for her and that flopped over her loose-fitting jeans, she made her head bristle with braids that went off in every direction and wrapped three scarves around her neck.

"You're gorgeous," her father told her.

To Alexa it sounded like mockery. She nearly asked if she could drive, changed her mind. If her father found out that she knew how to drive, there'd be an investigation.

They crossed the river, got onto the highway towards Montreal. Ten minutes later they took an exit that brought them to a narrow, bumpy road lined with bulrushes and bushes. The restaurant was hidden by a little woods. You couldn't see it until you'd parked the car in a pine grove and followed the path covered with pine needles that led to a pergola softly lit by Chinese lanterns. Alexa was immediately enchanted by the place. And mystified. She stopped under the pergola and asked: "Where are you taking me, Papa?" As there was no reply, she looked up at her father. The face that appeared to her, that of a child divided between pleasure and fear, moved her deeply. She took her father's hand and squeezed it in her own to reassure him. Then felt stupefied by what she'd just done.

As if he had suddenly wrapped himself in the cloak of a magician who is about to snap his fingers and bring a new world into being, her father gathered momentum and pushed open the door of the restaurant. All the tables were occupied except for one reserved for them. The hostess led them to it; it was near a window, at just the right distance from the fireplace, where a crackling fire sent shadows to the ceiling. Voices, footsteps, sounds were muffled. Music played softly in a pleasant setting. What had pushed her father into the dining room as if he were going onstage? A mystery.

Alexa smiled at the delighted child sitting across from her, who smiled back blissfully. It was another world, truly, a new world that must be infinitely fragile, if you saw how carefully the child—

her father—handled every object: glasses, napkins, menu, the olives and almonds that a young woman had brought to the table. François! Alexa called to him inwardly. Don't die before I can tell you! My father is a child!

"We'll drink!" exclaimed the child as he looked for the wine list on the back of the menu, his tone of voice calling on Alexa's complicity to defy a prohibition.

"Papa! Please! We've played enough. Let's eat now."

Her father took on the very disappointed look of a child who's been caught out. Slowly, he shook his head, looking down. He crossed and uncrossed his fingers, rolled up his napkin, sulked again before declaring that he was hungry, that he was ready to order. He wanted the rabbit terrine and the salmon trout.

Alexa hadn't read the menu, she felt like crying, she felt tired and lost. She couldn't follow what was going on. She didn't know this man who'd just metamorphosed into a child across from her, and she had no idea what role she was supposed to play. She told the waitress: "The same thing, I'll have the same as my father." She had emphasized *my father* to make him go back to being the father she could recognize. As for him, he reacted first by looking her up and down, then by gazing at her as if he were taking his distance, as if he were leaving the harbour to sail away in search of the Promised Land.

The terrines brought him back from his long journey. "Your father," he whispered, straining towards Alexa, "is the father of three girls, but he's not the child of any mother! He's the child of a test tube made of whalebones! Don't tell a soul! And you, Alexa, the second of my three girls, I promise you, on the head of Glenn Gould, who as we speak is playing the Goldberg Variations in this dining room, that you'll become a test-tube mother too if you can't tolerate the fact that the world doesn't exactly match your vision of the world."

"Be quiet! Please, Papa, that's enough!"

Her father sat hunched on his chair like Glenn Gould and drummed on the table while he hummed to himself.

"That's enough!"

"It's sublime!" he said. "Those words are sublime when they're spoken by a would-be rebel who wants to know her maternal grandparents."

"That's enough!" Cut to the quick, Alexa burst into silent sobs.

The child didn't care. He savoured the wine, clicking his tongue, wolfed down his terrine and his trout, applauded the arrival of the chocolate cake, which he didn't cut into until he decided that he'd had enough to drink. He tried to read the time on his watch. In vain.

His eyesight is getting weaker, thought Alexa to herself, he's forty-six now, soon he'll be fifty, he'll lose more and more hair and he'll die. She didn't know this Thomas Saint-Arnaud. She no longer knew why he was more her father than any other of the men sitting at tables in this restaurant; he was, though, more than any other man, of that there was no doubt, since she bore his name, since she was sitting across from him, waiting to be told the reason for this tête-à-tête. Or this one-on-one. Or was it a heart-to-heart? Even François Piano couldn't have put her through such an ordeal. She wouldn't have allowed it. She would have left the restaurant, she'd have been ready to do anything to get home—hitchhike, call the police—rather than spend two hours across from a François Piano who'd started to behave like a child with her. What was he hoping for? She had no idea what went on in the head of Thomas Saint-Arnaud. She tried to make a mental list of what she knew about him. She discovered that she wouldn't even be able to write his obituary. Meaning that she had just spent the sixteen years of her life with a total stranger.

"You didn't notice anything," her father suddenly reproached her.

Alexa chose not to reply. She only wanted this to be over,

wanted this evening to never be mentioned again. Wanted her father to become once more the stranger she'd been used to since her birth.

She raised her eyes. The child had disappeared. Her father asked if she'd heard that he was seeing a young girl the age of his daughters. Yes, Alexa thought she remembered some such reference, but she absolutely couldn't care less, it had nothing to do with her.

"I told you a while ago that I had three daughters. Three. The young girl," said her father wearily, "is not my mistress, she's my daughter, and your half-sister. Her name is Macha. She's going to join us for coffee."

Alexa struggled against dizziness. She wished that she could undo at the speed of light every one of the braids on her head. She who was wild about stories, all stories, suddenly shrank back, barricaded herself to keep from hearing any more. She just didn't feel like listening to the lament of her old man, that yak, actually, that orangutan, finally. He's going to introduce me to my half-sister without wondering for a second if I have the slightest interest in meeting this half-sister; and before that, does Mama know about her? Another daughter? That's ridiculous! He doesn't know how to make a son, or what? She looked all around the restaurant in search of this Macha, who maybe was already there, waiting for a signal from her father.

"It's like some soap opera," said Alexa in a quavering voice that she couldn't control. "Now you're going to tell me that Nathe's the daughter of the Immaculate Conception."

"I'll let your mother tell you about that."

"Are you crazy or what? You didn't even ask if I was interested in these little stories."

"No, what I really wanted was a celebration. I'm an idiot. It never occurred to me that I should ask permission first, because I don't see how I could have got permission to tell you a secret without revealing the secret at the same time, can't you see? If I'd said, 'Alexa, may I have your permission to tell you a secret?' surely you'd have wanted to know what the secret was—wouldn't you?"

"Not at all, absolutely not," Alexa protested, "I'd have said that I prefer parents to keep their secrets to themselves and just let us breathe."

"You say that! You've never stopped bugging your mother to tell you the secret about what drove her away from her parents, what drove your grandmother away from hers. *You* refuse to know a secret? You've got to be kidding!"

Alexa stifled a nervous laugh. It was so ridiculous, the way she and her father would fight without making waves, clenching their jaws and whispering and muttering so that their exchange wouldn't overflow to the nearby tables. If they'd gone to the bank of the river they could have gone at each other all they wanted, the way she and François would go at each other, I love you, I hate you, dimwit, without playing father, you see, never.

"I don't get it," she admitted, aware that she was fighting a losing battle.

Her father summed up. The love in question had hit him five days before he married Émilie. An impossible love that had lasted for five days and from it had come Macha, born around a month before Alexa. And I, thought Alexa angrily, I can tell him what comes next, but I'll wait for him to tell me. When she was twelve or thirteen, Macha started threatening to let it all out if her mother wouldn't tell her the name of her father. And the mother, on the advice of a psychologist, went along with Macha's demands.

Alexa curbed the flow of her thoughts and asked her father if her mother, Émilie, knew and, if so, for how long. "No, she doesn't. I only found out about Macha's existence a year ago. Her mother and I never saw one another again."

"And you didn't tell Mama anything."

"It didn't strike me as useful. Your mother . . ."

Alexa bristled: "My mother? What? What, my mother?"

"Your mother is a child," said her father calmly. "If you've never realized that, it's simply because it would be unbearable for you, just as right now you couldn't stand another few minutes of putting up with the child that I can be just for myself, that I only allow myself to be when I'm absolutely alone."

Alexa's gaze was lost in the night that was pressing against the windows. Counting Émilie then, that made four daughters in all. "So you seem to think it's useful to tell me. Not Mama, me." At once, the impression that she'd imitated the smug tone of the psychologist announcing that Vanessa had died made her blush. She mumbled an apology.

"No," said her father, "don't apologize, it's Macha. Macha said that she wanted to meet you."

Alexa tightened her arms against her chest. "What about Nathe? Doesn't Macha want to see Nathe?"

"Not for the moment."

A shadow was heading towards their table. Alexa closed her eyes. The voice that said simply, "Papa, here I am, I'm free," was that of the young girl who had served them.

———————

Alexa checked to see if Nathe was asleep or just pretending. She was pretending, as usual. Alexa waited for her signal. Nathe stuck out one foot, raised it and spread her toes in a fan. Alexa sat on the edge of the bed and started to undo her braids. Nathe told her that she stank of fried fish. Alexa replied that there hadn't been fish on the menu.

"Did Thomas Saint-Arnaud confide in you?" Nathe whispered.

Alexa took Nathe's foot in her hands and warmed it, then put it back under the covers.

"Ulysses phoned. If he goes away again, I'm going with him," whispered Nathe.

"Do you think he's handsome?" whispered Alexa.

"He isn't Chinese," said Nathe.

"He's mixed race," said Alexa.

"He's Québécois," said Nathe, thinking it over.

"I think he's very handsome," said Alexa.

"Me too," said Nathe, "with his skin."

"Would you have liked it if Mama were black?"

Nathe, astonished: "Black?"

"Yes," said Alexa, "then you and I would have been mixed race too."

"Is this about breasts?" asked Nathe.

"About breasts, neck, mouth, nose, waist, dancing—especially dancing," said Alexa.

"I always forget that Mama used to dance," said Nathe. "Actually, forgetting is a kind of storage cupboard, not the void, because things come out of it, do you see what I mean?"

"Yes," said Alexa, "it's clear. And in your opinion, could Thomas Saint-Arnaud have married a black woman?"

"Say *adore*, instead," said Nathe, "he would have adored, yes."

Alexa laughed to herself. "Sounds like you know what goes on in Papa's head."

"No, I don't, we aren't allowed to rummage around in our parents' heads," said Nathe, turning her back on Alexa. "You ought to take a shower, you know, you really do smell like fried fish. Good night, little darling."

"Sweet dreams, dimwit," said Alexa.

"Don't let the bedbugs bite, bright wit," said Nathe.

Alexa sat at her desk and gazed at the blank computer screen, at the keyboard, the mouse, the speakers of her Walkman, the case that held the Peter Gabriel CD, *Passion*. She had given one of her three scarves to Macha. She untied the other two and wrapped them around her fingers, then let go of them and booted the computer. The screen lit up. She typed in bold the words that were flaying her, burning her skin: "If you can't for one second put up with the fact that the world isn't always exactly the way you conceive it." She picked up the camcorder and filmed the words, counting the seconds up to sixty. Then hit the Delete key on the computer and switched it off. As François would say, I'm losing it, she said to herself very softly. She smiled bitterly.

She turned the camcorder towards her and filmed herself. Speaking very slowly, she said: "The world as I conceive it." She shivered. "The world as I give birth to it," she went on slowly, "doesn't always exactly conform with the world that others give birth to. An example: my mother as I bring her into the world doesn't always conform exactly with my mother as she brings herself into being, day after day." She pleaded: "Papa! You had no right!" She was indignant: "Now what am I supposed to do? If the world exists just as it is and not the way it's constantly being created, Papa, why was I born? And Macha? And Nathe?" Alexa allowed her tears to be recorded till she was overcome by a fit of giggles. It was too funny, too wacky, too weird to record her own tears. But she went on filming: "Filming your own tears is a sacrilege that deserves stoning. I can't stone myself, so I'll hang myself. There's no other way to stop conceiving the world the way I do, Papa. I conceive the world as a huge pile of steel wool shaken by electric and magnetic and telluric and psychic fluxes, do you see? No, it can't be seen. But I can feel it going up and down this spine that you managed to break tonight with your monstrous child huddled on his imaginary piano stool, with your monstrous child who popped up like a jack-in-the-box, who softened me up and then blew up in my face, then spit in my face that my mother is a child and then, to make your daughter Macha look better, not a mother or a child but a mixed-blood goddess, daughter of a Senegalese goddess from Dakar and Thomas Saint-Arnaud, and why should I believe either one of you?"

Then Alexa heard her father's voice saying over and over, "That's enough." She dropped the camcorder and rushed to open her window. She inhaled as much as she could of the night, of the glittering stars, the rustling leaves. She saw herself again as she offered Macha her blue scarf, after noting her phone number and email address. She'd promised to write her. She took refuge in her bed.

For the first time in my life, Alexa finally admitted to herself, I have wanted to be in someone else's place, in Macha's place. Suddenly I wasn't the eldest, wasn't the first. I'd become replaceable, already replaced. When I finally looked up, when I discovered that Macha was the girl who'd served us, whom I'd neither seen nor noticed during that hideous meal, I was filled with a terrible shame. When Macha said she was working to save up for medical school that she would start in two years, when she said that she'd then go to work for Médecins sans frontières, when she said that she'd had to hold back the feeling of urgency that would have made her go immediately to Sudan, the more cramped inside my own destiny I felt and the more I wished I'd been born in her place, not mine. The pang that I felt then must have been jealousy. I wished that I, like Macha, could look at my father with that same straightforward and direct gaze, with the same respect and the same gratitude. I wished that my father would look at me in return as if I'd just been born, convinced that my birth would give a meaning to something that otherwise wouldn't have had one.

She curled up and moaned softly: "Mama?" The question stayed floating on her lips, consoling her by making her forget the abyss that had been opened in her by the words "Your mother is a child."

ÉMILIE, SEPTEMBER 14

WHILE SHE WAS TRYING to remember the title of the novel in which a character described a dream identical to one of hers, Émilie had let hers slip away. All that remained were some shreds of images—it's winter, she is travelling on a train, sharing a room with Nathe, Alexa is asleep in the dome car. There's a snowstorm. The car sways, creaks, comes to a standstill. Newborn babies with AIDS are brought to be nursed. Émilie discovers that the breasts of Alexa and Nathe are overflowing with milk, unlike her own, which produce only a trickle of India ink that blackens the snow piled into the luggage rack, but no, it's only feathers from her mother Fabienne's eiderdown, and they are suffocating her. Émilie reproaches herself: "I shouldn't have tried to remember the title of that novel. But maybe I started looking for it before I woke up." She had stopped short over a laminated press clipping: DOCTOR DUMONT CLEARED. She read "CLEANED" without noticing that her eyes were playing tricks on her, she tried to stick together the outs from the film. She swayed on the edge of waking and dreaming while she hummed "Madame Blancheville launders money." With bleach? Whiter than white? But isn't money already white? Is it whiter, then? It was lugubrious, she was in a foul mood, felt as if she'd just lost her fortune in a casino where you gamble not with money but with time.

She went outside, intending to have a coffee on a terrace. The neighbourhood seemed to be a single gigantic stone monument erected in memory of Stéphanie where she couldn't find even a small place to sit. She walked across Joyce Park to the pharmacy. The sight of Antoine bent over the Saturday papers behind the counter in the dispensary filled her with despair. She turned around and went to prowl with the dogs in the wooded area around the Sanctuaire. She was back at the apartment a little before noon. François would be there soon.

———————

Two hours later, she'd hoped twice rather than once that François had died in a tremendous pileup on Highway 40, but he must have taken the 20. She'd decided not to answer the door or the telephone, she'd transformed the apartment into a second-hand clothing store. Trying on everything in her suitcase had wiped her out. She had never known how to manage her femininity. Did she even have femininity? There wasn't one scrap of cloth that wasn't totally ugly and grotesque. Now she was ready to take off—in the final acrobatic act of the dancer she hadn't become—from the top of the fire escape that opened onto the lane, stark naked under her mink. If she decided, because of her appalling inability to break the commitment to sleep with this Piano man once and for all and put an end to it, that she would open the door to him anyway, it would be in order to tell him, right away, what she had decided, with him as witness, and then act by straddling the kitchen window to get onto the fire escape, which would be her springboard to the back lane, and splash.

When she finally noticed the telephone and remembered how one could use it, she'd dialed the number of François's shop. As luck would have it, Catherine answered. Never mind, she asked for Nathe. Catherine had been aloof. Émilie had barely recognized her voice. Catherine hadn't seen Nathe, but Alexa had dropped in and then left. The usual pleasantries and that was it. So Catherine hadn't gone to Les Éboulements after all, meaning that François hadn't been able to get away and hadn't thought of a way to let her know. So much for the facts that should have been a letdown for Émilie. On the contrary, she felt liberated. Waiting had exhausted her desire, if desire there had been. This was nothing new. Actually, it was routine: how many times a year did she get ready to go out and, just as she was about to leave, realize that the mere idea of going out—which had driven her to take a shower, then do her hair and makeup and perfume herself, pschtt, pschtt—had satisfied her? Take for instance her sessions with Mister Quaker. Each one was so much more fascinating when she was making them up while she got ready to go there than when she dragged her feet into the office. If she'd had a session that day, would she have been able to tell him about the evanescence that characterized her desire?

"Evanescence?" he would have said, echoing her.

"I feel no desire for my desire, and I have no memory of ever having the slightest desire for my desire."

Quaker would not have held back his reaction in time (hairsplitting, wool-gathering), Émilie would have retreated, agreeing with him, but without delaying another fainting spell. Even when she let François embrace her, she didn't want to, it didn't work, but because she'd gone that far she forced herself to play out the whole sequence. Pathetic. Émilie finally told herself, To alleviate the repetition of those small disasters that ended up forming the ultimate disaster of desire, I would have to go over the film again frame by frame. I'd be bound to discover that subliminal images had been inserted—but by whom? by what editor other than herself?—to undermine, corrode and abolish desire at its source.

There are those images, but why not fit some sounds into the soundtrack too, that give the order for a crushing defeat, let's be clear, in the form of a slightly sour, slightly acid smell, that I struggle against but that finally gets the better of desire all down the line. And who could know if Émilie had passed on to Alexa and Nathe this same system for wiping out desire? It was horrible. Horrible to anticipate that she, their mother, might have contaminated Alexa and Nathe, horrible to imagine her daughters at forty searching for whatever it was that was stealing from them the full possession of their desires. Horrible to imagine them adrift, isolated in a suburban bungalow or an armoured downtown loft or a grimy cellar, slumped in front of a TV soap, waiting for a response to their inertia.

Stop! Stop! Émilie reasoned with herself, just because I'm going through some turbulence, it doesn't mean that what I've accomplished will collapse into limbo. But she opened her hands and saw that they were empty. She had to slap her head to make her memory take out of mothballs the name of the worker— which was the only word acceptable, unlike *attendant*, or *helper*, or *drudge*—she had been, still was, would be as of the next day if she went back to Carouges, so that her memory would consent to remind her with what patience, what care, what zeal, what pleasure she'd carried out her triple task of wife, mother, accountant. If she added up the thousands of deeds she'd done to ensure the daily well-being of Thomas and the girls, would she see the shape of an accomplishment that was recognizable as her own? Or did that accomplishment, which consisted of thousands of acts, have as its ineluctable destiny to disappear night after night into a chasm of invisibility that was deaf, mute, weightless, that left no trace, no proof? If there were any chance of re-creating even a rough draft of that accomplishment, she would be assailed by the snickers of Stéphanie and Carole Monty: "Unwind and rewind the cord of the vacuum cleaner, the toaster, the iron, the kettle, that's your great accomplishment!"

Émilie rebelled. What about them, what was their great accomplishment? And what did it matter if there was an accomplishment or not? But her protest didn't take off, it became breathless, struggled, fell; dust motes fluttered through the rooms without freeing her of the dread caused by the vision of her daughters grappling with depression, collapse, death. Faced with the Carole Montys of this world, Émilie stumbled, spun around, so dazed that she felt dizzy; she saw herself on a stretcher, speeding down the corridors of *General Hospital*. She would die there, intubated for good. She was going to be carried away in the flow of commercials and presto, zapped!

The telephone had rung. As she hurried to answer it, Émilie had thought it was another dream.

"Has your Pi-a-no come yet?" Antoine teased her.

Let him tease her as much as he wanted. "He hasn't come and he won't be coming," said Émilie.

"I see, and how do you feel?"

"I don't feel anything at all."

"Have you got any plans, I mean for tonight, have you made any plans? Would you like to see some dancing?"

"No," said Émilie, "but don't worry about me, I'll be fine."

"I'm inviting you anyway, if you want we can have supper with Jérémie on the terrace at Paris Beurre."

"I don't know him," said Émilie.

"I didn't think you would," said Antoine.

"How should I dress?" asked Émilie.

"If you can, leave behind your mink," suggested Antoine.

What a fool, Émilie laughed after she'd hung up, what is it about my mink? Could he be ashamed of it? What a fool, that brother of mine, he's losing his hair, he's gaunt with melancholy.

It suits him fairly well, it certainly gives him some charm, but if he doesn't do anything, if he decides not to react, if he stays there stagnating in his dispensary, bent over his newspapers like his father, his grandfather, his great-grandfather, all of them bent over their newspapers until *bam!* a heart attack, they land with their heads in the newspapers, each in turn, they crash into the ink of their newspapers, that's where they were going, that's where they all go, where they all end up, with their photos in the papers, like Stéphanie for that matter, who finally had her photo in the papers. Melancholy, that's what Antoine is, it may not look like it but I adore him, I hope he'll be cured of his melancholy. It would take away some of his charm, though, and then, how do you fight against the only thing you have left? If the gifts he wasted were transformed into an insulating bubble from where he can watch the world become iridescent with floating glitter, nothing would make him give it up. He would go on bending over his newspapers as if he were bending over a dying man for whom he could do one last thing that no one else would have thought of.

Émilie felt better and was now going around in circles, trying to think of some way to help Antoine. She took down from the wall the photos of *the man who'd been cleared* and slipped them into a beige garbage bag, look, these bags are beige, not green, I wonder why? She tied the bag and went down to throw it into the garbage cans of a nearby building in case it should occur to Antoine to get back those bits of debris when he realized they'd disappeared. And what else could she get rid of to help Antoine begin his struggle against melancholy? What on earth had he locked up in that chest? Where would he keep the key? A scruple made her abandon her search.

They met at the restaurant—Émilie, Antoine, Jérémie. Antoine introduced Jérémie: "Jérémie is a computer engineer. He invents programs for companies that want to rationalize their operations."

Émilie wanted Jérémie to explain in concrete terms what *rationalize their operations* meant. He offered as an example distributors of mineral water. "Suppose you have three brands of mineral water to distribute to five thousand retail outlets on the Island of Montreal."

Jérémie broke off to let the waiter take their orders. Émilie was willing to imagine whatever anyone wanted. She'd had no trouble choosing what to wear, she'd simply closed her eyes and put on the dress her hand had caught, the cornflower blue with sage green, made of rayon that glided over her skin. Antoine couldn't decide between the *magret* and the *ris de veau*. Émilie suggested the *magret* because she had chosen the sweetbreads, she'd give him half of hers, he'd give her half of his duck. Antoine took a resigned look at the plates on nearby tables, trying to figure out how to stabilize the table.

"So, five thousand retail outlets," Émilie repeated, "then what?"

"In what order to load the delivery trucks to correspond with the orders for delivery to the retail outlets so that handling costs the company as little as possible?"

"Fantastic!" said Émilie dreamily. "I should have become a computer engineer. I had no idea they were involved in solving such specific problems, I congratulate you!"

Antoine burst out laughing, mimicking Émilie: "I congratulate you! I congratulate you!"

Jérémie slowly bent his head towards Antoine: "What's going on with you?"

"What do you mean, what's going on with me?"

"Who are you speaking for? Are you expecting somebody?" asked Jérémie quietly.

"What do you mean?" asked Antoine, showing his empty palms. "Have I committed a crime?"

"Not at all," said Émilie, "it's my fault, I should have remembered that most people don't say 'I congratulate you.' It's a family tic."

Antoine pinched his forehead and yawned, stretching his legs out under the table. They were reduced to silence by the thumping bass coming from a car pulling into the lot behind the terrace. They lowered their heads, knives and forks in suspense, like all the diners.

Antoine, Émilie mused, thinks that everything I do, including breathing, I do against him, he thinks I could behave differently: talk differently, dress differently, smile differently, look differently, so that I wouldn't get on his nerves. He invited Jérémie to act as a buffer between us. Neither Antoine nor I, thought Émilie, seems able to accept what either of us represents for the other. My presence is a blatant reminder to Antoine of everything that he hasn't been able, or known how, or wanted, to become, just as his presence reminds me of what I haven't been able, or known how, or wanted, to become. There's only one thing I want and that is to get out of here, leave them to their universe, I have no business in their universe, there's just one way out, which is to complain of a malaise, a malaise, brilliant, a malaise it will be, I sense that I've got one that's already making me light-headed.

If I were president of the universe, thought Émilie, I'd have all the woofers in the world destroyed, that would be my first contribution to humankind, the destruction of bass speakers; my project would be the destruction of leaf blowers, electric guitars and woofers, I can see myself, round-shouldered, receiving a medal from the nation. I'm still young, I have time before I start on such a project, generally speaking, forty is the perfect age to think about becoming president of the universe. Except that if I let myself get carried away by my fantasies about omnipotence that Quaker has denounced but not eradicated, I won't be able to manufacture for myself the malaise that I need if I'm to go back to the apartment. At this moment I can see the silhouette of a female diner taking shape at the restaurant bar. If I were a choreographer, if I were a dancer-choreographer, I'd go over and persuade her—regardless of her age—to come and work with me. Each of her footsteps takes root at the same time in the ground and in whatever direction she goes. Each of her footsteps has repercussions all the way to the ends of her hair. Immediately, the air expands and you can see the dance. It's dancing. I should tell Antoine to look at that woman, she's dancing, why look for dancing anywhere else? But I'll say nothing more to Antoine, not a word, I'll leave him to his own universe, I'm going to follow that woman. Here she is, she's coming, she'll come close to our table, even if she were blind she would go on dancing, everything takes place inside her, I'll vote for her. I don't dare look at her, she's too close now, I can't stare at her, after all, but I can see, she's Stéphanie's age, what is she doing? She's stopping. Jérémie knows her. Antoine knows her. They stand up, embrace her, this would be a good time for my malaise. Who is she? From very far away I can hear Antoine calling me.

"Émilie? Émilie? Do you remember Carole?"

I hate surprises. Surprises repel me. Practical jokes, bad ones, I also hate. Carole? No, I don't remember any Carole. Carole Monty, yes, but otherwise, no, I don't understand.

Antoine tries to refresh my memory. "Well, Émilie, it's her, Carole, it's Carole Monty."

I don't even look up. I'd be surprised if it were Carole Monty—Carole Monty the coach? The coach who coaches you for death? I don't believe you. What I want to know is, can you know if you've gone crazy, if you've really gone crazy? Me, for instance, I really do see a diamond-like glitter deep in Antoine's eyes, and that shifting, elusive brightness proves to me that yes, it was Antoine who set the trap and is driving me crazy, that's clear. To break out of the trap I mentally toss a coin with the intention of consulting the I Ching. It's very pretty, but heads and tails merge, a safety pin opens and pricks the tender skin of my neck, my fingers trace the outline of the collar of my cornflower blue dress, I remember that it was the other dress, the fuchsia one, that had a collar I pinned on, so the open pin is actually that of a brooch that was lost somewhere and now has opened. It must have been fastened to the mysterious fabric that's torn by sadness.

"Yes, it's me, and I'm very moved to see you again, Émilie, and grateful that life has made it possible."

I don't know what other people do to keep from fleeing the present moment. What they call the present moment is a blank space where the dance cannot be deployed. You can't dance the present moment if you aren't dead. You need the entire history of the earth beneath your feet if you're to dance. I want to, I'm going to watch her. But don't tell me, Mister Quaker, that the eyes that are going to see haven't already seen. You can't empty your eyes of what it is that makes them see. You can't start them over, there's no present moment. There is the story. And I look up and see the woman I thought I'd vote for two seconds ago because she is advancing from the centre of the earth, from the fiery core that is the centre of the earth. I don't recognize Carole Monty. The woman I see is familiar with pain. She shivers as she hugs her shoulders, brushes snow from the folds of her skirt. The woman I see is a dancer who knows the sequence of steps from death to life of every move she makes.

"I confess, Antoine," said Carole, "but of course you know, that every time you make a date with me, I think that I'm going to see Stéphanie again and that she'll forgive me."

I personally love the kind of voice that's unsteady and that crumbles a little on the vocal cords. Not that those voices are hoarse or smoky or smell of wine, no, it's the slowness of the meaning that bruises them and gives them an oblique and late-day clarity. "Stéphanie refuses, she always refuses," said Carole. And I can hear Antoine echo her, repeating after Carole that Stéphanie always refuses, saying it as if Stéphanie weren't dead. I just look at the table. I saw that woman, I didn't recognize Carole Monty. Maybe Stéphanie's Carole Monty was masked after all, it's hard to know. I can see that Antoine is polishing his knife with his napkin, that Jérémie is handing Carole the menu so she can order, I can see the tremor of life beating in Carole Monty's hands. I'm not as crazy as I was a while ago, I'm on my guard. I don't dare to understand what Antoine did. No, I don't dare admit it.

"Do you know, Émilie, that I went to Aiguebelle in the hope that your parents would give me some clue about where Stéphanie is hiding? Do you know, Émilie, that when I realized that your parents thought she was dead I was horrified, horrified, Émilie, at such a settling of scores, Antoine remembers, when I came back from Aiguebelle I was shattered, do you remember, Antoine? I asked you a hundred times: Are you absolutely sure that Stéphanie is alive? And a hundred times you answered yes, you answered that you didn't think it was such a major settling of scores to pass yourself off as dead in the eyes of the people who thought you were dead, do you remember, Antoine?"

It's like Schubert's music a few hours before he died. I adore Schubert a few hours before his death. He heard the Fantasia and transcribed it. After thirteen years Carole Monty thinks that Stéphanie is alive, I understood that, I understood perfectly well. I'm not the least bit crazy, Émilie reassured herself. They're the crazy ones—Antoine, Stéphanie, Carole, who doesn't take her eyes off the menu, so that it seems as if she is reading what she says. What she pronounces. What she dances. Antoine had told her that the death of one of their children could not affect those who'd never thought of them as anything but guinea pigs on whom to perform their educational experiments.

"What I still don't understand," said Carole in her voice of a reader who stumbles here and there over the way words are spelled, "I don't understand a word of your stories about the Dumonts, to me it's gobbledygook. What's important is how, how on earth could they think she was dead if they hadn't seen her body? I'm just going to have dessert, I'll have the crème brûlée."

Corpse and crème brûlée inevitably launched the emergency assistance that is the absurd mental calculation in relational triangles, where it's a matter of establishing for x persons the number of relational triangles that are formed. Three (3) persons form one (1) relational triangle; four (4) form four (4); five (5) form ten (10); six (6) form twenty (20). If nine (9) persons form eighty-four (84) relational triangles, how many relational triangles do ten (10) or x persons form? I haven't seen the body either. Until today I've only seen bodies on TV. Antoine and Christine Musse were the only ones who saw Stéphanie's body. If I were to focus for a quarter of a second on the hypothesis that Stéphanie isn't dead, that she'd chosen to disappear, to change her identity (name, sex, passport), helped along by Antoine, I can't imagine what would happen to me or what would happen to Nathe. It can't be. I'd rather count, count anything at all, so why not triangles? But I give up counting. I refuse. I won't be party to it. That's it. I've had enough.

As if he had a premonition that I was going to defect, Antoine put his hand over mine. He calls me in a voice like Turkish delight, "Milie?" The texture of his sweetness that brings silence belongs to Stéphanie: "Milie." I recognize it and there is no doubt, Antoine is urging me to be quiet. Beyond Stéphanie and Antoine today, that tyrannical sweetness also belongs to our mother, Fabienne, and probably to old Blanche as well, if we go back in time. Stéphanie corresponded with old Blanche at the end. She'd become infatuated with Blanche through letters.

Carole strains her bare face towards me, tilted slightly and held back, like someone who has received her share of slaps and is expecting more: a face as bare as the bare hand of a beggar, as the face of a girl who's become a woman and who calls her mother to ask if that really is all, if that's all there is and nothing more. Antoine crushed my hand. I mustered my strength against Antoine and Stéphanie. I told Carole that Stéphanie had died of an aggressive cancer thirteen years before, that she'd been cremated, that Antoine had scattered her ashes in the Louvicourt River so the water would carry them to Hudson Bay, I meant to the sea, to the Hudson Sea.

I can hear my voice. Perceive it. Each of us perceives our voice, yet when we hear it recorded, even on an answering machine, we don't really recognize it as the voice we hear, as the voice we perceive. I haven't taken on a murderer's voice. I wanted the woman I'd have adopted right away when I saw her enter this place to be set free, because she was the captive of a lie.

Carole's face is still strained towards mine. I would like to press my hand to her cheek and stroke it. Carole turns towards Antoine and pleads: "Is that so?"

Without answering her, Antoine orders champagne. I see Carole's face subside, fade, dry up, wrinkle, switch off, fall, disappear. I in turn reach out towards that absent face to beg for my share: "Why?"

Fugitives

The violet eyes become dark and wet. Carole's lips are swollen as lips are when you've cried or made love for seven days in a row non-stop. "Because," says Carole, "after she was admitted to the bar, Stéphanie told me that it was over between us. And I tried to find a way to hold on to her. If she didn't love me, there weren't very many, and I took the one that there was—blackmail. Maybe she hadn't altogether respected the terms of our financial agreement, but I'd held on to the evidence of everything, of the prostitution. For a long time I'd told Stéphanie that it had nothing to do with prostitution, you know, we were just showing off, and it paid well. But as for the blackmail, what I did was threaten to smear her reputation."

The champagne arrived. I too wanted champagne, sparkling with helium bubbles. I too wanted someone to tell me the truth, to tell me what dead woman really was dead and what living woman I might really become someday. Antoine raised his glass, he looked at me, I couldn't tell if he was killing or thanking me. Carole drained her glass in one gulp, she said that the world had totally changed in twenty years, that prostitution didn't bother anyone now except halfwits. I asked her if she was still practising law. She broke into quiet laughter. Of course she was still practising law. More seriously, she said that she and Jérémie were working to help street people. Then she asked me if I was well, if my daughters were well. It was weird, but the champagne had sobered me up completely. I was able to give her ready-made answers without feeling the slightest dizziness. My daughters, thank you for asking, were very well, Thomas too, still working for the government, still writing reports about reports on projects, while I was, yes, very well. Jérémie and Carole excused themselves. Their day

148

was far from over. They had appointments with some street people. Antoine and I stayed to finish what was left of the champagne.

———————

I hate surprises, was what I told Antoine. If he had any more for
me, he should bring them all out together. Antoine swore that
he'd only carried out Stéphanie's plans, that it was her plan to
respond to Carole's blackmail. He had made a promise and he'd
kept it, but when he'd seen the state I was in the night before, he'd
thought to himself that he'd had enough, that maybe I would free
him from the pact without his having to ask me. He thanked me.
I asked him who had told old Blanche that Stéphanie had died.
"No one," said Antoine, "no one told her. Did Mama? I don't
know; all I did was write 'Left with no forwarding address' on
the letters that kept arriving from Victoria and put them back in
the mail."

I'd have liked to know what became of Christine Musse, whom
Antoine had hired as a handywoman, that's right, a handywoman,
for Stéphanie: "Was she a midwife, yes or no?"

"Her mother had been, I think, in Brittany. Christine had
learned everything from her. She'd just arrived in Montreal. She
placed an ad in *La Presse*. 'Handywoman.' She was shrewd. I'm
sure she managed very well."

"I would like her to be dead, I don't know why, it seems to me
that Stéphanie would be even more dead if Christine Musse were
too. She hated me."

"No she didn't," said Antoine, "she wanted to persuade you
to bring Nathe once, just one last time, to see Stéphanie, because
Stéphanie was asking for her."

"I couldn't do that to Nathe."

"That's what I thought," said Antoine.

Fugitives

We went back to Antoine's place. He wasn't thrilled to know that I was leaving for Aiguebelle the next day. He tried to talk me out of it. He said that there weren't any answers, neither for him nor for me, up there. He told me that I was liable to get lost, even more lost, if I tried to find answers where there weren't any. I told him that I wanted at least once in my life to travel that road, the long road to Aiguebelle, by myself, and that I would leave the next day if he was still willing to lend me his car. He asked if I wanted the map for getting to his island. No, I wouldn't go to the island. "You'll see," Antoine told me, "my car is almost a mother." I didn't quite grasp what he meant by that. Actually, I didn't understand a thing. Increasingly, I think that my brain is more clouded over than other people's, because of a fog that won't dissipate.

FABIENNE, OCTOBER 27

STÉPHANIE, ÉMILIE, ANTOINE. Over the years each one in turn has asked the same question: "Mama?"

Stéphanie left for boarding school, was she sixteen then? Sixteen or seventeen, I don't remember. Émilie followed her, then Antoine. He should have gone to college in Aiguebelle, but events—his father's arrest, accusation and trial—made us want him to go away too. Until they turned eighteen, the children came home for Christmas and New Year's. As soon as they'd turned eighteen, we never saw them here again. Only in Montreal. Never where they lived. Never at the apartment on Joyce Street, never at the house in Carouges. Always in a restaurant, on the occasion of an ENT meeting or a history symposium or to see a doctor. Xavier and I took the opportunity to shop for shoes. To have a massage too, I forgot that, for me of course. Not that we lack masseuses in Aiguebelle, but I'm too shy. I wouldn't want the masseuses in Aiguebelle to see my body, to disclose my body. But my children never came to Aiguebelle. They couldn't stand us anymore, neither me, their mother, nor Xavier, their father. It wasn't hatred, at least I don't think it was, from the way they behaved with us, like rejected lovers, with their sighs and their pleading looks.

When it was time for the goodbyes, Stéphanie, Émilie and Antoine in turn, and in secret from the others, would murmur the same eternal question: "Mama?"

―――――――

Stéphanie died at the age of twenty-nine. Twenty-nine is already old, in astrology it's the age for the Saturn Return, I say it just like that, I repeat it, without the slightest idea of what it means. Still, it's more restful to say that Stéphanie died of the Saturn Return than to say that she died of an aggressive cancer. Given two vague causes, you might as well opt for the one that cuts short the hell of endless repetition. Be that as it may, she left us without warning, without finding an answer to her eternal question—"Mama?"— and without understanding that the answer to the question absolutely couldn't come from me, any more than the answer to the question "God?" could never come from God.

―――――――

When Émilie turned up unannounced on September 15, a Sunday, with her mink over her arm, I felt a rush of panic, but nothing happened. It had been more than twenty years since she'd set foot in Aiguebelle. At least she'll be able to admire the autumn while she drives through the Laurentians and the inland seas of La Vérendrye park. What was it she'd come looking for? I answered her questions. Yes, I was honestly glad to see her in Aiguebelle, yes, I missed her a lot, her daughters Alexa and Nathe too, even though I've never met them, I'm not complaining, she can do what she wants. I miss Antoine too, I told her that. Yes, you were a wanted child. Yes, we loved you. Yes, we did the best we could. Yes, we were wrong. Yes, you're right. Yes, we could have done better. Yes, you're going through a difficult period. Yes, we'd like to help you get through this crisis, tell us what we can do.

———————

"We, we and we, can you just stop saying *we* and start to say *I*?" said Émilie. Of course I could try, of course. Actually, there's a crisis every ten years. Life passes in blocks of more or less ten years, with one crisis per block, no more, no less. Maybe it's seeing a sum below the line we draw that provokes it. Normally, the crisis at turning forty isn't too severe. It's statistically less severe than the crisis of turning fifty. Émilie wanted to see Blanche on her own. Why, of course you can go by yourself, to see Blanche in the hospital, who would stop you? She'll be delighted. Yes, you can call her Blanche if you want, you can call me Fabienne if you want, you can call your father Xavier if you want. Yes, she's blind, she's completely blind now. If she weren't completely blind she wouldn't have left Vancouver Island. But since she's completely blind now, she had to leave Vancouver Island. Yes, it's her age and nothing else that caused her blindness. Yes, it's incongruous that you want to offer your mink to Blanche. The hospital is overheated. Blanche will never go any farther than the end of the corridor. But if you absolutely insist, what can we do about it? I assure you, though, darling, it's not the most brilliant idea. I did all I could to appear open and laid-back. It must have made me sound high-strung and inscrutable. Too bad.

———————

What shocked Émilie was finding out that the walls of the bedrooms had been knocked down to make one big music room, plus the library, plus the two computers. She shivered in all her limbs, she snuggled inside her mink. She's too thin. What does she eat? Really, darling, you wouldn't want me to turn your bedrooms into a temporary mortuary and burn candles and incense there, would you? Émilie left in tears, behind the wheel of Antoine's car. A beautiful car, a Volvo. He hadn't told us he'd bought a new car, a Volvo. That's just like him, these little wipers for the headlights! That's just like Antoine, he's a child, and so kind, he would lend Émilie his car. Why was Émilie crying? She shouldn't have given up dancing. It was the right path for her. It had all been laid out. But then she had to become a bookkeeper and spend her life glued to a computer. Today she's going through a crisis, that's how she described it to me. What can anyone do? She wanted to talk about her psychotherapy. I told her to stop. I didn't force her, though. If you want to talk about your psychotherapy, be my guest. She fell silent. She could have talked about it if she'd wanted. You know, more and more patients have the guts to ask Xavier if he thinks their asthma or ear infection or tinnitus could be psychosomatic. He tells them, Look, I'm just a specialized mechanic. Do you ask your mechanic if a flat tire might be psychosomatic? Of course Xavier doesn't talk to his patients like that. He just thinks that he does. Xavier doesn't say anything to the patients. Especially since you-know-what, Émilie. Since he was cleared. An ordeal. You never sent a note to your father after he was cleared. I can hear you, don't shout, I'm well aware that you were away at school, that you had other things to do. Only Antoine called to say he was relieved that your father had been cleared. And he was away at school too. Only Antoine. Antoine alone. We only have Antoine. We've just got one child and it's Antoine. You and Stéphanie left and never looked back. Isn't that right? Did you look back, Émilie? "I don't know who you are," Émilie replied. "I don't know what you're thinking. You're constantly on my mind, but I can never know you. That has to stop." Then she left to visit Blanche in the hospital.

———————

People think that simply by talking to one another they will find the answer to the question "Mama?" In the hospital, on the floor for the bedridden, every morning, every evening, the dying ask the same question: "Mama?" In all sorts of versions for the bedridden: "Are you angry, Mama?" "Where is Mama?" "Mama! I'm hiding under the covers! Mama! Come and look for me! Mama, why aren't you looking for me?" They dissolve in tears, they kiss their own hands, murmuring, "Mama, Mama, Mama." That's all I can do, Émilie, you'll just have to understand it on your own.

———————

"Your mother absolutely doesn't call her mama," said Émilie when she came home from the hospital.

"That's because she calls God," I told her, "or the Virgin."

"You're wrong," said Émilie, "Blanche doesn't call. Not God and not the Virgin. Or her father. Or you, for that matter. Blanche doesn't call anyone. She's delighted that you faithfully bring her champagne every Sunday. 'Every Sunday,' Blanche told me, 'your father and mother come and drink champagne with us.' Blanche told me: 'Touch me some more, darling, stroke my head, it feels so good, your hands are so soft, is Stéphanie happy?'"

Émilie concluded that I hadn't told Blanche Stéphanie was dead. "What about you, what did you tell her?"

"It's not up to me to tell her," shouted Émilie.

———————

Émilie can still cry. Can weep. Can therefore enjoy herself. When you can no longer cry or weep, you can no longer enjoy yourself. If you've never cried or wept, then you've never enjoyed yourself. Émilie still can. "Enjoy! Enjoy!" Émilie exploded. "Always that same dribble filling your generation's bib."

———————

Émilie has become a minefield. Is it possible for so much aggressiveness to be lodged in someone so frail? "Sorry, Émilie, forget the word *enjoy*. I only meant that it's still possible that the tone of a voice, the indentation of a sky at dawn or dusk, that the silkiness of a perfume, an aroma, a taste, the taste of a cheese, a Cantal, for instance, which evokes grass fires and their smoke that hovers in the cool mountain mist, along with the odours of stable, foamy milk, hair—all these things make you one with life. Or maybe it's your younger daughter, Nathe, who offers you her hair to breathe in, how old is little Nathe now?"

"You've forgotten," said Émilie without watching her chair, which she banged against the wall as she got up from the table, "that I've hated cheese since I was very young and that you get on my nerves when you talk like a cultural journalist, those words, your diction, your poetic phrases like 'indentation of a sky' distress me. It was Stéphanie who liked cheese. You don't even know which of us is dead. Where are the photos, I'll show you which one is dead."

———————

Émilie deplored the fact that I'd destroyed the photos. "You're monstrous! Monstrous!" Is it because she hadn't had time to come and get them? It took us years to decide to start the major work here. After that, the flickering glow of a night light was all we needed to realize that certain species colonize finished basements as well as damp cellars. Sleep lets in illegal immigrants, what can you do? Of all kinds. Fat ones that make you wonder what they're doing there, emaciated ones from all over that travel by satellite. That the flies which eat their faces have perished during the crossing is all you can hope for. What can we do about all the survivors who take advantage of the night to grope for switches? Eventually they orient themselves and make their way to the freezer. When they lift the cover, a light comes on automatically.

Xavier's bed is empty. He took off by hydroplane at dawn to close up the chalet for the winter before Alexa arrives. There's no road to the chalet. Only the hydroplane, which was what Xavier wanted. Normally the chalet is closed up on All Saints' Day, but we're expecting Alexa. Alexa has said that she's coming, Alexa will come, no one knows exactly when, but she will come. She wants to meet us. Let's wish her good luck. Xavier is going to stow his boat under the gallery. From where I am I can hear the water lapping against the sides of the boat, the belly of the boat sliding across the sand. When the children were around, a chalet was out of the question. After the children left, the only reason for having one was to reconstruct ourselves. We hold on, we collapse, we rebuild ourselves. Xavier is alone, horribly alone. He held on, he collapsed, he rebuilt himself. He was born alone, he built himself alone, he collapsed alone, he rebuilt himself alone. I stand by him. I don't want him to die the way he was born, after losing his parents in a train derailment. He lost his parents before his birth. He was taken out of his dead mother. When they told him that, he realized that he remembered waking up at night with his head full of the screeching of metal. So that was it! It's all clear now! But once everything is clear, most often it immediately gets dark, you see.

When he moans, I join him in the twin bed and I take him out of the derailment.

Émilie accuses me: "You only loved him out of pity." I don't see what that's supposed to mean. I'm just beginning to realize that feelings pass through me, so why not pity, if pity is a feeling? Or is it an idea? I don't know yet. Pity could just as well be only a suggestion. Émilie wraps herself around my ankles like a hungry cat: "Did you love him, yes or no? Did you ever have an affair? Any amorous thoughts, any rush of emotion, any daydreams for, I don't know, the dentist maybe or your doctor or one of your colleagues at the college? Stéphanie thought you were frigid. Are you frigid? Do you feel anything? You never wanted to snuggle, you'd go stiff, you'd pull away, let me touch you."

When Stéphanie died, I felt nothing. Nothing at all. Can I decently say such a thing to Émilie, who wants so much to know me? To anyone? Who? Xavier had spread the newspaper across the table the way he does at noon every day while he waits to be served. I don't know what to make of Xavier, who has continued— as if his innocence hadn't been published once and for all—to buy and read the papers after the trial, after he was cleared, after the horror. Xavier said: "Look."

I bent over the page and saw the photo. I looked at the photo and the name. The name and the photo. Stéphanie Dumont. Xavier turned the page. On the reverse side, a furniture store was advertising a pre-Christmas sale on leather sofas. I served the leeks. Leeks au gratin. Xavier ate them without making his utensils screech. So, I thought—now there's a thought, if anyone wants to know my thoughts—Xavier knew how to not make his knife and fork screech against his plate. I pointed out to him that the notice didn't say of what.

"What, of what?" said Xavier.

"What Stéphanie died of."

I thought it was a deliberate act of revenge by Stéphanie that Xavier and I hadn't known she was dying and that we'd learned she had died in a newspaper obituary. Pathetic. Antoine and Émilie were only obeying one of their sister's last wishes. Pitiful. To shame us? But who would know? No one.

I said to Xavier while I poured the scalding tea into cups, "Aside from less than five percent of the twenty thousand inhabitants of Aiguebelle, and in that five percent I count the Knights of Columbus, the Lions Club, the Richelieu Club, the Rotary Club, the Daughters of Isabella, there are the millions of Chinese, East Indians, Europeans, Americans, Africans, Australians—in other words there are a fair number of individuals on the planet—all the people who play hockey, soccer, football, who drive racing cars, who win medals for every possible achievement, I won't list them all, all those politicians, men or women, those community workers, miners, those who work in wood, in textiles, men and women, surely you don't want me to list them all—who'll never suspect that the Dumonts found out that their daughter Stéphanie had died through the obituary in the paper. So we can perfectly well survive that notice and end this day, this October 17, as if nothing had happened, because nothing has happened to all those people I've just listed and to all the ones I won't list, today or any other day, world without end, amen."

Xavier's eyes were still riveted on the ad for a sale of leather sofas. His shoulders were still slumped. He dragged himself to the living room, turned on the TV, watched the one o'clock news. I followed him step by step for fear his legs would give out. He'd had sturdy legs until the acquittal, and at that moment his legs gave out. He strengthened them by swimming in the lake. They could have given out again after he saw Stéphanie's photo in the paper. They didn't. He left for the clinic. He went out of the house, got into his car, fastened his seat belt. It took him forever to start. Back up, forward, now he's moving. I closed the paper and folded it. You'd have sworn it hadn't been opened. You could have sold it as if it were new. In any case, what was new, even newer, was that I couldn't remember what had happened from one second to the next. You'd have said that a child was amusing herself by opening and closing a switch in my head.

I dialed Stéphanie's number. Antoine answered. I asked him what Stéphanie had died of. "Cancer," he replied rather tersely, surely from grief. I didn't want to dwell on it. He had things to do. Time was short. But I still wanted to know if there would be a funeral and if she would be cremated or buried. "Cremated, Mama, she'll be cremated."

I hung up and drank my tea in little sips. Whom could I tell? And yet I'm not a criminal sipping her tea after a murder. I'd started to imagine a scene with journalists gathering in front of the house. One of them would boldly ring the bell. I'd open the door calmly, wait till all the mikes were pointed at me to declare: "We have nothing to be ashamed of." I corrected my declaration: "I don't think that we should feel any shame." Later: "Fuck off!" There, the summary was done, the tea was cold, I like it just as well when it's cold. I yawned. It was time to give my class on the American Civil War.

———————

In the days that followed, not one second, no breathing space to make room for an emotion or a feeling. Concrete details filled my mind completely. How Stéphanie wore her hair, for instance. Her shoes. I wondered what object she'd held in her hand until the end. A tissue? And if it was a tissue, was it a Kleenex? And if it was a Kleenex, was it a two-ply or three-? And if it was a handkerchief, what size? Embroidered? Plain? What colour? Above all, the cremation. What was it like? Do the clothes burn? Is there a pillow, a comforter? At least a blanket, I hope. And the teeth? Do they burn too? The ivory of the teeth? I should have asked, but I didn't. I avoided asking. And there was the smell of fingernails that followed me everywhere, that I couldn't blow away. The smell that fingernails give off when you file them. I repeated: "My daughter is dead, my daughter is dead." Sounds with no echo. Oh, my whole being was strained in expectation of an echo. What did I say? My whole being? I don't know what that means. Émilie's visit left oh's and ah's in the air.

I don't remember the exact number of victims of the Polytechnique massacre two weeks later. But I do remember December 6, 1989, and the days that followed. I didn't take my eyes off the TV. I plunged as if into a mirror into the features of the mothers of the murdered women students, in the hope that I could imitate what they showed of their feelings. The thought that those women were surrounded by microphones and cameras which they obeyed, which they didn't avoid, that they agreed to expose the most intimate experience they would ever have, wiped out my efforts. I had tried. I had failed. If they had come to interview me, I would have cocked Xavier's rifle and I would have fired. "That's it for my tears," I'd have yelled. "That's it for feelings." Of course, they would have kept filming me in the name of freedom of the press. "Get used to it," Xavier would have said. "Give me that rifle, don't speak to the press like a Fury."

"I'm not aware," I would then have said contritely to the free press, "of the difference. My daughter only died because her time had come. No one murdered her. No one raped, butchered or murdered her, thank heaven. You must understand me. Between death and absence, I don't really see the difference. My children left home very young, for their education. Their father's parents died before he was born. My own parents exiled themselves five years after I was married, when my father retired. They settled at the other end of the continent, on Vancouver Island. You have to understand. My parents were still my parents, my very dear parents, and like everyone else I wished for their death a little when I couldn't put to death the part of myself it was impossible to live with. I won't change anything. Stéphanie, Émilie or Antoine will always be welcome in their home."

"You'd better stop right there," Xavier would have suggested, "they're going to cut you off in any case, they're going to chop you up in the editing to give you feelings that are statistically normal, stop working."

———————

I don't like the way I sound when I'm being interviewed. My diction seems false. As soon as I think about the word *diction*, everything seems false and closely monitored. The word *diction* makes other words ridiculous. Paying such close attention to diction always makes the news sound ridiculous. Besides, I can never decide what to wear for the interview. Anyway, there wouldn't be any interviews. No one has ever tried to interview us, neither me nor Xavier after he was cleared. Even before he was cleared, no one ever asked me what I thought. I was the only one. I found myself in such a state of dilapidated isolation that I invented hallucinations that had me being followed by a pack of journalists hungry to know what I felt about the allegations hanging over

Xavier. Actually, the whole city set itself up as a hungry mob that hounded me wherever I went and to whom I, like Xavier, offered only my silence to digest.

———

A year after Stéphanie's death came the visit of Carole Monty. It was the first time we heard that Stéphanie had a friend named Carole Monty, but we showed her in. I can still see quite clearly the colour of her suit—eighty-six percent chocolate. Just one of Stéphanie's friends. She didn't say *the friend*, but *a friend*. A lawyer. "Are you related to the Montys from the Monty garage?" asked Xavier with his usual ENT mechanic's irony.

"You remember me? I was very young," said Carole.

"No, no, I don't remember you. Should I?" said Xavier.

Carole's lips began to quiver. "I'm looking for Stéphanie, the death notice is just a hoax Stéphanie orchestrated so she could disappear."

———

"A Martian, that one," Xavier observed. We watched her not decide to get into her car.

"We didn't see the body, we didn't see the body! Did she see the bodies of the six million—"

"Stop," Xavier pleaded, "don't start your history lesson, no, she didn't see them any more than you and I did, she's finally getting into her Honda, she's leaving now, let her go."

———

Stéphanie's death really happened to me through the death of Lady Diana. It was Diana's death on August 31, 1997, then September 1 and the days that followed, that snatched Stéphanie away from me, something I never should have confided to Émilie. Some confidences are extorted from us by our own anxiety because we can't find a way out of deadlocks. Émilie's brief stay consisted only of a series of deadlocks.

"That doesn't surprise me, coming from you," said Émilie, "you've always been a megalomaniac. As far as you're concerned, the Dumont family occupies summits that are inaccessible even to death. Observing ants never taught you anything."

I said: "Meaning?"

She said: "We'll never know if some ants have a phobia about the soles of shoes, do you follow me?"

Where did she want me to follow her? I was very careful not to tell her anything more. In fact I spent hours parked in front of the screen with the words "My daughter is dead," which, this time, devastated me. Not death at first. The words themselves. Rapacious words that tore me apart and fought over my skin. I ran into the garden, I offered my face to the harsh September sun, I opened my mouth so the rays would fall onto my tongue, into my throat, my lungs. But the sun's warmth was receding from my body. I wished I could call someone for help, but that someone did not exist. I had to hold on tightly to myself, as usual, but it was me, me and no one else, who was hiding from myself and who was running away. I went back inside, defeated, to freeze in front of the TV screen.

"What exactly are you up to, in front of that Mercedes?" Xavier finally growled in his voice already hardened by irony.

I murmured: "It's Stéphanie, she's dead." And finally I howled the way real mothers howl, the way you must yell, the way howls are born in the guts and slice through them: "She's dead!"

Xavier stood there riveted to the wreck of the Mercedes. I went back to the garden, threw myself to the ground, rolled in the grass as if I were in flames, and I was. My skin was on fire. I stayed there on my stomach, pulling out the short, yellowed grass, and I waited for the sky to disintegrate and fall, for it to topple with me into the pit that was growing inside me, until a desperate entreaty took shape in my mouth: "Forgive me! Forgive me! Stéphanie, I beg you, forgive me!"

Xavier held out his hand. I refused his help. I was swollen up. It was late. After all, we had to eat, didn't we? Xavier opened a jar of herring. I went into all the rooms in the house. Nowhere did I see what I wished would appear. I went back to the TV. Xavier unfastened the antenna from the back of the set. I hit him as hard as I could. I rushed at him and hit him on the chest: "It's you! It's you who killed her!"

I no longer slept. "You're getting worse and worse, you're just skin and bones, take sick leave, retire," said Xavier. Every day I tried to find the strength to ask for help, but whom?

One night in December that same year, someone knocked on the front door. I couldn't not answer, the house was all lit up, I'd just come in from shopping, I hadn't even pulled the door shut behind me yet. I had never seen the woman in Aiguebelle, very short silver hair that danced around a plump face with sparkling blue eyes and charm. She gave her name: Christine Musse. She spelled

"Musse" very quickly so as not to waste any time. She was collecting signatures for a petition about trees, against clear-cutting trees in the heart of downtown. She had a distinctive way of making the words ring out as if she were inventing them along the way, as if they'd never been used before. I told her: "I would have called myself Musse too. But not Christine. Marie. Marie Musse, that's what I'd probably have called myself," and I had no problem putting down my name, address, postal code, phone number. She watched me sign. Studied my signature. It seemed to speak volumes and to amuse her. I felt the blood circulating in my legs. A very surprising sense of a new beginning. Nearly embarrassing. It was Christine's voice that created it. I thought: blood really is warm, so warm, such heat! And I thought: blood that's cremated? And I said to her: "Blood that's cremated?"

"Well," said Christine Musse, intrigued and apparently ready for anything.

"Sorry, my head's taken off. Blood burns, do you think so?"

"Look," Christine Musse said, "may I call you later? I really can't deal with it tonight—a head that takes off, blood that burns—I have to collect at least a hundred signatures in the neighbourhood, I'll call you."

I told her not to bother, I'd get over it, what had got into me, to lose it like that? She insisted. She was enjoying herself. I told her it would be best if she waited for a few days. She wanted to know why she ought to wait, if blood was burning. I lied. I've never had any trouble lying. I've always enjoyed lying. I told her that my daughter Stéphanie was here for a brief stay.

"What does that mean, a brief stay?" asked Christine Musse. I didn't know any more than she did. "All right," she said, "here's my number. Call and let me know when I can call you."

Christine called me before I called her. Between the moment when we'd arranged to meet and the one when I dressed in black from head to toe to meet her, I experienced a hope, a violent and terrible hope, of which I couldn't pinpoint the objective but that had been stirred by a promise made audible by Christine's voice. Something was going to be given back to me. There was no way I could curb the excitement that made me sift through my memory in vain in search of whatever it was that had been hidden from me and that was going to be given back.

The area was called Black Blood, on the low hills along the river. I had to wait in my car for Christine, shaken and lashed by gusts of wind. It was pitch-black. I was as frightened as a child who understands that the groping in the car will never end, will start up again forever. I was slowly becoming that child, in the dark, in the car, and I didn't ask myself by what path I was becoming her. I maintain that there are bound to be airlocks between ages that aren't airtight at all.

Christine honked her horn, then switched off her headlights. It startled me. I thought about the police. About denunciation. About prison. She shouldn't have honked her horn. It made it seem as if we were good friends. It killed through familiarity. I put the key back in the ignition. I was going to turn around. I stayed. A gust of wind made Christine twirl around just as she was stepping out of the car. I waited till she'd found the keys and opened the door before I joined her. She was waving her arms excitedly, as if we were already accomplices. The wind rushed inside her house along with us. She said "What lousy weather!" while she was taking off her boots. She'd been stuck in an interminable meeting at the Conseil de la Culture. She tossed her coat onto a bench in the hall, rushed to her answering machine to listen to her messages.

Her lipstick had stained her pink scarf. Now she was nothing like the woman gathering signatures for a petition. She was someone else who was agitated, driven by emergencies regarding her accountant and Revenu Québec. I had taken off my boots and put on shoes. She made an urgent call while showing me where to hang my coat. Then collapsed, out of breath, into the sofa cushions. "Have a seat, Fabienne, is it okay if we use our first names?" She held out her hand, saying that she hadn't forgotten anything: "The head taking off, the burned blood, tell me about them."

I don't say that I'm not a little crazy. That I've never had hallucinations. I simply say that I've behaved properly enough in the course of my life to pass for someone who's nearly normal, in spite of the fact that very early on I'd lost hope, but hope in what? At the precise moment when Christine Musse called me Fabienne, the hope that something would be given back to me, if not hope itself, vanished into thin air. I certainly wasn't going to be all that friendly with Christine Musse. I didn't want her to hold on to my hand, which she was trying to keep in hers. I had nothing to say to her. I talked about one of my students.

"Never mind your students," she said, "why are you all in black? Come upstairs with me, you can try on one of my dresses, I've got one with sunflowers."

I hate sunflowers when they're real. I like seeing them from very far away, floating in the mist, or when they're slightly faded on a print or a painting. But I followed Christine upstairs, into a boudoir actually. All the same, she brought out the sunflower dress. She dropped it onto the wing chair, laughing: "I know plenty about you already, I've been living in Aiguebelle for quite a while now, more than ten years. You don't appear in public very much, do you? Of course, you do such a good job of looking after your old mama, and then you've got your classes to get ready for, to give, but we never see you at the theatre or a concert. Don't you like music? Aren't you going to put on the dress? Let's go and eat. You impress me, you know. All that black impresses me. Scorpios love black. Are you in mourning? Come on, don't deny it. I know you're in mourning. Here, take off your shoes, I'll put the soup in the microwave."

I wouldn't say so, but it was still brutal. I'll never understand why I obeyed her. I obeyed her, but I already wanted to leave. I struggled. I was cold. It was cold in this house that was plagued by raging winds which came down from Hudson Bay, it's the sea, say the sea, Hudson Sea. I started crying from the cold. It was ready, the sorrel soup was ready. "Quarrel soup," I said. Laughing, she said I was crazy. My madness seemed to excite her more than anything else in the world. "But? You're crying? Why the nasty tears?" With one leap she was at my side, wiping away those nasty tears.

How is it conceivable that I let myself be led into such a grotesque scene, a woman of my age, mother of three, mother of a dead daughter! I pushed Christine away. Violently. But only in my mind, because I never take action. In my mind, I saw her head crash onto the yellowish-brown tiles. Mentally, I killed her. Very violently. There you go, I've killed her. But I've never been able to kill in actual fact. I've always dreamed of being able to. There has always been in me a mind-boggling violence that could have killed had I not been paralyzed. I had been paralyzed very young, I don't know why or how, it's not me who would have told Christine Musse. She would have taken advantage of it. She told me that I was scared. "You're scared." In reality she wanted to play don't-be-scared. She was nothing but tricks and spitting in the wind, I should have known from the first minute. She fed me my soup. I opened my mouth like a little girl. Swallowed it. She was enjoying herself. She opened some wine. Made me drink.

"The head taking off, the blood burning: I want you to tell me about them," Christine ordered. I was disgusted with myself, I was convinced that I was starting to smell bad, me, with my dead child inside me, me, out of my mind because of a vanished hope. I wanted to leave without explaining. She held on to me by force, with both hands, forcing me to sit down again. I had no choice. "What is it that's making you resist so hard?" How could she have known that without such resistance she'd have been found dead the next day, her head shattered on the kitchen floor tiles? I was silent, but I couldn't stop the tears that gushed from my eyes. "Make yourself comfortable, I'm going to read you a couple of passages from some letters I've had in my possession for quite a while now."

She reached up to grab from the top shelf of her bookcase what appeared to be a book bound in light brown leather but was actually a box, from which she took a bundle of envelopes that had been carefully opened with a letter opener. "My dear child," Christine read, "you cannot imagine how your letters warm my old heart. I wish that I could answer all your questions about what our lives, your grandfather's and mine, were like. You beg me in terms that touch me deeply. With the passion peculiar to your age, you believe there must be some revelation that would end your suffering. What happened to your mother? You wish there were facts that you could lean on. I'm going to disappoint you, poor child, when I tell you that what happens most often is something invisible, whose signs we can see all too well, from the blooming of roses to their inevitable devastation, signs we can never take by the throat to demand an accounting.

"Till she was thirteen your mother was a wonderful child whose parents pampered her and adored her. When she was around thirteen, she took up a position behind an unassailable wall of perfection on which she hung her prize medals. She became inaccessible to us for good. When she met your father, when she followed him to Aiguebelle, when she had you—you, Émilie, and Antoine—we thought that matters might improve, but we were wrong. Your mother didn't want to have anything to do with us, not me or her father. George became so sad that he couldn't bear it. That was why, when he retired, we went to Vancouver Island and started a new life, instead of waiting for our daughter to become again the source of joy and delight that she had been for us throughout her childhood. But it was already late for George, who, as you know, was several years older than me. You would have adored your grandfather, just as he adored you the rare times when he could sit you on his knees and listen while you related the deepest thoughts of a four-year-old child. You don't remember. You'll realize later on that memory is an incredibly sophisticated organ, on a scale far beyond our own simple history. Don't let yourself stop, darling. Though your memory refuses to give you access to them, all the answers have already been given. You'll hate me, I know you will, but let me add that it's up to you to invent what is missing. It is vain, pointless and harmful to wait when we have inherited the gift of invention."

From the first lines of the letter that Christine was reading, the film of a tremendous rage that was first unleashed in boarding school was rewound in my head. In the dormitory. If it was the dormitory, I was thirteen or fourteen. Meaning that I hadn't had a chance to rewind the film? The objects were going back into my dresser drawer, the chairs were resuming their position in front of the dressers, the pillows, the heads of beds. The curtain was sewn up again. The dormitory doors closed softly. I went backwards down the staircase that led to the music room. In a practice booth in the music room, the piano. Sitting on the piano stool, a blonde midget with her hair in a ponytail. Christine's voice as she read the letter kept me from grasping the words that the midget was swallowing because the soundtrack was being rewound as well. I managed to isolate the sound "lifodep" that went into her mouth like spit. "Lifodep?" I snickered inwardly. Why keep the photos if the films are intact in the deep-freezes of oblivion? When Christine stopped reading, I waited. I knew that something was going to happen to me and I wanted to see what it was. The blow was dealt. On the face. I hit her. I mean I slapped her very hard. I was as surprised as she was. I was amazed at what I'd done.

I ran outside. I brushed the snow off my windshield. I drove to the airport to calm myself. It's a small airport that stays open in winter so the medevac air ambulances can take off and land. Between the hangars the wind was howling. Impossible to land in such weather. The word that the midget pounded and swallowed again lit up in my head. It was blinking. "Lifodep." I didn't get it. Until finally "pedophile" was spelled out. The midget was swallowing the word "pedophile." I turned around. Stormed back to the house in a rage. As soon as I'd parked the car, opened the door and stamped my boots, I felt nothing. Nothing had happened. I smiled at Xavier. He thought that I looked as if I'd had a pleasant evening.

Summer of '98. I was swollen up, matter-of-fact, tough. Xavier: "You're only skinny and dying." I left to spend a month in a rented place in Saint-Irénée, on the North Shore of the St. Lawrence. I left Xavier to his pilot's lessons, to his isolated chalet on a nameless lake, to cans of tuna and herring. For five summers I returned to Saint-Irénée. I even went back these past two summers, despite Blanche's arrival on the hospital floor for the bedridden. "You go to the hospital every day, all year, you can certainly take a holiday, I'll go to see Blanche every day during the week," said Xavier. The first time, the journey from Aiguebelle to Saint-Irénée was merely an abstract number of kilometres to cover. A long flight with no breathing apparatus. Starting in the second year it became a migration, beginning at dawn with the crossing of the inland seas of La Vérendrye park, as far as the first stop at Baskatong. Then the descent through the Laurentians to the river at Portneuf, the second stop, where already I was no longer Fabienne Dumont but an anonymous woman driving to the spot where you could glimpse the bay at Saint-Irénée. The reason for the migration: to achieve my own anonymity. The sun slipped into the folds of the mountains. I didn't recognize as my own the rare words that I wrote in the notebook. I didn't ask them for their ID.

The sky encloses me, burns me like its incense, I want.

I have no hopes. No sign, not even one coming from me.

The sky falls from the sky, the river turns in your shroud,
I make my way towards the forgiveness granted by dawn,
Feet bound to the leash that is studded with shards and grapes.

I could see myself biting the blazing rail between the cliff and the river.

Hands open to the frenzy of the ivy that binds the wild roses, I surrender.

I went back to Aiguebelle after the night of the meteor showers. I closed the notebook and went back to teaching. My students were Alexa's age. I spoke to them as if they were going to die within the hour. I gave them only good grades. I didn't correct their grammatical errors. I wouldn't let them try to make friends or to call me Fabienne. I went on thinking that I'd have liked my name to be Marie Musse. Then I would have allowed the students to call me Marie.

I got along well with Xavier, he got along well with me, we'd bought twin beds. He had introduced me to the computer. We got ready for some major work. The major work got under way. I gave the toys to the Daughters of Isabella and I burned the photos. Xavier didn't need them either. We often held hands while we watched the snow fall. At Christmas I decorated the tree for the children and we waited, alone, hand in hand, for midnight. We shared an orange on Christmas Eve. Xavier removed the peel in a single strip. We got into the car and drove around to look at the lights. We embraced with our eyes closed on New Year's morning and birthdays. When we spoke to one another, we opted for caution. We were silent about what was most important. It was just as well. Our memories sometimes lit up at the mention of a reminiscence: "We're snobs." Our eyes got wet. You would have said we were already old. It didn't stop anything—Xavier from taking off for his island in a seaplane, no road goes to his lake; me by car for the St. Lawrence River. But I won't go back there, to my retreat in Charlevoix County.

That summer I took an excursion to Île aux Coudres, as I did every year. I had just climbed out of the hold onto the deck of the ferry. A couple with a young daughter of twelve or thirteen drew my attention. I could only see them from the back. They were virtually motionless, absorbed in the starting operations. At the very moment when I saw the three of them, I felt overwhelmed, feverish, on the verge of tears. Each one in turn, the man and the woman, the father and mother most likely, wrapped their arms around their daughter's shoulders, gripped her arm while they pointed to something or other, replacing a lock of hair, straightening the shoulder strap of her dress. Wasps. Wasps excited by the first signs of autumn. Wasps that the girl did not push away, seemed not to feel, did nothing to drive away except through the extreme tension in her body. I thought: Those two are having a fight to the death over their daughter. I thought: Those two are waging a battle to the death in order to possess her.

I was hypnotized. The more unbearable the scene became to me, the less I was able to turn away from it. I should have fled. Instead, I went up to the ship's rail, quite close to them. They fell silent. They were gazing at the sky where dense black clouds had formed that would tip over into the windy slipstreams between coast and island. The white silk sails of a sailboat swelled and the boat was driven towards the sea.

I was about to move away from them when the girl turned her head in my direction. She looked at me intensely. She broke away from her parents and approached me. "Aren't you feeling well, madame? Would you like me to help you?"

Those words! That child! That voice! I'd have sworn it was Stéphanie. The same dark blue eyes of rebellion. I started shaking from head to toe and mumbled some kind of excuse or other in a foreign language, a language that I didn't know and that the girl didn't recognize. I fled into the ship's hold and locked myself in my car. "Would you like me to help you"! But she was the one who needed help! She was the one who was grappling with a couple of vampires who were draining her of her youth.

I didn't disembark on the island. I went back to Saint-Irénée. I had a fever. I should have told her: "Yes, yes, I would like you to help me. Help me understand why I've never been able to do anything for any child prisoner, for any captive child, for anyone, ever, not even my own children." For no child, ever. As if each child would take me back to the child I was myself, frozen in the terrible rigidity of an icy heart, the terrible rigidity that takes over forever your body, your soul and your thoughts. The ghost of Stéphanie that I saw on the ferry didn't let go of me. I fled. There is no answer.

Fugitives

Today, we're expecting Alexa and I'm afraid. I dread her visit. I imagine it was Alexa on the deck of the ferry to Île aux Coudres. I'm so ridiculous, I want Xavier to come home as soon as possible. When he's there, I am safe from my own thoughts.

Émilie wanted to know if I'd ever cheated on her father, if her father had cheated on me. I sighed. She said: "You empty your accordion."

I told her: "The accordion is not an instrument our family's familiar with."

She said: "I know a Frenchman." She burst out laughing. Her laughter did me good. I laughed with her. She said: "Well?" I rolled my eyes. She said: "You're closing your fan."

I said: "Do you know a Japanese?" We both laughed, and there was no one there to ask why. I said: "Children tend to feel more betrayed if their parents have affairs than the parents do themselves." No reaction. I added: "What do you think?"

She thought it over. She said: "Nathe, for instance, maybe. Alexa, absolutely not."

I asked: "And you?"

"Me?" said Émilie. And burst into sobs. She wailed. Really, she wailed.

I said to her: "Darling." She wailed that I wanted to stop her from wailing. She wailed that she needed to wail. I told her: "You've always had this terrible need to wail."

I should never have said such a thing. It was even worse than if she'd found out I'd cheated on him with a woman. I said to her: "Your father will be home soon, there won't be anything to eat."

We went out to buy groceries. At the meat counter, everything disgusted us. We bought eggs. I said to Émilie: "I love to go shopping with you."

Émilie huddled against me and I didn't go tense. She looked at the sky, which was discharging its red and its mauve, she furrowed her brow, she said: "Mama?"

I said: "Yes, darling."

She said: "Blanche told me that she had loved a woman."

I said, laughing: "Oh yes, it was me, I imagine, her only daughter."

Émilie said: "No, Mama, not you, a woman."

———————

We went back to the house. I opened the egg box, an invention of one M. Desgagnés from Île aux Coudres who'd bought himself a white grand piano and a condo in New York with the royalties. I took out an egg, sent it flying into the sink.

Émilie said: "Mama?"

And a second and a third, and all twelve—I sent them flying into the sink. I asked Émilie: "Now do you know me?"

Émilie said: "I'm sorry, I couldn't imagine that you didn't know."

I shouted: "Yes, you could imagine it. You didn't want to. You can both go out for dinner, that's all."

———————

They went to a restaurant. I went to the hospital. I told Blanche: "Too bad euthanasia isn't legal yet. You'd be gone before midnight."

Blanche said: "Sweetheart, what are you talking about? What's going on in that little head that has too much talent for just one person?"

I said: "There's no little head, you can keep your confidences for your Eskimo woman who doesn't understand them. Leave my daughter alone."

"Your daughter Émilie is adorable," said Blanche.

I said: "Either you calm down or I'll put a hanky in your mouth instead of champagne." I threatened: "And a pillow over your face."

Blanche said: "Fabienne, darling, about you I said nothing. But about me, excuse me, but I can, I want to, and it's one last pleasure, a brand new one, that I can't refuse, I've been silent long enough."

I said: "How can you talk about yourself without talking about me?"

That's not true, I said absolutely nothing to my mother, Blanche. I only said it to myself. My mother will never give in. To whom, to what? No way of knowing. I was content to go on reading the life of Theodora. I didn't lose my mind.

I came home from the hospital, my head cool. They weren't back from dinner yet. In the sink, the eggs had dried up. I cleaned it. There was no trace of broken eggs when Émilie and Xavier came in. They hadn't told each other anything. They had eaten. Émilie asked why I was so weird. Weird? Like someone who's just won at chess.

That was the night Émilie asked if she could give Alexa permission to visit us. "We've always wanted to know your children, Émilie," said Xavier. Émilie's face became tense and she started to cry again. She didn't stop shedding tears until she left. Most of all, I would like Xavier to come back. The house is ready for Alexa. I myself am ready to adore her.

BLANCHE AND AANAQ

B LANCHE would have preferred to be buried on Vancouver Island, next to George. She would have preferred a death that takes you with one swing of the scythe, on the same day, at the same time, leaving behind nothing but some golden pollen to fly out the window, which was what had happened with George. She'd neglected to make the necessary arrangements. She'd allowed herself to be distracted. At every moment, she had forgotten that she in turn was going to die, and if she did think about it, it was so intense, so joyous that it was still immortality. Even when she'd sold the big house, shut up the rooms one after another, when she'd emptied the cupboards, the sideboards, when she'd given to anyone who wanted them the books, the scores, the records, the tablecloths and embroidered sheets, when she'd burned in the one fireplace where she still made fires the photos, the letters, all those bundles of letters with their strings and ribbons—those from Fabienne, from George, from George's mother, and after that George's manuscripts, all his manuscripts—may George forgive me, so much ink that fights back before melting into flames—and last, the letters from her granddaughter Stéphanie in which the promise to help her die if necessary was written in black and white, she had felt liberated and madly excited, as she'd been at twenty when she left normal school, at starting a new life now that she was over eighty, in her little house with its tangle of rose bushes and honeysuckle. Every day, there was so much to do—groceries, mail, gardening, reading, bridge games with dear friends, visits to the less fortunate, to the most desperate invalids—that it was impossible to imagine that the universe would soon have to get along without Blanche. Some time later, Blanche had been forced to admit that she couldn't really see anymore, and that even with a magnifying glass she confused kings and jacks, twenty-dollar bills with tens or fives. Why worry, though? One could lose one's eyesight at any age. In fact it was a good thing. It was not thrilling to see oneself in a mirror. It was well thought out. And anyway, one gradually gets used to seeing clearly in a different way, thanks to the kindness of others, thanks to the continuous murmur of the earth, the sky, thanks to the texture of things and the hum of one's life. There were still the scents of salt, of roses, of fruit, of Sarah, her last nurse, to envelop and caress her. Smiling, she drew her shawl up over her chest. No one was going to catch her. Yes, that was the immortality Blanche had invented for herself. She would have preferred that the end would come from just one swing of the scythe, but. But a bad fall, a dislocated shoulder, and Sarah had decided that the time had come to appeal to Fabienne. Only then had Blanche remembered that she'd forgotten to do what was necessary to die on the island.

———————

A few days later, Fabienne had landed. Blanche's suitcase was ready. "What about Papa's manuscripts?" Fabienne had asked. Blanche had answered, as if she were speaking to a customs officer, that everything was in order, that she wasn't leaving anything behind, no clutter. "Mama, tell me that you didn't get rid of them," Fabienne had pleaded.

Blanche calmly brought her fingers together as if to pray. She was quite innocent. "If I'd ever imagined that someday you'd be interested in your father's manuscripts, I wouldn't have burned them, I certainly wouldn't have burned them."

"Dear Mama," said Fabienne, "you did exactly what you wanted. As usual."

Blanche had wrapped herself in her shawl, thinking that if she'd really wanted to be buried on the island next to George, she could have simply stopped eating before Fabienne got there. At least she'd finally thought of that ultimate refusal of food as a way to go gently if life ever became intolerable for her.

Once she was on the plane from Vancouver to Montreal, she'd tried to explain to Fabienne why she had destroyed the manuscripts. Fabienne had refused to listen, but then proved to be a darling, paying very close attention so that during the flight Blanche would not suffer as a result of her blindness. They had spent the night in a hotel near the airport. The air conditioning had bothered them, they'd pretended to be asleep. The next morning Xavier met them at the airport in Val-d'Or. When they got to Aiguebelle, Xavier and Fabienne drove Blanche straight to the hospital, without stopping at the house. If she hadn't thought a few hours earlier, when she allowed herself to be caressed one last time by the merciful air of the Pacific Ocean, that she could simply fast in order to go gently, Blanche would perhaps have lost her mind under the shock caused when she was admitted and then when she was moved to the floor for the dying.

She hadn't imagined anything. She hadn't expressed any wish, but without even realizing it she had taken it for granted that Xavier and Fabienne would fix up a little place for her, at least for a week or two or a year or two, under their roof. She would have been discreet. She wouldn't have got in their way. "And you'll have a companion, Mama," Fabienne had said in the elevator, "you'll be more secure with a companion. She's an Inuk called Aanaq. She doesn't speak French or English, you see, but since that's the case, she won't disturb you too much either."

While Fabienne was unpacking the suitcase and putting away the contents in the closet and the little chest of drawers on the side near the corridor, Blanche had recapitulated her situation to prevent the breakup of her outrage from sweeping aside what was left of her immortality. Obviously a blind woman wouldn't be easy, but she'd got by fairly well anyway, she wasn't incontinent yet, she had all her faculties, or rather, no, she'd never had all her faculties, but then who did? She was losing her independence, obviously. To put an end to this spiral of protests that were liable to take away her wits, Blanche had called on a poem by Baudelaire that she and George had memorized along with some others after seeing the film in which all the books were being burned. *Behave, my Sorrow! Let us have no more scenes,* Blanche had prayed in a quavering voice, *Evening is what you wanted, Evening is what you desired—Evening is here.* Fabienne had shown her the bathroom, the call buttons, the lever that controlled the angle of the bed, and the uprights of the bed. *Come away, my Sorrow, leave them! Give me your hand.* If she'd known what was waiting for her, Blanche might have figured out a way to starve to death.

———

As soon as Fabienne and Xavier had left, Blanche groped her way to Aanaq's bed, located her hands, felt them, squeezed them. They were smooth, strong and firm. They gave off a gentle, penetrating warmth. Blanche closed her own bony, dry blue hands inside Aanaq's broad palms. Energy flowed through her to the soles of her feet. After that, Blanche placed her balding head in those hands. The Inuk stroked it and produced a cheerful growl. Then it was Blanche's turn to feel the Inuk's head, to smooth and comb with her fingers the scattered tufts of hair on her bare skull. The Inuk didn't shy away. She continued to deliver her slow cascade of laughter when Blanche started to explore her features by touching them lightly, then her body by feeling it, until she realized that she was dealing with a giant, something like a big, warm, smooth-skinned bear that the narrow hospital bed could barely contain. With the warm, fleshy tips of her fingers, Aanaq explored Blanche's face, then clasped it gently between her palms and drew her to her chest, while offering slight chuckles that spread in little waves of sparkling salt.

"You smell," Blanche told her, "of baked apples and rosemary."

Aanaq rubbed her nose against Blanche's. The covenant was sealed. For a long moment they didn't move. Aanaq indicated to Blanche, by cautiously releasing herself, that it was time for sleep.

Blanche went back to her bed on the corridor side of the room. Without using the step to help her up, but gripping the mattress like a cat that has never been domesticated, she hoisted herself onto the bed. Beneath her pillow she discovered a rosary. Fabienne, Blanche imagined, thought that I'd lost mine during the move. It was very thoughtful of her to give me a new one. Blanche pulled at the chain until it broke. The rosary beads flew through the room like a soft scattering of nocturnal hailstones. It was the only sign of rebellion that Blanche allowed herself. "And we'll say no more about it." Lying on her back, she carefully pulled the smooth flannel of her nightgown under her backside, then laid her open hands flat on her stomach, thumbs and tips of forefingers touching. She breathed in and out, matching her breathing to Aanaq's.

The next day, Blanche tried to find out more about Aanaq. Where did she come from, what was she suffering from, did she have any visitors? Fabienne thought it was inappropriate and pointless to conduct an investigation. What could they do with the information? And if they couldn't do anything, of what use would it be? "What we do know," said Fabienne, "is that 'Aanaq' means grandmother, that she's nearly ninety and that she's a runaway." The veiled contempt with which Fabienne had said "a runaway," much as she would have said "a slut," amused Blanche. "Why are you laughing?" asked Fabienne.

Blanche quickly searched for a good response. "The thought that your father is looking at us," said Blanche. "He adored you. You were his favourite."

"I'd like to know how an only child can be the favourite," said Fabienne sadly.

Blanche held out her hand: "Fabienne, my dear little girl, those are old quarrels."

"Quarrels," Fabienne repeated bitterly, then changed the subject: "Tell me, did you have a good sleep?"

"I had a wonderful sleep," said Blanche, "everything's fine, don't worry, there are no problems, the people are sweet, already they're calling me Blanche."

"Oh, Mama, please . . ."

"But I assure you," said Blanche, "I assure you—except for one little thing, if I may say so. I wish that I could make them understand, without offending them, that I'm not deaf."

There was nothing that Fabienne could do. The thought that old people—but it was better to say "the elderly"—were deaf would always win out because, statistically, it was true. The best solution would be earplugs. Blanche didn't tell Fabienne she'd found herself a new nurse in the person of Aanaq.

The room provided just one armchair, designed for people the size of Aanaq. It stood next to Blanche's bed. Aanaq filled it. Blanche got lost in it. Aanaq sat Blanche on her lap and rocked her while she sang *Taka taka taka*. Blanche followed the heartbeats of Aanaq, whose breath was gradually filled with rhythmical hiccuping and panting that ended in bell-like laughter.

———————

Fabienne would arrive for supper at half past five, bringing fruit, chocolate or a piece of cake. She helped Blanche eat her meal. Aanaq had wolfed down hers before Blanche had even started. She didn't stop clucking while she watched Fabienne feed Blanche. She began to wish that she was in Fabienne's place. All that Fabienne had to do was clear the trays. Aanaq had her tea in the armchair. Fabienne took the folding chair: she set it up between the beds and read a few paragraphs from the biography of the Byzantine empress Theodora. Thanks to Fabienne, Blanche was not losing the notion of time.

———————

Xavier came with Fabienne on Sunday. He brought champagne. He offered a glass to Aanaq, whom he called "grandma." "Here, grandma." In one gulp, Aanaq drained her glass, looked astonished, blushed, chortled and sneezed very loudly. The meal-service carts were clattering down the corridor and the supper trays touched down on the bed tables. Blanche made her champagne last until dessert. Xavier poured her a second glass and Blanche thanked him and paid him compliments: "You're the greatest ear-nose-throat specialist in the universe, aren't you, Xavier?" It was as solemn as a ceremony at which medals are bestowed. Fabienne carefully washed the glasses and stowed them in the chest of drawers at the head of Blanche's bed. She reported to Blanche on every move she made. Often, Blanche felt as if she were following a play on the radio.

As soon as the door had closed behind Xavier and Fabienne, Blanche and Aanaq had some fun. Aanaq danced while making the sounds of birds that Blanche didn't know. Blanche beat time with her hands. Blanche felt as if she'd been freed from all the old quarrels. Ah! It was good to be rid of them! She and Aanaq invented a language that could not include old quarrels. Depending on her mood, Blanche would call Aanaq "Dolly," "Kachina," or "Big Teddy Bear Lady." When Aanaq made a new sound, Blanche came running. "Did you call me? Are we going?" When Blanche heard Aanaq becoming agitated at the window, opening it and sniffing the air, she couldn't help scurrying over to her. She attached herself to Aanaq's hands. If she could not resist running away, well then, she'd just have to bring Blanche along. She, Aanaq, would be the eyes and Blanche the ears.

Aanaq moved around silently, like a bear in the forest. Every morning after breakfast she took Blanche for a walk down the long corridor of their floor, all the way to the picture windows that looked out on the forest on one side, on the city and the river on the other, as Xavier had explained it to Blanche so that she could orient herself. Now and then Aanaq stopped short in front of the elevator doors. Blanche would squeeze her hand tightly and lead her away. One day at the end of their stroll, they met a woman who stopped to talk to them. She insisted on telling Blanche that she and Aanaq reminded her of a blind woman with her dog and that they were a very moving sight. She asked Blanche if she was the mother of Fabienne Dumont. Blanche was reluctant to reply. The woman had the impassioned voice of Edna Thiffault. Edna Thiffault was the woman Blanche had loved more than anyone. More than George, but for a shorter time.

Blanche had a dream about Edna. She was able to look at her as much as she wanted. Her mass of blonde hair was tumbling down. Her gaze was exhausted from joy. Nothing was left of the scenes of criticism. The harmony of their thought was intact even though Blanche couldn't hear the melody that Edna was playing on the violin. Powdered rosin was scattered in the light. Blanche woke up and was blind again. Every morning Blanche had to suddenly become blind again, because every night she was not.

At the first snowstorm, Blanche tried to find Aanaq, because she couldn't hear her breathing. She discovered her with her face flat against the window, her whole body trembling. She copied Aanaq. She pressed her forehead against the window and she began to tremble. Aanaq raised the window a crack and opened her hands to the snowflakes. She closed the window and held out her hand for Blanche to lick, repeating, *U! Uu!* Blanche began to shiver. Aanaq lifted her in her arms, carried her to her bed. After that she collapsed into the armchair. Blanche could hear her sobbing. Blanche copied her and wept.

Blanche disliked having to leave Aanaq when she went to be bathed. She wished she and Aanaq could take their baths together. She was afraid that Aanaq would have disappeared after the bath. And she didn't like the fact that it was a man who bathed her. The old humiliation was awakened and managed to burn her. She didn't confide in Fabienne or in anyone else. Anyone would have guessed that it was because of the old humiliation which would only disappear with death. She came back from her bath exhausted. She sat on the floor next to the big armchair and rocked gently back and forth.

———

For Christmas, the woman with Edna's voice set up a crèche on the windowsill. Fabienne came that evening and declared that it was very pretty. She praised the good taste of the volunteers. She described the baby Jesus to Blanche. It was a big Chinese baby. Blanche asked, as she explored it with her fingers, if the figure might represent an Inuit baby. "Quite possibly," said Fabienne. She had brought two wreaths of balsam fir, which she hung above the chests of drawers. She opened the folding chair and read a page about Theodora. Theodora was the daughter of a bear keeper in Constantinople, but as her story progressed, Theodora became more the daughter of her mother, who introduced her to the dance. She had lived in the sixth century. She had experienced a grand destiny. Fabienne read a second page because she was on vacation over Christmas. Her visits had been a little longer since it had snowed. She had to include the time for unlacing and lacing up her boots, for shaking off her coat, scarf and gloves.

As soon as Fabienne had left, Aanaq took down one balsam fir wreath and set it on Blanche's head as a crown. Then Blanche crowned Aanaq. Blanche scurried to the windowsill, found the baby Jesus and placed it head down on Aanaq's stomach, then let it slowly slide and land on the sheet between her legs. Aanaq gasped, let out an *Aa ta taa!* of pain, and grabbed the infant and placed him at her breast. Blanche started again. Aanaq stopped her after three times. "Three, you had three children," Blanche told her. Aanaq took the Jesus away from Blanche while releasing a long moan, followed by a second, desperate one. "Two of your children are dead," said Blanche. Aanaq went to the window, flattened her face against the cold glass pane and stopped moving. "The third will be coming to get you," said Blanche, pressing herself against Aanaq's back.

———

Fabienne brought Blanche some flowers from the garden. Snowdrops, daffodils and narcissus, the first tulips, lily of the valley, lilacs, irises. Later, lilies and gladioli. After Fabienne left, Aanaq put them under the nose of Blanche, who was dizzy from exhausting their scents. Blanche saw herself treading barefoot on the lawns, saw herself nibbling on the stems of sweet, mauve vetch, saw herself standing in the middle of a field of white clover taller than she was, saw herself walking along a dark forest. She slowed down and scrutinized the shadows until she spotted the flute of a datura standing on its long calyx. Hypnotized by the poisonous flower, she stopped moving.

———

Xavier gave Blanche a radio incorporated into a pair of headphones. Since she'd become unable to distinguish broad daylight from pitch-black night, Blanche needed to use her ears to orient herself in space. So as not to disappoint Xavier, she feigned enthusiasm. Then she rushed to join Aanaq in her bed and the two women shared the headphones. Blanche didn't stop chattering: "Where are Inuit buried? Do they freeze to death? Do wild animals devour their corpses? Do the northern lights carry their souls to heaven or are they buried in stone, to be brought back to life by a sculptor? Do you know a song for the dying? If I die, will you hold me in your arms until the pollen of my soul has flown away?" Aanaq made the sound of a big mother bear. Blanche pressed herself against her and fell asleep. The radio batteries were dead.

To celebrate their first anniversary of living together, on May 26 Blanche obtained permission to go down to the main floor with Aanaq and get some fresh air with her in front of the hospital. The volunteer who accompanied them was the woman with Edna's voice. Her name was Christine. In the elevator, Aanaq's hand suddenly became lifeless and damp. Christine guided Blanche onto the sidewalk. Blanche wanted to walk on the lawns. She'd assumed there were lawns all around the hospital. Christine told her there was nothing but asphalt for cars. Blanche hoped to embrace the trunk of a tree. There wasn't a single tree nearby, only a narrow strip of grass between the sidewalk and the parking lot. Aanaq knelt in the grass and began to pull the leaves off dandelions and eat them.

The second summer arrived and Fabienne went away, as she had the first summer, to spend July on the shore of the St. Lawrence. Xavier came every day. Aanaq adored him. To prove it, she pretended to scrape the back of her hand against his shaven cheek, she swallowed in a single mouthful the cakes that he brought, while making her *Am! Am!* sound. Blanche called Xavier "Dr. Dumont." Dr. Dumont didn't sit down, not in the big armchair or on the folding chair. He stood at the foot of the bed, knocking his wedding ring against the metal post.

Around the middle of July a violent storm burst while Xavier was there. Xavier loved violent storms. He described to Blanche the streaks of lightning that fell into the river. Aanaq howled with laughter. Blanche remained huddled on the chair with her legs drawn up and her arms hugging them. The storm died down. From her chair, Blanche told Xavier glumly that he had been cruel to his children, did he remember? Why? Why had he been so cruel with his children? Xavier replied at once, as if he'd been asked the question a hundred times, that he didn't know he'd been cruel, that he was hearing it today for the first time, from Blanche, and that he really didn't know what to think of it. In his opinion, cruelty was a phenomenon whose definition varied depending on the culture. If Aanaq could speak, she would no doubt say things that to her were absolutely insignificant but that would make Blanche's hair stand on end.

"You don't know, then," said Blanche, her voice barely audible, "that George and I put four thousand kilometres between ourselves and you and Fabienne because we were appalled at your cruelty towards your children, our grandchildren, and by our own inability to step in."

"I didn't know," said Xavier. Blanche sensed defiance in his voice. "I thought," Xavier went on, "that you went there because Fabienne was afraid that you and George . . ." He choked and stopped short. As if she had sensed that another kind of storm had just erupted, Aanaq had pulled her sheet over her head and lay there like a recumbent effigy.

"Be brave," said Blanche calmly, "try to finish your sentence." She had unfolded herself and was now sitting upright on the edge of the armchair. She was persistent.

Xavier moved slightly so he could rest his back against the wall. "Because Fabienne and I were afraid," he said in an even, courteous voice, "that you and your husband, George, would abuse our children, particularly Antoine, the way George had abused at least one child before you married him."

Aanaq sneezed, quite uninhibited, like a Tibetan monk expelling the first signs of a cold. Blanche heard Xavier's wedding ring strike the bedpost.

"I'm an old woman," said Blanche. She lowered her head and opened her hands, holding them out towards Xavier in a sign of surrender. "Forgive me," she said, "forgive me, it's the storm that made me lose my head."

"I don't think," said Xavier without raising his voice, "that you lost your head, not when you broke off with Edna Thiffault and not when you burned George's manuscripts."

Again the clink of his wedding ring. Blanche crossed her fingers and began to laugh softly. "Well, well," she concluded, drawling, "finally a good conversation! My dear Xavier, I really had no idea that you knew so much about your in-laws. It seems that my trial took place without me and that I was sentenced. The reduction of my sentence was rather nice, but now I have to pay. Wouldn't you like to get me that one little pill that puts you to sleep?"

Xavier stopped clicking his wedding ring. He told Blanche that he wouldn't repeat a single word of this conversation to Fabienne. He wished her good night. Blanche called Aanaq.

Aanaq emerged from her hiding place, went to the bathroom to wet a towel, wiped Blanche's face and hands, put her to bed and fussed over her tenderly, growling and murmuring.

Fabienne was calmer when she came home from her vacation. She worried about Blanche's weight and suspected that she had stopped eating. She arrived fifteen minutes early in the evening so she could be sure that Blanche was eating properly. Theodora had grown up, she had been repudiated by her lover, she was taking a perilous journey around the Mediterranean. Fabienne promised Blanche that Theodora would meet the emperor Justinian before Christmas.

———————

In mid-September, Blanche had a surprise visit from her granddaughter, Émilie. Aanaq's comings and goings between the room and the corridor alarmed Blanche. Émilie was both intrigued and amused by Blanche's concern: "You can't see her, Grandma, but I'm not kidding, it's my mink that's got her so worked up. It's much too small for her, so she winds it around her neck and struts about with it. She's fantastic!"

"Keep an eye on her anyway!" Blanche pleads.

"I won't take my eyes off her, I promise," Émilie laughed.

Peace and quiet don't return to the room until the lunch trays arrive. When Blanche had finished her meal and settled in for her tea, Émilie asked her why she'd destroyed her grandfather's manuscripts. Annoyed, Blanche pushed away her table. Her tea was cold. Could Émilie get her another? When Émilie came back with two scalding cups of tea, Blanche told her that she found it painful that Fabienne was having her daughter conduct her investigation. Émilie protested. Blanche thanked her for the tea. It was boiling hot, the way she liked it. Finally, since Émilie had said nothing else as she waited for her to say something, Blanche jumped in. "You know better than I do what a poor dancer is, and you know that tragic story. An untalented dancer, an untalented actress, if you ask me it's still the same thing, still the same tragic story. One that strikes not just bad dancers but also every bad artist in the world. I call it the drama of being under heavy surveillance.

Those artists keep constant watch over themselves and everyone else. They're captives of their own surveillance and nothing and no one will ever be able to stop them from doing it." The roar of Émilie's laughter interrupted Blanche. "What's wrong with you, what's so funny, is Aanaq carrying on with your mink again?"

"No, no, I'm sorry, Grandma, you're the one making me laugh, with your pouting and your funny faces and your little gestures—you must have been a fantastic actress in your day!"

"Oh, I had a small talent maybe," Blanche conceded humorously, "but it was all tangled up with the heavy surveillance, I'd never have got anywhere. Unlike your grandfather, I knew that very early on."

"Me too. I knew fairly soon, I stopped dancing," said Émilie.

"You did the right thing," said Blanche, "after the childhood you had, I can't see how you could have overcome such close scrutiny."

Émilie took Blanche's hand and traced the blue veins with her finger. "What about Grandpa?"

"He kept watch over language. Your grandfather was an entire bureau of linguistic surveillance. He treated it like someone afraid that his inheritance will fade away before his eyes. He got that from his mother, his grandmother, his great-grandmother. They'd all spent their lives watching over language, their own and their children's. As if another language, you see, were nestling in their neurons, just waiting for the signal to start howling. As if a crime, a monstrosity, some kind of defect were liable to free itself from their words and reveal itself. As if language were liable to betray them, to denounce them at every moment. Why are you laughing? What's so funny?" said Blanche as she pushed away Émilie's affectionate hand.

"I don't know," said Émilie, "I think it's your hint of an English accent that makes me laugh. You must have picked it up on Vancouver Island."

Just then, Aanaq, with her head in Émilie's mink, began to snore like an airplane. Émilie laughed even harder. Blanche mulled over that laugh, was about to denounce it as an expression of the heavy surveillance she'd just talked about, but began to pat Émilie's hand. Émilie apologized again and begged Blanche to go on.

"That's all there is," said Blanche, "and it's very simple. If you really want to know, your grandfather watched over language the way he watched over his attraction to young boys, in order as he said to sublimate it. He had made the mistake of not sublimating it at the beginning of his adult life, when he was twenty-nine. The boy he'd loved, once he was of age, threatened to denounce your grandfather. Do you understand? George's manuscripts were just pages and pages of heavy surveillance, and in the end they were nothing but the record of an imaginary trial from which he emerged exonerated, because he showed that one inflicts on others only what has been inflicted on oneself."

This time Émilie was silent. She was stunned and profoundly upset. And even more when she realized that Blanche knew nothing about the accusation that had been levelled at Xavier. She asked Blanche if she'd known when she married George. Blanche knew. And George knew that Blanche, for her part, had loved a woman. "We were happier than most," said Blanche.

Émilie told Blanche that soon she would send her great-granddaughter, Alexa, to see her. Blanche asked if she was Stéphanie's daughter. Émilie said that neither Stéphanie nor Antoine had had children. Blanche was surprised. Very surprised. She was certain that she'd had a letter from Stéphanie one day announcing the birth of a little girl. But she'd burned all the letters. If she hadn't burned them, she could have shown Émilie the letter. "I never understood why Stéphanie went away without leaving an address or why there's never been another sign of her. She made me a promise that it would be wise for her to keep."

Émilie came back to say goodbye to Blanche early the next morning. She offered her the mink. Blanche didn't know of what use such a coat could be. Aanaq, though, had plenty of ideas; she had no intention of parting with it.

Over the following days, Blanche became inaccessible. She got up, she walked on Aanaq's arm, ate properly, spent hours standing, elbows on the windowsill, she was polite, even with Fabienne, but she didn't allow any access. She's daydreaming, she's planning her revenge, thought Fabienne. "Mama," called Fabienne. Blanche turned her blind eyes towards her daughter and held out her hand to be stroked. "I can't wait for Theodora to get married. Do you think she'll ascend to the throne before Alexa comes to visit?" Fabienne gently stroked the tense hand and repeated: "Mama?"

THE FINAL DEPARTURE

"WAIT," Nathe says to Ulysses, "I can't think as fast as you, I can't recapitulate. What will there be to eat?"

"When a prisoner escapes," says Ulysses, "he doesn't ask questions like that."

"That's because he has a gun," says Nathe. "We haven't got a gun."

"Not true," says Ulysses, "he hasn't got a gun when he escapes, he finds one afterwards. Believe me, Nathe, there's a gun on the island, Antoine explained everything."

"Is there any rice?" asks Nathe. "With rice we can survive, no problem, a few grains of rice don't take up much room, I'll put some in my bag."

"The most important thing is for you and Alexa to make up your minds. You have to decide right now. Otherwise I'll go by myself."

———

Everything was happening too fast. Nathe couldn't recapitulate anymore. Events kept shaking her up. First of all, her mother. Her mother had come home from her "brief stay" that hadn't been a stay at all but several days, not at the clinic in Borigine but in Aiguebelle, where it wasn't the least bit cold, not cold enough for a mink, anyway. She'd come home completely cured. Nathe preferred her the way she was before. Not quite so cured wouldn't have bothered Nathe. Her mother didn't stop openly loving her and Alexa. After those tons of love, she'd wanted to force Nathe to make her happy by resuming her violin lessons. The answer was no, once and for all. "But what's happened to all of you!" exclaimed her mother. "I've only been gone for a week. I can't recognize my husband or my daughters!" Yet Nathe was doing all she could to appear stable and the same. Alexa calmed her mother by showing her that she'd actually been away for more than a year if you counted from the first time she fainted, and that her absence hadn't kept her daughters from growing.

Then, Alexa. After asking for ages, she'd finally got permission to go to Aiguebelle and meet her grandparents and her great-grandmother, Blanche. She would go on All Saints' Day. She pestered Nathe: "Come with me, come on! We'll celebrate Halloween with Blanche, Mama says that Blanche loves parties." Alexa couldn't see herself making the journey, hours and hours alone on a bus. She told Nathe that if she hadn't decided not to see François Piano again she would have borrowed his car. She knew how to drive.

"But you need a driver's licence," Nathe had said.

"You're so stupid, I know you need a licence, but with François I always drove without one and nobody got killed."

"What can we do?"

The two sisters thought it over. "We could just pretend we were taking the bus but go by car," Alexa had said.

"I'd be too scared," replied Nathe, who was trying to shed the fear that haunted her more and more. Any idea that strayed from the school timetable and program terrified her. In the end, everything frightened her too much. The entire universe was under the influence of dormant cells that could waken and blow her up without warning. And what if it snowed, she thought, what if it started to snow? And what if we got lost in La Vérendrye park, she wondered, and what if the water in the inland seas started to rise and washed the road away? The worst thing would be to get arrested by the police and submit to an interrogation.

———

Finally, Ulysses. He too had changed since he'd come back. On Yuck's advice his parents had revealed to him that they'd bought him in Brazil for thirty thousand dollars. The price of a Volvo, according to Ulysses' calculations. The price included a guarantee that the child would be white. But as the precise makeup of a person's race can't always be detected at birth, his parents had taken him on the plane from São Paulo to Montreal as White. It wasn't till he was six or seven months old that they'd realized their child was neither white nor pink, but yellow, black and white. Ulysses had been angry at Nathe because she'd asked if his parents had shown him a photo of his Brazilian mother. He'd called her stupid. That's what had changed. Ulysses could call Nathe stupid. How could she have known about the existence of surrogate mothers in Brazil?

To win forgiveness for her stupidity, Nathe had told Ulysses everything about François. She shouldn't have. He was even more indignant than if it had happened to him. But it was the only way to make him understand why she would never set foot in the Faubourg again, why she was afraid, why she was stupid. She didn't want to run into François ever again. It was Ulysses' opinion that, on the contrary, Nathe should go on taking revenge, that she should put his back to the wall. Nathe wasn't sure what specifically the expression *put his back to the wall* might inspire her to do. She didn't want revenge. It was simply her desire to make everything go away that had led her to do the worst. All she'd wanted was that there no longer be a Nathe Saint-Arnaud on the planet. You didn't have to be a genius to understand. But neither did she want to die.

"I'll learn how to drive soon, like Alexa, and then I'll go to the other end of the world, I'll camp underneath a giraffe, because a kick from a giraffe will split open the heads of any hyenas that want to eat the baby giraffes."

Finally, Ulysses smiled. "Does Alexa know how to drive?"

"François taught her."

"François? You mean François raped Alexa too?"

"No, not at all, certainly not, I swear that's not what I'm talking about. Who said anything about rape?"

————————

The words were too scathing. Nathe didn't feel like talking anymore. She felt like learning absolute silence as Ulysses had learned before he ran away. The more she said, the more she was liable to slip up, to make curt remarks that she shouldn't make. She bitterly regretted that she'd spoken. You have to be totally silent if you're afraid that you can only be partially silent. The words that came out of her mouth became disfigured when Ulysses repeated them to her. She'd had enough.

————————

The plan that had taken shape in Ulysses' mind was simple. Since she knew how to drive François's car, Alexa would borrow it from him. She would also borrow the money for gas.

"No way, forget it," Nathe had said, "if she borrows money she'll have a debt."

"Don't be so scared," Ulysses had said, "we've got nothing left to lose once we decide to run away. You'll go to François's place and you'll blackmail him, okay? Either he lends his car to Alexa along with some money or you'll denounce him to the police."

"I can't, I'm too afraid of Catherine."

Ulysses couldn't know why Nathe was afraid of Catherine because Nathe hadn't said anything about her. Nathe didn't know why she hadn't told Ulysses anything about Catherine. She'd only told him about François. Quite simply, that was the way it had gone: on the one hand, everything had been said, on the other hand, nothing had been said.

"Yes, well," Nathe said, "François will turn me in to the police for trying to kill him."

"The cops will laugh, a thirteen-year-old girl tries to kill an adult, and they'll ask why."

"You're the one who told me how to kill somebody, it won't make them laugh."

"Then I'll call Antoine," said Ulysses. "Antoine could lend Alexa his car, he could even go to Aiguebelle with you. Maybe Alexa should phone Antoine."

"All Alexa wants is her independence, I know that, she won't want Antoine to be involved, do you think he'd let her go without a driver's licence? Never, she's his niece!"

"If you'd stop putting up obstacles to every suggestion, I'm sure we could do it, I know where to go," Ulysses said.

He was going to settle on Antoine's island, on the river that runs through the village of Louvicourt then changes its name and goes up to Hudson Bay, which is actually a sea. His parents had warned him that if he ran away again they wouldn't look for him. They wouldn't tell the police or anyone else. They'd had their fill of Ulysses. They were at ease with their conscience and their self-esteem. Ulysses would have to take care of himself. The timing was right. It was what Ulysses dreamed of. Nathe didn't try to reason with him, only to be reasonable herself. She would join Ulysses only for the four days when Alexa would be in Aiguebelle. Alexa would take them to Louvicourt, they'd follow Antoine's instructions to the island, but she, Nathe, would come back to Carouges with Alexa, leaving Ulysses alone on the island.

"But you won't tell Alexa till the last moment that you're coming to the island with me," said Ulysses.

"I won't decide till the last moment," said Nathe. "In fact, I won't know what I've decided to do till I'm actually doing it."

"Whatever, but now is when you're going to call François," said Ulysses.

Nathe thought that she should talk about it with Alexa first. Ulysses thought that Alexa should be filled in once the deed was done. Now when Ulysses talked, Nathe felt as if he was giving her orders. She obeyed, but only halfway. She called the pet shop and asked to meet not with François but with Catherine.

Catherine refused. "I've seen enough of you."

Nathe lost her temper: "You haven't seen the end of me."

"What's that supposed to mean?" said Catherine.

"I'm going to tell on you," said Nathe with conviction. "You abused me sexually and if you don't know what that means, the cops will explain."

"I see," said Catherine. "When do you want to come?"

"I don't want to see François."

"Then come at noon on Wednesday. He should be out, I think he's meeting your mother," said Catherine.

Nathe agreed and hung up. The last part of Catherine's remark made its way with difficulty to her brain. *I think he's meeting your mother?* When she realized what that meant, she lost all self-confidence and went looking for Alexa. Alexa told Nathe that she was sorry she had told her she'd been François's mistress. But that was no reason for Nathe not to go on seeing her friends: "You get everything mixed up, I didn't want you to lose your friends because of me. I should have kept my mouth shut."

"That's not it," said Nathe, "I just want to know what Catherine meant when she said 'I think he's meeting your mother.' It's sick, that remark. Imagine François telling Mama that you were his mistress because you wanted to be, because you gave yourself to him: then what will you say?"

"Don't listen so carefully, Nathe," said Alexa, "and quit being so crazy. Stop fiddling with your sheets and listen to me. Ears can be locked, you know, no matter what people say. It's more important to learn how to lock your ears than how to be quiet. You quite simply didn't hear that remark."

Which is easier said than done! Alexa didn't even know that Nathe was about to blackmail Catherine, Alexa didn't know a thing. On Wednesday, then, Nathe bravely climbed the stairs to the bookstore and had no trouble asking Catherine to lend Alexa her Camry and the money for gas. Catherine didn't defend herself, didn't make excuses, barely looked at Nathe, dug around in her papers: "Is that all? And who do you intend to poison up there?" Nathe locked her ears. Catherine would pick up Alexa and Nathe at Carouges at seven a.m. on the twenty-ninth and drive them to the bus station. And then she'd take a taxi or get home some other way, it was up to her. What's more, she was to lend Nathe her cellphone. "My contract is up," Catherine said.

"You can take out a new one," Nathe said coldly. But she'd been shaken by how easily she had got what she wanted. She had armed herself with insensitivity for a struggle that hadn't happened. By not putting up any resistance, Catherine had trounced

Nathe and kept her from sharing the enthusiasm of Alexa and Ulysses when she announced the results of her shopping. She left it to Alexa to tell their parents they wouldn't have to drive them to the bus station, that Catherine would pick them up very early in the morning on the twenty-ninth.

———————

Alexa was driving. She'd put on just enough makeup to look older without appearing to be coming on to clients. She absolutely looked old enough to be driving. And actually was, almost. Ulysses was acting as navigator, they could have been setting off on safari. Are there safaris in Abitibi? No, there are hunting parties, they kill moose. Was the hunting season over? No one in the Camry knew. Alexa had told Ulysses not to wear his lime-green cap until he was on the boat to the island. Ulysses had wanted to wear a black headband. "Don't put anything on your head, they mustn't spot us."

Nathe was curled up on the back seat, waiting for disaster. The car was going to roll over and over, the universe would be extinguished as easily as a firefly. There, nothing to it, the universe was going to be extinguished like a candle, like a fire, like a forest fire, like a star, the papers would run their photos, all covered in blood and stuck in the wreckage.

Ulysses was giving orders: "Stay on the right! Now the left-hand lane, speed up a little, we'll never get there! Look in front!"

Alexa must have locked her ears, she didn't reply to Ulysses, didn't beg him to keep quiet. Maybe François behaved like Ulysses when Alexa was driving, who knows?

"What are you doing? Cut in! There's somebody behind you."

"Ulysses?" said Nathe, intending to tell him not to distract Alexa. Ulysses didn't hear. "Alexa?" said Nathe.

"It's okay, Nathe, it relaxes him, we're already at the Laurentian Autoroute."

"Already!"

"Yes, we're already far from Carouges. You can sit up, you know. Absolutely nobody's interested in us."

"Yes, but what will Fabienne say when she sees us pull up in a car? Won't she yell?"

"Can't she be quiet!" Ulysses shouted.

Alexa gripped the wheel. Nathe buried her head between two knapsacks.

———

They filled up with gas at L'Annonciation. "The name is connected to the mother of God," Alexa explained.

"God doesn't exist," said Ulysses.

"Too late," said Alexa quietly, "you named him, so he's just come into existence. What doesn't exist doesn't have a name."

Ulysses and Alexa had two hamburgers each, plus fries, at Pierrette's, right after the gas station. Nathe couldn't get anything down. She kept an eye on the car. Alexa looked at the map, counting the kilometres left to go—more than three hundred to Louvicourt—while Ulysses looked at the map Antoine had drawn for him. Just as they were about to leave, Alexa asked Ulysses if he realized that he'd yelled at Nathe in the car. Yes, he was well aware of it. Nathe had been getting on his nerves, Nathe and her fear. Without raising her voice, Alexa explained to Ulysses that if he yelled in the car once more, just once more, he'd have to hitchhike the rest of the way, no matter what good excuses or good reasons he came up with.

Nathe's anxiety went up a notch. Everything was her fault. And was Alexa going to become a different person too, someone who was going to order her around? Because she couldn't imagine leaving Ulysses at the side of the road, she'd die of grief, of shame, of helplessness, she'd go crazy. But she couldn't back out now, and what kind of mess had she let herself get mixed up in? Always, she let herself be sucked in, but she could never stop events from leading to consequences. And at night? At what time would night fall? Had Alexa thought about the night?

She stared wide-eyed, she could see perfectly well that it was still daylight, yet her nerves told her that night had fallen. She remembered that in *The Anatomy Colouring Book* for medical students, the nerves were yellow. She tried to follow the course of her own nerves in yellow. She got lost in the network of her nerves and gave up. She started to count her teeth, helped along by the tip of her tongue. The vise in her chest loosened, letting out a word that Nathe didn't want to hear: "Mama." She had lied to her, she'd lied to everyone, now the three of them were liars.

No, thought Nathe, I didn't lie to my mother. My mother left for Borigine. The woman who came back to our house isn't my mother. She's someone else who looks at me as if she'd bought me and was trying to tell me, as if she couldn't do it. Next time I see her, if I ever do see her again, I'll tell her. I'll tell her she can confess to me that she bought me from a surrogate mother. That she must have hoped I'd turn out to be yellow. She was the one who lied. All we did was to repeat what she taught us, to lie.

———————

The night rose from the forest and quickly ate away at the pinky-grey sky. It's ugly, thought Nathe, as ugly as fear, it's shaggy, there's nothing but claws everywhere, the claws of trees. She was very careful not to say it aloud. They got to Louvicourt. Ulysses followed the detailed map that Antoine had given him. It was all there—the hotel, the bridge, the river, the boat and the trailer sheltered under the high gallery. At the hotel reception desk, Ulysses picked up the key to the shed where the motor was stored. He filled a can with gas at the pump. Alexa and Nathe helped him slide the boat across the grey sand, connect the motor—a 35 h.p. Johnson, it was written on it, Alexa translated "John's son." Together they pushed the boat into the water. Ulysses put his cap back on and started the motor. Success! It all worked! Now they only had to travel for fifteen minutes or so up the river to the island.

Ulysses gestured to Nathe that she should take her bag out of the car. Nathe came back without the bag but with the cellphone, which she held out to Ulysses. "Take it and leave it on till we come back, I can't do it, I'm scared, I'm too scared, I'm sorry, Ulysses, I'm going with Alexa."

"Of what? What are you so scared of?" said Ulysses, fuming.

Nathe plugged her ears and ran to the car to take refuge. The boat opened a passage in the icy black water. The phosphorescent lime green of Ulysses' cap seemed to blink like a firefly, then disappear into the night.

———

Alexa got back behind the wheel. They were still a hundred kilometres from Aiguebelle. Nathe couldn't replace Ulysses as navigator. "Don't worry, little sister," said Alexa gently, "everything's fine, everything's going to be fine. Thanks for not abandoning me. We'll have a fabulous party with Blanche."

Alexa was being so nice, thank you, thank you, and it was incredible what a good driver she was, not impatient at all. Nathe could catch her breath. Downtown Val-d'Or wasn't very reassuring. Even though it was well lit, you could think it was a town in the Far West, with its low houses and no trees, and that bullets were going to start whistling through the air. "Keep your eyes open anyway, there must be policemen all over," said Nathe.

Alexa smiled without taking her eyes off the road. She had no trouble finding the junction for Aiguebelle. "Here we are," said Alexa.

"We're a long way from Carouges," said Nathe.

"I'd love it if you'd sing something," said Alexa. "I'm afraid of forgetting this day forever. I'm afraid that someday this day will have disappeared from my memory. But if you'd sing something, I think it would keep the day from being totally erased. Every time I heard the song I would remember this day."

It took quite a while for Nathe to choose her song. She found the one that Fabienne had taught Émilie, their mother, and that Émilie had taught to Alexa and Nathe. *Someday I'll have a goat, Inch'Allah-ha, I'll take it to the Sahara, Inch'Allah-ha, Someday I'll have a tent, Inch'Allah-ha, I'll pitch it in the Sahara, Inch'Allah-ha, Someday forgetting the earth, Inch'Allah-ha, I'll fly away to the land of Allah-ha, Inch'Allah-ha, Inch'Allah-ha.* That's what a double life is, thought Nathe while she was singing, we drive through the forest at night in the cold and we pitch our tent in the Sahara of our minds. Now that I've finished singing and I have the goat in my mind, in silence, Alexa says that she adores me, that for the rest of her life she'll never forget this trip. Now that I've finished singing, Nathe thought to herself, now that I'm alone in my tent in the Sahara of my mind, I can feel the gulf of Catherine's absence starting to open in my heart. So it's possible to have wanted to kill a person and still feel the gulf of her absence in your heart. I have to resist the intoxicating effects of absence, I have to take off slowly all the way to the deaf and blind being I've created up there. I have to lock my ears to the snickering of the hyena of shame, the hyena that could eat up the goat in the Sahara.

When I ground the devil's tobacco seeds and mixed them with the coffee beans, I doled out enough for three. There were three cups. One was for me. I would have drunk mine if my father hadn't come to drive Mama to the station. But when he showed up, Nathe thought to herself, I ran away like a murderer. If Catherine had had the coffee analyzed in a laboratory, wouldn't the results have shown that I really wanted to leave with her even though I'd run away? Now, thought Nathe, we're driving into the town of Aiguebelle and I want to run away, run away like a murderer.

I couldn't make up my mind to follow Alexa, to get out of the car and follow her, to ring the bell and wait for someone to open the door, it was dark, the house was set back behind a hedge taller than us, barricaded in front by trees much higher than the roof and by others too, behind the house, that reached up above the roof to get a look at us, there's a gate, it's open, but you don't even know if they have dogs. Alexa turned onto the drive that led to the house, I said there must be something wrong with the engine, it was back-firing so much. "Your ears are hallucinating," said Alexa, and got out with no hesitation and rang the bell firmly, lights came on all over the house, my grandmother Fabienne came out, I saw her kiss Alexa, I saw that she wasn't expecting her to be that height, it's true that Alexa is tall, she stands one metre sixty-three, which is not an Olympic record for a sixteen-year-old, but Grandma was still expecting her to be shorter. Alexa waved frantically to tell me to get out of the car, she had just told Fabienne that I was there, it's true, I was there in a sense, but again it was something double, because I wasn't there either, I'd taken refuge without knowing why far outside myself, up there at the top of the ropes and cables that lead to the being I've created that was of no help to me when I had to poison some people to get out. Alexa is so passionate that it sometimes makes her icy. So I obeyed, I got out of the car and I made myself recognizable. Result of the running around: my grandmother fainted. She fell on the front steps, right into the

arms of Alexa and the arms of my grandfather, who happened to
be coming along just then, luckily. That's what I am trying to say:
I didn't do anything and my grandmother fainted. Which goes to
show that the absence of a cause can have an effect. So Halloween
was me before my time, and as I'd predicted, it turned out badly,
there was a razor blade in the apple and tar in the candy kisses.
Stop saying *kisses*, there's no such thing, say *sweets*. *Sweets!* The
first time my grandmother sees me and *wham*, she collapses. My
grandfather patted her cheeks and pulled off her turtleneck, my
mother hates turtlenecks but she'd love to wear them, actually
she wishes she could *stand* them, she wishes she could stand to
be strangled by a turtleneck, but she's the wrong sign. My grandmother was wearing one, lime green, not phosphorescent but in
the same range as Ulysses' cap. My grandfather did a good job of
pulling it off her, he's so sweet, it was as if he'd been practising
all his life, I'd like it if someday someone would take my sweater
off the way he took off my grandmother's. We had time to catch
a glimpse of the fantastically feminine bra my grandmother was
wearing, there were golden flames embroidered on it that burned
her breasts, you could see that hers were very nice. At her age I
thought they'd be dried up like prunes, that's what people had told
me. Well, it's not true at all, not at first sight anyway, they looked
more like languorous little melons, I didn't say watermelons. I
wished I could say to Alexa: "What a beautiful woman!" "What
soft skin!" "What beautiful breasts!"—that kind of thing, but
out of tact, because Alexa is still waiting for breasts, for her own
breasts, I said nothing and we moved on to serious things because
my grandmother had recovered and put her clothes back on, she
brought out food and she didn't look at me again except in little
whiffs that were immediately turned into fumes. Alexa was in fabulous shape despite the day she'd had. Right away, with no transi-
tion, she became an intimate of my grandparents, she went out
of her way to charm them, it came to her naturally, it was inborn,

actually it came from them if you want, because whatever is inborn comes from our grandparents, she laughed and smiled all sorts of things at them so they'd forget that we'd come by car, and they forgot that we'd come by car because it hadn't occurred to them to ask how we'd got there. No one would ever have guessed when they saw us that we'd never met till that evening, that we'd never hugged one another, that never before this evening did our grandparents have a chance to help their granddaughters take advantage of their knowledge, which I imagined to be tremendously vast. Alexa didn't hesitate to tell them how little we knew about them, without blaming anyone or Mama.

We slept in the guest room in their finished basement, close to the droning of the freezer. I would have liked to exchange impressions. Alexa declared that she was exhausted, that we'd talk tomorrow, and she fell asleep. I wanted to call Ulysses, I had to go upstairs, there was no phone in the finished basement. I went back up, groping for light switches, I didn't want to appear to be snooping, I didn't want to startle my grandmother or be responsible for making her faint again. But she hadn't gone to bed and I had to think up something to say so I told her that I thought she was a lot younger and a lot prettier than I'd imagined, even at this time of night, and that actually she reminded me of a woman I'd seen somewhere, but I couldn't remember where or when or how, maybe in a dream because in my dreams I get an advance look at lots of people. In the end she laughed and was able to look at me without getting the vapours. I took advantage of the moment to ask permission to use the phone. She thought that I wanted to call my mother. I let her believe whatever she wanted, but she wanted to have a word with my mother when I'd finished and I had to tell her that it wasn't my mother I wanted to call. She looked surprised, but not excessively surprised. Flustered, that's the word, she looked flustered. My grandfather called her, he was watching the news on TV and he needed my grandmother as a witness. Exactly like my father, who absolutely has to have my mother as a witness when he watches the news. And I could talk to Ulysses in a low voice.

He'd arrived safely, everything was the way it appeared on Antoine's map. He was furious with me for simply following Alexa to Aiguebelle. That was the reason he gave to explain why he'd decided to phone Antoine in Montreal and tell him he'd arrived on the island and that it was excellent, that everything worked the way he'd said, that everything was intact and excellent, which had persuaded Antoine to come up for All Saints' Day, for Halloween actually, and then on the Day of the Dead he intended to leave for Montreal at dawn, around five a.m., and he'd get to Louvicourt around noon. He would phone when he was twenty minutes from Louvicourt so that Ulysses could leave the island and pick him up in the boat.

Ulysses was more than delighted but still really mad at me, still hardened and cynical where I was concerned. I thought it was a lot more because he couldn't stand what had happened to me with François than because I'd followed Alexa instead of him. Pointless to tell him that the way he'd started treating me made me think he held me responsible for what had happened. The fact that I think this or that has no influence anywhere, doesn't jam any machine gun, doesn't suspend the arm of any terrorist. There's just one thing to do, then: tell myself that I'm not doing anything but what I'm doing, from one instant to the next. At least luck is nearly all on our side, it isn't raining, isn't snowing, nobody's sick, we have no money problems.

Yesterday was the day after our arrival, the eve of Halloween. Alexa woke up with her plan worked out. Her plan included soft-pedalling my sensuality, that's news to me, I'd never heard of that before, explain. "The way you pout and bat your eyelashes, your languid poses, your vagueness," said Alexa, "and come back down to earth." Once again, I was totally in the dark. "Even when you cough," said Alexa, "it's booming with sensuality." So now I'm booming. I didn't even flinch, the night before I'd witnessed her own seduction scene without sighing once, what did she want? Did she want me to stop breathing? "Figure it out," said Alexa. It was her plan for getting to know our grandparents that had her so worked up and that my sensuality was liable to cause to fail.

We went upstairs. I'd have loved a café au lait, the kind that Catherine Piano makes. I didn't dare ask for it. I told myself that, for Alexa, just the words "bowl of café au lait" might be the height of booming sensuality. Grandma warned us that Blanche had deteriorated a lot and that she tired very easily, that she couldn't follow the stories people told her, the story of Theodora for instance, well, she just wasn't interested anymore and she hadn't reacted when Theodora finally became empress, and that was just one example of what she'd lost, there were others, she dressed every day as if she were leaving, she didn't want to leave in night-gown and slippers, so every day she had to put on a dress and shoes, she'd asked for warmer socks because she didn't want her feet to be cold in her grave. Alexa was intensely interested in the story of Theodora, whom she'd never heard of. Grandma told her briefly about Theodora's fate, but it took all morning and there we were setting the table for lunch at the same time we were clearing the breakfast table.

Grandpa came home to eat, because he wasn't on vacation, and the conversation revolved around the senses of hearing, taste and smell. Alexa wanted to know about the medical field of ears, noses and throats now that she had ready access to a specialist. Above all, she wanted to know if Blanche could still identify flavours and tastes. Grandpa explained that Blanche defied the statistics, that statistically she could no longer smell or taste, but that they had to acknowledge that she could still smell, still taste too, and that her hearing was terrific, you didn't have to shout at her. Alexa said that she thought it was possible to taste through our thoughts because when she thought about biting into a lemon, her mouth really did fill with saliva. "If thinking about a lemon can make me salivate," said Alexa, "maybe Blanche can just think about tastes and smells and she'll be able to taste and smell." There was no end to it. If it wasn't booming sensuality to talk about saliva flooding your mouth, I'd have loved to know what it was. I was trying to figure out how to get rid of my stringy string beans. I asked Grandma if all the beans in Aiguebelle were sewn with dental floss. She agreed with me, I could leave them on my plate, certainly I mustn't force myself to eat them. The explanation fell flat: the bean season has been over for ages. Everybody, including Alexa, started talking seriously about the seasons and about asparagus from Chile on our plates in September. According to my watch it was past two o'clock and we hadn't taken one step in the direction of the hospi-tal. If it was dark by five o'clock, we wouldn't get there before nightfall. But there was no question of interfering with Alexa's plans, it was up to her to decide, and she had decided to go on with her seduction campaign, which was going very well. Now and then my grandmother looked at me as if I were someone else, I don't know who, maybe I reminded her of her daughter Stéphanie whom I'd never seen because there were no photos of her any-where. My mother says that she was as beautiful as a movie star. Even though I told her that some stars are so horrible and ugly that I'd be ashamed to walk beside them on the sidewalk, my mother still said that her sister shone like a star, that she had small, short, very straight teeth, a perfect nose with a little dip on the bridge, something like mine. There was absolutely nothing perfect about mine, it's a nose with two nostrils for the air to go in and out of.

I pulled on Alexa's sleeve, I'd had enough, but Alexa knew where she was in her organized timetable and told me to let her follow her plan. Ulysses was following his plan. Alexa was following her plan, and I went back over my life, thinking that Catherine followed her plan and François followed his plan, that my mother and father followed their plan, and I consoled myself with the thought that I too must be following mine, but without realizing it, the way Theodora had followed the plan that had brought her to the emperor Justinian without knowing that her plan would lead her to the Byzantine throne, as Grandma had explained to Alexa briefly but at length over the course of the morning.

———

At three o'clock Grandpa had gone back to the clinic, and Grandma took us to the hospital to introduce us to Blanche. My heart was pounding in my eardrums, I told Alexa. She was nice, she gave me some advice: to stop listening to myself if I wanted to remember what we were experiencing. Waiting for the elevator, I pointed out to Alexa that she had a booming blue vein throbbing just under the skin on her temple. As soon as the elevator doors had opened, Alexa turned all affectionate, making me feel as if I was the sick person she was bringing to the hospital. I had already noticed, when I went to see Ulysses during his silent period, that in certain individuals, walking into a hospital can provoke mood swings that make them docile and very affectionate. The problem was, it made me suspicious. My grandmother had put her arm around my waist and that also made me suspicious. Finally, she knocked on the door and the three of us entered the room.

My great-grandmother Blanche was sitting with her angora rainbow hat on a chair the same green as the chair in Ulysses' room. She even had her winter boots on, as if she were on her way to church. Aanaq, whom Mama had described to us a hundred times, was grinning from ear to ear and didn't have a single tooth in her mouth, which Mama had failed to tell us. For me, though, it was the smell, the smell of baby powder, that caught in my nostrils and made me want to cry, because at the centre of that smell I could hear a kind of gnawing away at a carcass. I shivered and Alexa whispered that I should get a grip and stop listening to myself.

Fabienne took off Blanche's hat and boots, before introducing her to Alexa. Blanche took Alexa's hands in hers, then she felt her face in order to know her, while she repeated Alexa's name. She asked who she looked like. Alexa said that her face was the shape of Mama's, oval, and that she had Papa's nose and mouth. Blanche asked if she looked like a movie star. Grandma said that Alexa resembled Theodora at sixteen. Blanche said that she didn't remember Theodora's face, that it had been erased. Aanaq had got out of bed and settled at the window. She was keeping an eye on the sky. Blanche asked what Aanaq was doing. "She's keeping an eye on the sky," Grandma told her, "stop worrying." Stop this, stop that, I'd already heard too much, I was already contaminated by decrepitude, all the way to my knees, which had started to tremble.

Blanche asked Alexa if Stéphanie had come with her. Alexa stroked Blanche's hair and told her very gently that Stéphanie had died of cancer, that it was Nathe, her little sister, who'd come to visit her. Blanche was silent for a long moment. She was trying to find her conclusion. "So Nathe," Blanche concluded, "is Stéphanie's daughter."

"Émilie's," Alexa corrected her.

"Émilie's," Fabienne repeated, asking me to move closer to Blanche. I moved closer, did the same thing Alexa had done, I put my hands in Blanche's and let her touch my face.

"Dear Stéphanie," said Blanche.

"Nathe, Mama, she's Nathe," said Grandma.

Blanche pulled me close to her face and whispered in my ear that she'd been waiting for me, that she was ready to leave now. "Above all, don't say anything to your mother."

I didn't wait for her to ramble on into my ear about what not to tell my mother, I backed up and left the room, it's not hard to understand why. "Above all, don't say anything to your mother." I'd been hearing that all year, I'd heard it too often, I can't listen to it anymore. It was as if Catherine or François were speaking through Blanche. Vertigo tried to draw me into its abyss, I left the room to avoid falling into it.

I took refuge at one end of the corridor, in front of the picture window. I would have needed François Piano's compass to orient myself. I'd have liked to be oriented by an expert. I know that the Muddy flows into the Hudson Sea in the north, Xavier had explained to a stunned Alexa that the waters of North America began to flow towards the Arctic starting here, that in Aiguebelle we were on the Continental Divide. So the north was at the other end of the corridor. So I was taking refuge to the south, and if the sky hadn't turned leaden I could have spotted Ulysses to the east. A fight broke out in a room, but I realized almost right away that it was on TV. It was a common room. It was empty. The TV was on. I switched it off and looked towards the west. I told myself that the west was there, it was ridiculous, it meant nothing to me, I went to the windows and I recognized the west. Black, sooty, dejected, merciless—the west was there and a woman came into the common room.

She didn't give me time to be wary, right away she told me that yes, that was the west, it had been for a very long time, that it was the west all the way to the Pacific Ocean. I succumbed right away to her voice, it was like a lifeline, she'd never seen me in Aiguebelle before, was I in Aiguebelle on a visit, how do you like my little pumpkins? From a black burlap shopping bag she extracted some little pumpkins and the candles that would light them up, here, do you see? She lit a candle with a wooden match, stuck it into the centre of the little pumpkin and she went into ecstasies and may I ask who you've come to visit? My grandmother, and then I corrected myself, my great-grandmother, and again I sank even more deeply into my abyss: I burst into tears. The woman set the lighted pumpkin on top of the TV and made me sit down, still with her life-saving voice, sweetheart, little girl, but no, it's nothing, that's all, that's all.

She was right, that was all. My wariness had regained the upper hand. I apologized so I wouldn't seem like a tease and took off. But she grabbed my arm and held me back. I would have torn myself away if she hadn't said my name. "Nathe?" So then my hand dissolved with fright into hers. "Nathe, great-granddaughter of Blanche, granddaughter of Fabienne, daughter of Stéphanie"— so she declared after she'd anaesthetized me with her floating voice that I didn't want to succumb to again. Luckily, all of a sudden a steadier, firmer hand settled on my shoulder, made me turn around, steered me into the corridor. It was Aanaq. She muttered all the way down the corridor as she pushed me into Blanche's room.

Grandma and Alexa were waiting for me at the door, livid. "She's agitated, she wants to see you, just you, by yourself," Alexa told me as if she herself were contaminated and at death's door. I protested that I hadn't done anything. Alexa said that they were helpless, that Blanche was mistaking me for Stéphanie or for her daughter, it was unclear, and that she wouldn't say anything to anyone until she had spoken to me. Aanaq was beating the time with her feet and didn't let go of me. She pulled me into the room and the door closed on Alexa and Grandma. Aanaq guarded the door, growling.

Blanche ordered me to sit on the arm of the chair. She no longer looked anything like a dying person, she'd passed on her death throes to Alexa and Grandma, that was the explanation because an explanation was needed. "Let me recapitulate," was what she said. "Stéphanie is dead, I understand that. If I were a few years younger I would shed all the tears in my body, but I'll be joining her in a few hours so I'm not crying, I'm demanding. I must have misinterpreted the dream, I thought it would be today. In her letters, Stéphanie promised on her soul that she would rescue me in my final hours. The soul does not die. You are her daughter. You have to keep her promise. You're going to take us out of here, me and Aanaq. Aanaq has to be with her own people, according to her own rituals, and I according to mine. Find a way to do it. We leave tomorrow. We're going to take advantage of Halloween to leave. Do you understand? You mother hated fear. You'll come and get us tomorrow. Go now, go and get ready, think it over carefully. If you let us down, if you betray Stéphanie's vow, the vow of your mother, Stéphanie, I predict that you'll be separated forever from your destiny."

Crazy old woman. Old wreck. Old ruined witch. Old broom. You won't get me. I'm not the dead woman's daughter. Nobody's going to get me. You should have talked to Alexa, she's already on the track to her destiny, she's the one who would have been frightened by such a threat. Again and again, threats. Orders and threats. Their plans.

I was able to leave the room when the meal trays arrived. Grandma and Alexa were telling each other stories, maybe the story of Theodora again, at the end of the corridor, in the west. I showed my empty hands. I hadn't just appropriated some inheritance in the form of old jewels that Blanche might have slipped into my hand.

"What did she want from you?" was Alexa's only question.

I said: "She's delirious, that's all."

"Why are you shaking like a leaf?"

"Because delirious people make me shake like a leaf, that's all."

They went back to the room to give Blanche her meal. I said that I'd had enough, I was going to walk back. I left the hospital. I thought of hitchhiking to go and join Ulysses. Night was falling, the horizon was delirious too, with green and mauve strips pinned to the tops of the spruce trees, with webs of helmeted spiders dangling all the way to Hudson Bay. I could have phoned Catherine. Catherine, help me. Catherine was all I had, I realized, only Catherine could have been my partner in crime. Or maybe François? Yes, that was it, only them, because I still had a fair amount of devil's tobacco seeds in the pouch of my backpack.

I hadn't gone twenty feet when a car slowed down and stopped. The same woman with the pumpkins, Christine Musse, that's what she said, invited me to get in, she knew where my grandparents lived. Sure, let her pick me up if it made her happy. I wasn't going to ask her to drive me all the way to Louvicourt, was I? "Don't wonder if you can ask, just ask!" Alexa would have said. I did up my seat belt without a word. Christine Musse. It smells good in her car, what is it? It's her odour, I no longer have the strength to identify it. I don't have any strength.

We drive down the hill, I can see that we're driving down the hill, we cross the bridge over the river, we drive along the river, I can see that, it's this, it's that, that's where your grandmother teaches, oh really, and then we drive up some small hills that enclose the river, oh really, and this is where Christine Musse lives, so we're going to her house because she's going to make me a hot toddy, you need a hot toddy, she says, you're running a fever, you're shivering.

———

She made the hot toddy in a bowl, which was a really good idea. My elbows were chattering against my ribs. Everything was tense, everything was trying to hold together the pieces of me, a pile of pieces that kept trying to stay in a group.

"What's happening with you, what's happening?"

That obsession of theirs with repeating questions! I shouted that I was not the daughter of Stéphanie Dumont. "I'm the daughter of Émilie Saint-Arnaud and that's that!"

"Yes, yes," said Christine Musse, "of course." Two yeses and one of course. So why had she declared to me, with her bag full of her pumpkin harvest, that I was Stéphanie's daughter? "Because you're Stéphanie's daughter too," said Musse, making her words undulate like a cold-blooded snake warmed by stones along the road.

At which I doubled up with laughter. In a flash I'd just pictured Ulysses in Brazil, looking for his mother, one among thousands, one name out of thousands of Portuguese, Chinese and African names. That was better. I told Musse that my mother's name didn't matter, what was urgent was to find a way to help Blanche, who'd decided to run away with Aanaq.

"Impossible," Musse decreed without thinking it over for a second. "You can't, it's impossible, it would be criminal, you have to tell on Blanche, you have to tell Fabienne and Xavier."

I pointed out that she'd just talked to me as if I were a baby and I knocked back what was left of my hot toddy. What had she put in it? The heat went straight to the marrow of my bones.

"Jamaican rum," said Christine, "the best."

So the best rum in the world had left Jamaica to stroll through my blood, climb to my brain and light me up. It was my turn to have a plan, and it was taking shape in my mind with growing clarity. Musse's face had been steeped in pleasure, as Catherine had said once—"a face that has been steeped in pleasure"—about a watercolourist who came to take courses in the summer. Anyway, it made me happy to realize that I hadn't lost Catherine altogether, because my memory kept some of her remarks intact so I could make use of them when the time was right.

I said to Musse: "You're going to do as I say or else I'll go to the Aiguebelle police and I'll tell them you forced me to get drunk so you could abuse me, they'll make me take a Breathalyzer test, they'll see that I'm not lying, I'll tell them you forced me to get in your car." I could see that she wasn't used to being infantilized by a child, but I didn't let go, it was all too clear in my mind. "Tomorrow you're going to wait for me at the hospital, in the TV room, at eleven a.m., and don't forget or you'll see what I can do to smear your reputation and the name Musse." Musse was horrified, I told myself, that's the face of a horrified woman par excellence, and I asked where I could make a phone call. I had to talk to Ulysses.

He answered. I could hear the 35 h.p. Johnson, chug chug. He and Antoine were nearly at the island. I told him: "Get ready for tomorrow, come and pick me up on the road, don't bring Antoine, you have to come by yourself."

"But you aren't leaving tomorrow, tomorrow's Halloween," Ulysses cried.

"If you aren't on the road tomorrow at the time I'll tell you, I'll call the police and tell them where you are and say that it was Antoine who put you up in Montreal."

"What's wrong with you, are you crazy?"

"You're going to change your tone of voice with me, Ulysses, it's my turn to tell you what you have to do, and don't even think about turning off your cellphone or it'll be the same thing, I'll call the police."

There was a silence, then Ulysses conceded, "Don't worry, I'll be there." I hung up. No question of weakening now that the solution was in the works.

Musse, who'd poured herself a glass of wine, glared at the last mauve shreds dissolving in the sky. She had a fantastic view from the picture window, which must fill up with northern lights at night. I'd have happily ripped it out of her wall and taken it to my mother in Carouges. "Is that a fine, expensive Bordeaux you're drinking?"

"Yes," said Musse. "Know what? You really are the daughter of Stéphanie Dumont."

Whoever you want, I'll be the daughter of whoever you want. Musse brought me back to the gate of the estate, at least I call it an estate since it's surrounded by tall hedges of cedars and Norway spruce, suit yourself. Suit yourself, whoever you want, I couldn't care less. I was about to undergo Alexa's cross-examination. I'd have to be armed to the teeth. But no, that didn't happen, it's not really approved of, my grandmother and Alexa barely wished me good night. They were deep in a feverish exchange about the U.S. Civil War, at the same time peeling vegetables without realizing it. I went down to the finished basement to sleep long before Alexa. I heard her slip between the sheets and sigh with bliss and contentment like some big fat lump whose throat will be cut by a commando during the night. I couldn't help asking her if I had lowered my level of sensuality to her liking. She told me to go back to sleep, but a few minutes later she wanted to get into bed with me because my warmth had already settled in. I didn't want any girl in my bed, but Alexa had whispered that she had a tremendous secret she absolutely had to tell me, so I gave in. I listened. She told me that Papa'd had a daughter by some woman other than Mama: her name was Macha, she was our older half-sister, she'd met her, she was in touch with her, I'd meet her too one of these days. What I heard was mainly the droning of the freezer that seemed to me excessively loud.

"You haven't got anything to say?" said Alexa, propping herself on her elbow.

"It sounds to me like the freezer's about to explode, can you hear it?"

"Maybe I shouldn't have told you tonight, but I thought it would take your mind off the fact that Blanche thinks that you're Stéphanie."

"You know what? You're too hot, I'm suffocating." I left her warmth. I went to sleep in the cold bed. I've got nothing against some alleged half-sister called Macha, but I'm simply against anything that's liable to disorganize me.

My grandmother and Alexa should have slept together, this morning it was as if they'd been lost to one another for centuries. I was entitled to a café au lait not in a bowl, without foam, they aren't equipped for making foam. I inquired about the program, was there a program? Alexa and Grandma were going out to buy groceries and masks for Halloween. No, no masks, poor Blanche, poor Aanaq. I understood. Blanche and Aanaq already had their death masks was what I said. Grandma Fabienne looked at Alexa, Alexa looked at Grandpa Xavier, and I looked at the jar of sugarless blueberry jam. I wanted to know why there wasn't a dog on the estate. No reason. Luckily it was Thursday, because I didn't see how I could have got rid of my grandfather. He left for the clinic. And what time was the party? Not until four o'clock. At four o'clock we were going to leave for the hospital as a delegation, with champagne and small black carnival masks. Excellent.

"What's with you, Nathe, what's wrong? Is it what I told you last night?" asked a worried Alexa while my grandmother was in the shower. I answered that I was trying to curb my sensuality. "You're stupid, you're stupid," said Alexa. I couldn't figure out this obsession with repeating the same sentence two or three times.

I went outside, I needed air so badly, they're terribly short of air around here. Catherine's car was gleaming like an insect in the sun. I sat in the car, it smelled of apples and almonds, Catherine's smell. I told myself that all I could do was not to do anything while I waited for the women to leave and do their errands. I moved the seat until it was horizontal and I dozed between my eyelids like a robber before a holdup, ready to draw his gun between the open car doors.

When the women had left, I went back inside, down to the finished basement, picked up my things, stuffed my backpack with everything I could find by way of pasta, rice, a bottle of champagne, plus two big green garbage bags, and made my way peacefully towards the hospital without even feeling the weight that I was carrying on my back, so heavy was the responsibility in my heart that was crushing me. Blanche was waiting for Aanaq, who'd gone for a bath. She was on tenterhooks. I told her to take off her hat and boots, that I'd tell her when to put them back on. The same for Aanaq, as soon as she came back from her bath I took Mama's mink away from her and gestured to her to sit down and eat. I folded the blankets and put them in a bag. Then the coats, and Blanche's and Aanaq's boots, which I removed from the closet and stowed in another bag. I took the bags plus my backpack to Musse in the TV room and told her to take them down, put the green bags in the back of her car and my backpack in the trunk, then come right back and join me in the room. I also told her that she'd forgotten to make up her left eye, that it showed. She had to fix her makeup.

At twenty past eleven, attendants with witches' hats and brooms brought the meal trays and I told Blanche to eat up, even the bread, even the cookies, even the crumbs. Volunteers dressed up like

Mafiosi, men and women both disguised as Mafiosi, it was the theme that year, handed out suckers and candies in the rooms. Blanche played her role perfectly, laughing like a loony and thanking the Mafiosi twice instead of once even though she couldn't see them. Aanaq was more restless than Blanche, she didn't feel like laughing, but she was starting to trust me. Musse arrived, it was only then that I noticed she was wearing flats. It made me laugh.

By noon the attendants had finished collecting the trays. Musse helped me disguise Blanche and Aanaq as veiled women, it wouldn't knock anyone over, they'd been seeing such things on TV all year, it had become a common sight, they wouldn't turn any heads, even though a panicky Musse was twittering that it would never work. We joined the volunteers but kept our distance. We had no trouble with Customs, we piled into Musse's car, Blanche and Aanaq in the back, me in front, Musse driving. That was a mistake, we had to seat Aanaq in front. It's not that there wasn't room in the back, the car was a Maxima and fairly roomy, it's just that Aanaq had got tangled up in her chador and turned it into a nightmare. I told Musse to turn onto the road to Val-d'Or and as soon as we could we made the switch. It was more practical. I gave Blanche her hat, I put on her boots and returned the mink to Aanaq, who started to hum louder and louder. *Taka taka taka*, the same *taka* three times, as if the record was scratched in that spot.

Poor Musse, I'd have liked to know where she learned to drive. She drives like my father, with a gun to the back of her neck. No danger of getting a ticket. It was not reassuring that we were constantly being passed, but it was incredible and I wasn't going to risk an accident by asking Musse to speed up. I could see her upper lip trembling with amazement. Fantastic! We'd get to Louvicourt well before nightfall. When the delegation of Grandma, Alexa and Xavier would walk into the room at four o'clock, we would already be on the island. *Taka taka taka.* I phoned Ulysses, he answered on the first ring, I told him I'd be there at two o'clock and if I was late he should wait for me.

We got there at two-fifteen. Blanche hadn't said a word, she just hugged me and hugged me and squeezed my hand. I was beginning to understand how useful it can be to repeat the same words two or three times, you did it to convince yourself that you weren't dreaming. Aanaq started to do a little dance on the sand and to plunge her hands in the icy water. Ulysses pursed his lips and avoided looking me in the eye. I didn't ask for explanations, neither did he, didn't ask any questions at the sight of Blanche and Aanaq. Musse took my backpack out of the trunk, and it was then, as she let out a cry of relief—"Antoine!" as if she were being held hostage and Antoine was going to pay me the ransom money— that I realized Ulysses hadn't come alone. Antoine ran to her, kissed her and held her in his arms. He looked as if he couldn't get over the sight of Musse. I realized that it had been a hundred and seven years since he'd seen her. As for me, I was observing Antoine, whom I'd never seen before; I thought he looked like the angelic side of François Piano, but I couldn't care less. He didn't scare me.

The icy wind off the Louvicourt River was already going right through us. I wrapped Blanche snugly in the blankets, put her very carefully into the boat, telling her where we were and assuring her that the trip would only last ten minutes. Then Aanaq got in and refused to sit on a seat. She settled herself on the floor of the boat, held Blanche against her in the mink and gestured that we should go. Quickly, I ran over to Musse, who was taking off again without even a goodbye, so that she wouldn't forget: "Don't say anything, you don't know me, you've never seen me before."

She took a brown leather-bound book out of her bag and thrust it into my hands. "Before she died, your mother entrusted this book to me and made me promise that one day I'd give it to you. Now it's done." She started the car, with a wave and a tight little smile for Antoine, who was sitting in the front of the boat so he could steer. Ulysses held out his hand to me, I got into the boat, he pushed off and heaved himself on board.

Now we are sitting face to face, Ulysses and me, on our seats, gazing at the 35 h.p. Johnson as if we were waiting for a light to come on to show what floor we were on, chug chug, *Taka taka taka*, there's absolutely nothing to do, the river is slipping along under our stomach, heading for Hudson Bay. Its water doesn't flow towards the south. Its water goes north. If I cry into it, my tears will dissolve into the icebergs. The book, I've slipped into my backpack.

It's now that things are going to happen. To take place. The wind stings our faces, warning us that it's now. Antoine has turned around, our eyes locked. I'm not afraid of him. Ulysses has probably told him that I'd threatened to denounce him. It's all the same. For the moment, I'm not afraid. The bridge has moved away, I can't see it now. Ulysses holds out his arm and points to two round frizzy heads in the distance that are drifting in the middle of the black water, the big head and the small head. I don't understand why my heart is breaking, but I do understand why I have to repeat three times, break, break, break. Things have started to happen. It's our own hair that is lashing our faces and nipping our foreheads to wake us up. For us it will be the small island, for Petite-Tête. It hasn't been baptized, this island of Antoine's. Petite-Tête, I'll call it. Dimwit's Island.

Antoine docks so gently that the water is silent and lugubrious. It's a quarter to three in the afternoon. Aanaq hoists Blanche onto

the dock, doesn't let go of her hand. They take tiny steps along the
path and the wooden stairs that lead to the door of the small red-
brick house, a cabin masked by the white birch and spruce trees.
As soon as you're inside, it's a safe place, with a cast iron stove that
spreads a gentle warmth. I take off Blanche's hat and boots and
I tell her: "Blanche, it's me, Stéphanie, I've kept my promise."
Blanche says: "What a wonderful trip, darling, what a wonderful
trip! Let's stay here, let's stay here until nightfall. And when night
has fallen I'll be ready to leave."

Aanaq has made a quick tour of the island, quickly spotted the
canoe on the rocky beach in a cove. She asks Antoine for the paddles. Antoine points to the sky and warns her: "Don't leave now, it
will soon be dark." Aanaq laughs with her toothless jack-o'-lantern
mouth and gestures that she won't leave without Blanche. She paddles between the two islands without a sound, between the two
frizzy heads that are drifting in the ink, *Taka taka taka*, disappears
behind Grosse-Tête. All you can hear now is the lapping of the
water and the rustling of the clouds. I'm afraid, I'm terribly afraid
again.

Antoine joins me on the dock. He says: "Hi Nathe."

I say: "Hi Antoine."

He says: "I've got bread, eggs, cheese, dark chocolate and wine,
and some fresh fish that hasn't been caught yet."

I say: "I've got pasta, rice, champagne and devil's tobacco."

He says: "Devil's tobacco? You mean *Hyoscyamus niger*. I've
got something a lot better than your lousy tobacco, but first I'm
taking Blanche to Aiguebelle."

I yell: "No!"

He says: "We have to, that's life."

I yell: "Blanche does what she wants to." Antoine doesn't reply. I'm not going to argue with him.

It's nearly four o'clock. The delegation will be arriving at the hospital. Around five, Alexa will think about phoning here. I go inside the little house. I find Ulysses making a soup with the fresh vegetables that Antoine brought. I say to Ulysses: "Alexa's going to phone, tell her that I called, that I was angry at the world, that I made my own way back to Carouges."

Ulysses says: "I'll tell her what you just told me, but I'd also like you to forgive me, please, forgive me for yelling at you because you were raped. You aren't the only person in the world who's scared."

I say: "I forgive you, but I forbid you to use the word *rape* when you're talking about me."

Ulysses carefully brushes the head of cauliflower before he tells me: "You have to use it. I have to use it too, for myself. I was also raped." I won't argue with Ulysses anymore either. I don't want to use any word that would weaken me.

Blanche has fallen asleep in the armchair by the stove, her face turned towards the window. I put my hand in front of her nose and mouth to feel her breath. I go down to the dock. Antoine follows Aanaq's boat with his eyes. Blanche has already begun her departure, her breath is coming to an end. The sky turns orange, then mauve. After that, the sky flings itself onto the ground and the light collapses onto the black forest. Aanaq comes back to the dock and calls Antoine. She makes more and more gestures and smiles to show him that the boat suits her, that it's a good boat, that she wants it for herself. Antoine nods his head and opens his hands to let her know that the boat is hers. Aanaq makes it sway when she gets out of it. She fastens it to the dock and puts her arms around Antoine. She goes back and forth between the cabin and the boat. Antoine gives her whatever she wants, everything she thinks she needs. Blankets. Waterproof gear. When every-thing is ready, Aanaq runs back to Blanche in the cabin.

———————

The wind is from the south. "If it were coming from the north," says Antoine, "it would be a lot colder." He says that he'll have to leave with Blanche right away, but he doesn't move, he watches the wind ruffle the dark water, he's thinking. I tell him that I'm going inside, it's time to drink champagne. He follows me. Blanche wakes up and tells us she dreamed there was a taxi waiting for her on Vancouver Island. She yawns and stretches with well-being. She would gladly have a sip of champagne. Antoine avoids popping the cork. He frees it very gradually and watches the bit of blue vapour escape from the bottle. He fills two glasses iden-tical to the ones I saw in the hospital chest of drawers. Blanche and Aanaq clink glasses, laugh and drink. Ulysses' phone rings. Ulysses tells Alexa exactly what I told him to say. Blanche savours every sip of champagne. The phone rings again. This time An-toine answers before I can stop him and I see him walk out of the house and down to the dock, waving his arms around. I realize that Musse and Antoine have betrayed me. Fear nips at me once more. Blanche seems to have fallen asleep and started dreaming again. As if she has sensed the threat that the latest phone call could represent, Aanaq hurries. She dresses Blanche in her hat, her boots, my mother's mink, then she picks her up. Antoine helps Aanaq carry Blanche to the dock, lay her down in the boat, wrap her in blankets. Ulysses gives Aanaq a big, carefully closed con-tainer of hot soup. Aanaq hugs me very tightly before she takes her place in the stern. "Bon voyage," says Antoine softly. He unties the canoe and gives it a push towards the north. Gradually the boat disappears into the last dancing lights, fades and disappears.

On the water there are only glimmers, but the sky is still vibrating, yellow, in the west. Antoine puts his arm around my shoulders and tells me that the wind is from the south, that it will help Aanaq as she paddles north. We stand there until I start to shiver. Then we go inside. I wish it were over. I wish that time would speed up, lift me onto its shoulders, take a giant step towards the future with closed eyes.

I take the brown leather-bound book from my backpack. I discover that it's not a book but a case that contains a bundle of letters addressed to Stéphanie Dumont. The first one I unfold begins, "My darling little girl." That makes me ache all at once. As much as I did on the beach at Les Éboulements. As much as if I'd swallowed some devil's tobacco seeds. It's as if Catherine's voice had crept into the words "My darling little girl," as if the abyss were about to open at my feet. My eyes race to the signature. "With lots of love from your grandmother." I put the pages back in the envelope, then I put the bundle back in the case and wait. I wait for the pain to die down.

Antoine is drinking champagne and pacing. Ulysses tells him to calm down, everything's fine, then he puts some wood in the stove. His mixed-blood face is peaceful. He brings down the cover of the stove over the flames that spring up. If I wanted to I could lift the cover and feed the letters to the fire. But I don't want to. So I replace the book in my backpack, vowing that I'll behave as if it weren't there. All three of us hear the roar of a small plane at the same moment. We stop breathing.

"It's Xavier's hydroplane," Antoine tells me, "get ready to convince him."

I say to Antoine: "You told on me."

Antoine says: "In exchange I'll tell you the story of your birth."

I say: "I don't want any birth."

Antoine says: "But you do want the story."

———————

Antoine hands each of us a flashlight, Ulysses goes behind the house as quickly as he can, all the way to the end of the island, I have to light up Grosse-Tête and Antoine is on the dock, signalling. The hydroplane appears from very far south, flies over our heads, continues on its way, disappears in the north, but returns to the island and lands. It comes ashore. Xavier gets out, then Fabienne and finally Alexa.

Xavier moors the plane firmly to the birch trees. When he's finished he says: "Where are they?" It sounds like a command.

Antoine replies: "There's hot soup waiting for you." Xavier shoots him an angry look. Antoine adds: "Nathe is the only one who can tell you."

———————

I thought that I had to gain some time. I ran ahead of them with Ulysses. We made the glasses, the champagne and the bowls disappear. There were no other traces. We busied ourselves finding placemats and setting the table. I thought to myself that each of us would have to choose their camp. Never had the world appeared to be so clearly divided into two camps. We were three against three. Three who knew where Blanche and Aanaq were, three who didn't.

At the table, the two camps faced one another. On one side, Xavier, flanked by Fabienne and Alexa. On the other side, me across from Xavier, between Antoine and Ulysses. Antoine cut the

whole wheat bread and handed out slices. We waited until Xavier
had taken his first spoonful of soup and I realized that it came
from my mother—the business of waiting till Papa had given the
signal to eat. I started to think about Mama. I thought to myself
that she'd be glad to learn that Alexa had achieved her goal, that
she'd finally met her grandparents, but my courage was flagging
because I'd let the word *Mama* go too far down the yellow course
of my nerves. I must have let out a sigh. Xavier took advantage of
it to look me deep in the eyes with his dark blue gaze. I thought
that my eyes were the same as his. Alexa once told me that the
violet spilled over from my eyes and made people think I wore
makeup. I let Xavier gaze into my eyes. I could have put them
on the table if he'd wanted. He could have dissected them to
his heart's content. He wouldn't have found either Blanche or
Aanaq.

I was playing for time. I could see the boat glide silently under
the Louvicourt bridge, I could see the wind pushing at Aanaq's
back, pushing the way that you're pushed by your father's or
mother's hand on a swing when you're little, pushing faster and
faster, higher and higher towards the north because that's where
they were going, these two old women who'd adopted one another to travel together to the north, to the northern lights, when
their time came. These thoughts that were keeping my mind busy
gained time for me, gained some ground for Blanche and Aanaq
against the opposing camp that claimed to know where and when
and how each person's life should begin and end.

Antoine brought out the cheese and opened a bottle of wine.
Without looking at anyone, Xavier said: "Do you by any chance
have some champagne?" He must have noticed the absence of
the bottle I'd brought. Ulysses winced, but then he pulled himself
together and didn't move a muscle. Antoine shifted the armchair
and lifted a trap door, went down and got a bottle of champagne

from a hiding place down there. Xavier said that it wasn't the bottle he'd hoped to see. They sipped some wine half-heartedly, it wasn't a drinking party but we were playing for time.

Xavier said: "It's too late to leave now, I won't go tonight, you're lucky that I'm a doctor, Nathe, for the moment, Blanche and Aanaq went out with us for the All Saints' Day holiday, that's how I explained their absence at the hospital a while ago, but on Sunday night they have to go back, or else."

More threats. I said: "Or else what?"

"Or else," said Xavier, "there'll be police, searches, TV, newspapers, headlines, names in papers, attention, scandal. You don't want to dishonour your grandparents, do you? I've been smeared enough," said Xavier, "you and Alexa didn't come to Aiguebelle to plunge us into another nightmare." He got up from the table and went out to meditate at the water's edge. A few minutes later Antoine joined him, they climbed aboard the hydroplane and stayed there, bobbing up and down in the water.

Fabienne and Alexa started arranging things to make room for everyone to sleep in such a small space. Ulysses was doing the dishes and putting them away. I wrapped myself in a blanket and went out to sit on the dock, not far from the hydroplane. I told myself that my grandfather now knew perfectly well that Blanche had gone away with Aanaq in the canoe. What else could he imagine? He was talking with Antoine. They got out of the plane, my grandfather went back inside without looking at me, Antoine sat beside me on the dock. He told me about Xavier's birth. His parents had died when their car collided with a train just outside Aiguebelle, before he was born. The ambulance attendants had taken him out of his dead mother's womb. I hadn't known. I thought it was horrible, but it didn't hurt me and it didn't scare me. We heard the sound of diving. Antoine was sure it was a beaver. I thought we should take flashlights and go out and look, in case something had gone wrong with Aanaq and Blanche. We couldn't see anything. It must have been a beaver.

Antoine asked if I wanted to hear the story of my birth now or if I'd rather wait. I told him I'd already gathered that, like Ulysses, I'd had a surrogate mother and that it was Stéphanie. For the moment I preferred to think about Blanche and to follow her all the way to the end. Antoine told me I had to know right away that Christine Musse had been present at my birth as midwife. Why did I have to know that right away? According to Antoine, that was what had given Christine the right to betray me, because she was the one who'd phoned Xavier. I shrugged my shoulders and kept them that way for a while so that my head could empty. Anyway, I thought it was weird.

We went back inside, everything was ready for the night. Fabienne and Alexa were bug-eyed from trying to see things clearly. Alexa was looking at me as if she'd never seen me before, as if I wasn't the one who'd been born, as if I were the brother she'd never had, who was cunning and silent enough to face up to the opposing camp. She went to sleep with Fabienne in the one bedroom. Ulysses, Antoine, Xavier and I lay down on the floor, close to the cast iron stove, and waited for sleep. I thought it must be like that in Algerian villages. Carpets would be unrolled out onto the bare ground and women, men and children, grandparents and newborns, great-grandparents and embryos, would lie down on them and wait. If they woke up alive, they counted the day they'd just gained.

In the middle of the night we were wakened by Aanaq's moans, *Aa ta taa! Aa ta taa! Aa ta taa!* We grabbed flashlights and rushed outside. There was no one. I knew that Blanche was really gone. I said nothing to the others and I let the canoe glide into my sleep so I could see Aanaq kiss Blanche's bluish forehead.

We woke up. Ulysses and I made coffee. Xavier told me that he and I were leaving. Antoine would drive Fabienne and Alexa back to Aiguebelle. I asked: "What about Ulysses?"

Xavier looked at Antoine and repeated: "What about Ulysses?"

Antoine said nothing. I don't know why I thought just then that Antoine was a coward. I gestured to Ulysses to follow me outside. He would have to decide what he wanted to do. Stay on the island? Go to Aiguebelle? Back to Carouges? "Don't let them take advantage of you, Antoine's a coward."

Ulysses protested: "Antoine is not a coward. Not when he's away from his father. And neither am I, I'm not a coward. I want to stay on the island, I'm going to stay on the island, and if I make it through the winter I'll be ready to leave for Morocco. And if I survive in Morocco, I'll be ready to come back and see Antoine and Jérémie in Montreal."

We held each other very tightly. We could have traded blood, so complete was our embrace. Xavier stepped out of the chalet. He was ready to take off. He wanted me to leave my backpack with Antoine. No way. I took my backpack. I won't let go of it.

The hydroplane took off towards the south, then a little farther on it turned and we followed the river. The din of the motor kept us from talking. Higher up we hit snow, snow that melted when it touched the wings. It was nothing, but we had to descend and fly even lower if we wanted to continue to scrutinize the shores of the river. We caught sight of Aanaq's canoe. It seemed to have run aground and been abandoned in the rushes. We continued flying over the river and the shores. We saw nothing, found nothing. We turned back and went to Aiguebelle. Xavier landed on the Muddy River, before the bridges. He helped me disembark. All at once he seemed so tall, I wished that he'd pick me up and make the sky spin around me. But things happened differently. I was the one who wrapped my arms around him and told him that it was nothing. "Don't be afraid, nothing will happen," I kept repeating, as if I were his mother. He smiled anyway and took my arm to lead me to his car. From the outside, you'd have thought I was under arrest.